THE URBANA FREE LIBRARY

W9-BCD-435

The Urbana Free Library

To renew materials call
217-367-4057

DISCARDED BY THE
URBANA FREE LIBRARY

	DATE DUE	
OCT 2 9 2007	AUG 14 2010	
MAR 1 6 2009		

Sabriya | Damascus Bitter Sweet

Ulfat Idilbi

A NOVEL

translated by Peter Clark

INTERLINK BOOKS

An imprint of Interlink Publishing Group, Inc.
NEW YORK

First American edition published in 1997 by

INTERLINK BOOKS
An imprint of Interlink Publishing Group, Inc.
99 Seventh Avenue
Brooklyn, New York 11215

Copyright © by Ulfat Idilbi 1980, 1997
Translation copyright © by Peter Clark 1995, 1997

Originally published in Arabic in Damascus under the title
Dimashq Ya Basmat al-Huzn, 1980
First published in English by Quartet Books Limited.

All rights reserved. No part of this publication may
be reproduced, stored in a retrieval system, or transmitted
in any form or by any means, electronic, mechanical,
photocopying, recording or otherwise without the prior
permission of the publisher.

Library of Congress Cataloging-in-Publication Data

Idilbi, Ulfat.
 [Dimashq yā basmat al-huzn. English]
 Sabriya: a novel / Ulfat Idilbi; translated by Peter Clark. —
1st American ed.
 p. cm.
 ISBN 1–56656–219–8. — ISBN 1–56656–254–6 (pbk.: alk. paper)
 1. Syria—Social life and customs—Fiction. I. Clark, Peter.
II. Title.
PJ7838.D48D5613 1997
892'.736—dc20   96–46045
                                                            CIP

Printed and bound in the United States of America

10 9 8 7 6 5 4 3 2 1

Translator's Acknowledgments

Sabriya is a translation of *Dimashq Ya Basmat al-Huzn*, first published by the Ministry of Culture, Damascus, in 1980. The edition I worked on was published by Dar Tlass publishing house, Damascus, in 1989.

I have received help and encouragement from many people, including Ulfat Idilbi and her son, Ziad.

Rana Saady guided me through points of Damascus women's Arabic and popular poetry.

Dr. Mounawar al-Sayed of the University of Damascus read the whole translation, comparing it with the original Arabic, and saved me from committing howlers.

Dr. Allen Hibbard and Theresa Clark also read the whole text and drew attention to inelegancies in an earlier draft.

Quotations from the Holy Qur'an are presented in the English of Mohammed Marmaduke Pickthall's *The Meaning of the Holy Koran*.

I am responsible for surviving errors and infelicities.

Peter Clark

Glossary

abaya: cloak

'Izzat Pasha al-'Abid: leading Damascus notable (1850–1931), former confidant of Ottoman Sultan Abdul Hamid

Abu Raghib: father of Raghib, familiar term of address

Ma'ruf al-Arna'ut: Syrian novelist (d. 1947)

'awwamat: dumplings made of flour and sugar

As'ad Pasha al-'Azm: early twentieth-century Damascus notable

baha: central courtyard of a prosperous town house

banafsha: flowering shrub, like dog-rose

fetta makdus: dish made with meat, eggplant, bread, yogurt, and tomato sauce

Gibran Kahlil Gibran: Lebanese writer (1883–1931) who lived in the United States and wrote in Arabic and English

al-Hilal: literary magazine started in Cairo in 1892, still running

kaffiya: man's cloth headdress

Ahmad Shakir al-Karmi: Palestinian journalist in Damascus (1894–1927)

Abdul Karim al-Khattabi: leader of the rebellion against the French and Spanish in Morocco in the 1920s

Khawla bint al-Azwar: heroine of the battle of Qadisiyya in early Islam; she assumed the clothes of her slain brother and fought on

kubba: meatballs made with burghul

kunafa: pastry served with nuts, baked in butter and soaked in honey or syrup

liwan: raised roof recess overlooking a domestic courtyard

Mustafa Lutfi al-Manfaluti: Egyptian writer and translator (1876–1924)

Mevlevi: Turkish Sufi order founded by Jalal al-Din al-Rumi (d. 1273), members of which are sometimes called whirling dervishes

namura: mouth-watering baked sweet made of cream, flour, sugar, and pistachio nuts

Nusaiba bint Ka'ab: heroine of early Islam who tended the wounded of the battle of Uhud between Muslims and Meccans in 623

Qais and Laila: legendary lovers famed in early Arabic poetry

Ahmad Shawqi: Egyptian neo-classical poet (1868–1932)

Umm Raghib: mother of Raghib, familiar term of address

George Zaydan: prolific Cairo-based Lebanese writer (1861–1914)

zilif: variety of citrus fruit

Khair al-Din al-Zirakli: Syrian poet and historian

Mai Ziyada: Palestinian-Lebanese writer (1886–1941) who lived mostly in Cairo

That spring the house was in an extraordinary state. The month of April had adorned it by elegantly scattering its tints, apparently at random but yet with an overall harmony.

Snow-white rose blossoms pour down the walls in frozen cascades. Red roselets climb up the arch of the *liwan*.

Yellow jasmine bounds over the trellis, weaving a multi-colored canopy of green and yellow.

In the pool is reflected the image of the moon, and the purling of the fountain produces a melodious rhythm.

A fragrance from the lemon and orange trees induces a sweet and relaxing restfulness.

The house seemed as if it had been prepared for a wedding party. Chairs had been set out in the spacious courtyard. Lights gleamed from the passageway that led to the *liwan*. Maybe that's how I imagined it because I recalled what a relative had once said to Mother: "It's as if your house was designed for parties and weddings. If Allah wills, you'll have your daughter's wedding party there and you'll all be very happy."

I would imagine a young bride and her groom entering from the passageway: the young man, slimly built, wearing a dark suit with a white rose in his buttonhole. Upon his arm a sweet, slender-waisted young bride, proudly walking with her fine white wedding dress as if she was enveloped in an autumn cloud. Without being aware of what I was doing, I would find myself feeling my waist to make sure that it was indeed slender.

Events do not happen as we wish or hope. I knew that the house that evening had not been got ready for the wedding party of my day-dreaming. It had been prepared for a ceremony to mark a death. It was as if the youthful imagination had adventures that echoed suppressed and perhaps embarrassing yearnings, yearnings that one might laugh at if they emerged from the subconscious, yearnings one would not want to be revealed to other people.

My mind stopped wandering when there emerged from the passageway not a bridal couple but ten elderly gentlemen in white turbans and dyed smocks. They were led by Abu'l 'Izz, a middle-aged distant relative. He seated them at the head of the *liwan* and talked quietly to them. It was clear that they had come to recite the Qur'an for the soul of the head of the house, who was my paternal grandfather, forty days after his death.

I had not attended funeral ceremonies before. It was not the custom at that time in our country for a fifteen-year-old girl like me to be present at funeral feasts unless she was married and the deceased was a very close relative. Even though the deceased was my grandfather, I was not allowed to attend. There were prescribed limits beyond which a girl was not expected to go. Otherwise they would quote the saying "The girl who goes out celebrating and commiserating and attending women in labor is the girl who will get all the blame." To avoid criticism a girl absented herself at such times.

When I was little I used to love to read and learn things, and I would retreat to a room from which I could look down on to the central courtyard which, in our old Damascus houses, we used to call the *baha*. I was able to follow what was going on and miss nothing. There was no better place than through the window of the small room halfway up the stairs. I called it the cubbyhole. From there you could see the entire courtyard. I was able to slip up there whenever I wanted to without any of the men knowing, because it was on the way to the upper floor, where the women gathered, together with my aunt, who was the principal mourner. She was Grandfather's only daughter, and my grandmother had died a long time ago.

The guests started arriving at the house. The men sat on the chairs laid out in the courtyard. Veiled women came in and at once climbed up the staircase opposite the front door that led to the upper part of the house. The men glanced from the corners of their eyes at the women as they went upstairs. I observed Father and my uncle sitting apart from each other. Both looked grim. Neither made any movement, as if the business of the ceremony meant nothing to them.

Meanwhile, Abu'l 'Izz never had a moment's rest. He greeted people and presented tea to the old men as if he alone was responsible for everything.

One of the old men cleared his throat, invoked the name of Allah, and started to intone verses of the Qur'an with a gentle voice that brought a reverent hush to the assembly.

I was distressed not to see any sign of grief on people's faces, not even on those of Grandfather's closest relatives or of his friends.

Was it because Grandfather had lived longer than he should have? He died at the age of eighty and had been paralyzed for the last ten years of his life. His nearest and dearest had longed for him to die.

I found myself asking Allah to let me die young. Was it not better for a person to die with some usefulness in him, so there could at least be some genuine show of grief?

There came to my mind an occasion which I will never forget as long as I live, even though I was very young at the time. I was five years old and one day Father came home looking very upset and unusually low in spirits. He was several hours later than usual. Mother was cross and said, "Heavens above, where've you been? I've been so worried about you. We've been hanging around waiting for you and have almost died of hunger . . ."

Father interrupted her.

"Leave me alone," he said sadly. "My father has been taken ill. He collapsed at the store after he heard that he had become bankrupt. They told us the news and we — my brother and I — rushed to carry him home. He's paralyzed. We sent for doctors. They told us that he won't get any better. We've left him with my sister, Sabriya. We don't know what we can do for him. I feel as if I'm in another world."

Mother began to weep and slapped her cheeks.

"The poor old man's paralyzed?" she sobbed. "Allah help us. There's no cure for paralysis."

She spoke as if she had made up her mind about it. Father curled his lips and said nothing. I did not really understand what was being said but her words obviously made an impression. I left my parents to carry on talking and went to the terrace to bounce my ball. I chanted the words as if they were part of a song:

"Allah help us. There is no cure for paralysis.

"Allah help us. There is no cure for paralysis."

Perhaps, I thought, it was a prayer or something like that. A few days later I went with Mother to call on Grandfather. I left her with my aunt, exchanging greetings and a few words, and hurried up to Grandfather's room. I stopped by his bed and said, very proud of my words, as if I was making a speech, "Grandfather, Allah help us. There is no cure for paralysis."

Suddenly he blushed. His muscles tightened and his face looked grim. He stared at me for a moment and his huge red eyes seemed to pop out of his head. He then grabbed my wrist with his good hand, drew me to him and said in an alarmingly imperious way, "Tell me, girl, who said that about me?"

"Mom," I said softly, with a smile on my face.

He dropped my wrist and turned to the wall.

"Bitch," he said tremulously, as if he was weeping. "What have I done to her that she wants me to die?"

I realized at once that I had made a mistake, and that what I had said was not a prayer but were words lacking in charity. I crept away from his room in silence, aware of the gravity of my offense. From that time on I noticed that Grandfather never again addressed a word to Mother. He would turn away from her whenever she came into the room. If she asked after his health, he would answer merely with a nod, without looking at her.

"What have I done to your father?" I once heard her say to Father. "I feel as if he hates me from the bottom of his heart. He hates me so much that he cannot bear to look at me."

4

Father moved his lips but as usual made no reply. I was the only one who knew the reason and, young as I was, I knew how to keep a secret.

I left the window of my cubbyhole and went up to the reception room on the top floor to see what was going on there. I found a large crowd of women, all in somber clothes, surrounding Auntie, who was in black. She wore a dark shawl on her head and a black-bordered handkerchief was in her hand. She was trying to hold back her tears, muttering sadly to herself, "What a disaster! What happens after Father? How can I carry on after you have gone, my dearest? If only you had stayed alive. If only I could have served you for the rest of my life."

She stood up in front of me, confused. I stared at her, amazed at her words. What were all these lies she was coming out with?

"Do you remember," I wanted to whisper in her ear, "the day I came to see you only one month ago? You were standing in the kitchen in front of a huge pile of washing. You were weeping bitterly and praying to Allah, saying, 'Oh, Allah. Either take him to you or take me. I can't stand it any longer.' When you saw me you exploded and said, as if I was responsible for it all, 'It is as if Hajj Abdul Fattah had no other children but me. One week goes by, two weeks, and I never see any of you. Where are your parents? Where's your uncle and his wife? Those with a conscience, those who knew the meaning of duty, have all died. Mother, my brother Sami. They left me all alone to carry this heavy burden and I can't bear it any longer. The only thing your father is interested in is leaving his work and going to the coffee-house to play cards with his friends. Your uncle's world is reduced to that sluttish wife of his. He can't see anything in the world beyond her. Look, I've just washed your grandfather. I've changed his clothes and his bedlinen. I then went to the kitchen to get his lunch ready. I'm never away from him for a moment without him summoning me. I run to him and find that he's wet his bed. Look at his pile of washing. I've only just washed an even bigger pile. My hands are worn out from washing. Was woman in this country created only for worry and chores? It's insufferable. I can't turn away from him for a second. I can't leave the house. I'm burried alive here. For ten whole years, day and night, he calls out, "Sabriya, Sabriya." When will Allah take Sabriya away from this agony? Did they call me Sabriya because it means

5

long-suffering? I am long-suffering. After such suffering, what is there left but the undertaker and the tomb?'

"I kept quiet as you spoke. There was nothing I could say. What you said was absolutely right, all of it. So why now do you grieve and weep when Allah has answered your prayer and done what you wanted?"

I heard one of our neighbors whisper to another, "How is it that Sabriya can weep at will? There can be no doubt that her father's death has come as a relief. Has she not serviced him for ten years? She has spent all her youth as a prisoner condemned to hard labor. He is at rest now and at peace."

"Don't say that," said the other in a hushed tone. "Whatever has happened, a father is a father. She's weeping not for her father but for herself, and what she's going to do with herself from now on. Unhappy the woman who never marries. She must feel bitter and humiliated when she finds that she's a burden to her brothers and her family."

"Allah, how right you are," the other said, nodding. "As the saying goes, 'It's tough for the women who rely on their brothers for their bread and butter.'"

I almost exploded with rage when I heard what these two, unaware of my presence, were saying.

How wretched are women in our country. They are not permitted either to learn or to earn. They are chained to custom and tradition. They are reluctant dependants and even then men are always complaining about them. I had been so dense. How could I be aware of what this old lady had gone through? I was about to criticize Auntie for weeping and to accuse her of hypocrisy. But I knew things that had gone on between her and her brothers that my Auntie, toughened over the years, did not know.

Ten days after Grandfather's death my parents met with my uncle and his wife in the reception room. Auntie had gone out to the cemetery to visit her father's grave and it seems that my uncle had taken advantage of her absence, for he said to Father, "What do you say to the idea of our selling up this house forty days after our father's death? I'll get an agent to find a buyer straightaway."

His wife, who had eyes that were constantly on the move, a sign of cleverness and also malice, said, "It's essential that we sell the house speedily. Property prices are high at the moment and we must seize our chance."

"If we sell the house," said Father, "where's Sabriya going to live? Allah knows, I wish our house was big enough for her to move in and live with us."

"I'd like to let you know," my uncle's wife put in aggressively, "that I'm not going to have anybody else living with me."

"Where is your sister-in-law going to live if not with her elder brother?" asked Mother. "You don't have any children and your house is big enough. We don't have room for an extra bed."

My uncle's wife turned to her husband. "The day your sister moves into our house is the day I leave it," she said in a way that did not invite challenge. "You know more than anybody else that I am nervous by nature and cannot stand having anybody else in the house. It's totally unacceptable to have to put up with some old maid."

"Steady on, woman," said my uncle. "Don't get upset in advance. We'll be able to rent a small house for her and she can live there by herself."

"What! Good heavens," she countered scornfully. "You're going to *rent* a house for her? Where are you and your brother going to get enough money for the rent? Two minor officials have no more than their salaries. Isn't it enough for your spinster sister to take a small room with one of the neighbors?"

"I can't see anything wrong with that idea," my uncle commented.

There was silence. It seemed that my parents were agreeing to this generous offer on the part of my uncle's wife.

I felt a sudden loathing for the whole lot of them. They were ganging up against this poor old aunt of mine after all her exhausting work, after her patience over ten long years. I was distressed and felt from the bottom of my heart a tremendous sympathy for her. I knew how much she loved that house. In her miserable life it was the only thing that had given her any comfort. She used to delight in planting rare flowers in the beds around the courtyard. She loved the trellis of vines, the orange, citron, and lemon trees on which she would hang cages for blackbirds, goldfinches, and canaries. And she used to feed the sweet little Damascus cats. She would fill the pool with fish of many colors. In all this she found enormous delight, solace in her solitude.

She would boast about it to her neighbors and friends, and hand out flowers, oranges, and citrons to them all.

How could they want her to live in a small room at a neighbor's house? She, the daughter of a distinguished merchant who had had standing among the people of the quarter, as well as among his brother merchants.

I wanted to take part in the discussion and offer my own view but I was afraid my uncle might hit me. I knew that he could be violent and rough. But he turned to me and said, "Get up, Salma, my dear, and make us some coffee. I like mine with plenty of sugar."

I got up and went to the door. Behind it I saw Auntie hovering, her finger on her lips, signaling me to keep quiet, which I did, for I respected her.

It seems that when she got back to the house she found them all gathered in the reception room. She stood at the door, eavesdropping on the discussion which was all about her.

She followed me to the kitchen. She was very pale. Her face was tense and she was shaking all over.

"Don't get upset, Auntie," I said. "I'll come and live with you wherever you are."

I hugged her and shed a few tears. She caressed my shoulders.

"You're a kind person," she said. "But where did your kindness come from? Don't worry about me. Let them talk as much as they like. I don't care about them one little bit. Believe me, I'm not at all surprised. I already knew that this was the end. They won't be able to get me out of this house of mine except as a corpse. You'll see how I get my own back. I'll get them talked about all over the town."

I was taken aback by the defiance, by the strength of feeling that possessed her all of a sudden. I felt somehow reassured and wondered what she was going to do.

These memories went rapidly through my mind and I decided to go back to the window of the cubbyhole on the stairs. I was afraid of missing what was going on in the central courtyard. I left Auntie mourning her father and the women around her whispering words of comfort. Meanwhile, Mother and my uncle's wife were dressed in black and grieving openly, for they did not want to invite any of the adverse comments that could be leveled without mercy against daughters-in-law.

8

The courtyard was filled with invited guests as well as the uninvited, people who seize such opportunities to gorge themselves. The space was large, with plenty of seating, but there was not a single vacant chair.

I observed that Father and my uncle were still in their places, from which neither had moved. It struck me that each was gazing at the other with a look of intense irritation, as if the whole ceremony had no meaning for them. Something apart from the guests was preoccupying them. I saw Abu'l 'Izz hasten to the door to receive the shaykh of the Mevlevi, accompanied by ten dervishes. My eyes fell suddenly on Father and my uncle. I saw amazement and puzzlement on their faces. I was both surprised and curious.

Abu'l 'Izz, the shaykh, and the dervishes proceeded to the *liwan*. A space was made for them. One of these dervishes by himself would not attract much attention, but when I saw them all together they were dignified and beautiful. They wore black-dyed cloaks beneath which could be seen smocks of a brilliant white. On their heads they wore cylindrical felt caps. With measured steps, the dervishes advanced decorously behind the shaykh, whose cap was wrapped with a green band.

The old men were still chanting the Qur'an. As soon as one stopped, another took up the chant until they had all recited what they were able to. They concluded the recitation with the prayer, "Oh Lord, censure us not if we omit an obligation or commit a sin." They delivered it together with the greatest enthusiasm, swaying their bodies forward and back in time to the intonation of the prayer. They then dedicated what they had recited to the spirit of the deceased, Al-Hajj Abdul Fattah al-Saruji. At the mention of his name my whole body quivered. I was seized by a tremor that was perhaps a sense of the presence of death. Tears unexpectedly welled up in my eyes, as if I was realizing only for the first time that Grandfather was indeed dead and had departed from this world never to return. I felt a sense of loss and wanted to see him. I looked out to the *liwan* and imagined I could see him sitting up in his bed, as if he was a piece of the furniture or one of its ancient trees. His clothes were clean and white, like those bedsheets that were always sparkling. His beard was also white, framing his innocent face. His head was shiny and bald, and kindliness poured out of his blue eyes. There shone a light from him as from one who was close to Allah. With his good hand he fingered prayer beads of yellow amber. The names of Allah were on his lips. He resigned himself uncomplainingly and without resistance, no longer concerned with the affairs of this world. It was as if he had already severed his bonds with this transient existence and had embarked on his journey to the eternal life beyond. But the road had been long, long. Every now and then he had shouted out, "Sabriya, Sabriya." His cry had been a call for help, as if he was pouring all his anguish into this cry. Auntie used to hurry to him, swiftly, energetically, and adjust his position, or place a pillow behind him, or give him something to eat or drink.

I was roused from these meditations by the melody of a raucous song that suddenly rang out. I thought for a moment that one of those present had gone crazy and had started to sing in the middle of this solemn memorial gathering.

"O Mary, who made the captain and the crew fall for you. May my time with you return."

I listened to the words of the song and realized that I had made a mistake. A man was reciting a eulogy to the Prophet and was shaping it to the measure of this well-known song.

The apparent frenzy and the expressive movements of his face as he sang confirmed that he was really singing a song of praise to the Prophet and was thinking of that Mary who made the captain and the crew fall for her.

As soon as that was over, another chanter started up. He seemed to be vying with his colleague and was also singing a song of praise for the Prophet to the rhythm and melody of a popular song.

"For blame, for blame, sweet one, tasty one.
You have brought us to the well-head and cut the rope, letting us fall."

To me it was all strange and fascinating. I had never thought that memorial ceremonies in our country would be quite like this.

When the singers had ended their chanting, one man started to beat an unhurried rhythm on a drum which gradually became faster and more animated and was joined by the clashing of cymbals and the strumming of lutes. Then all the old men stood up, along with some of the guests, and began to intone, "Allah, Allah, Allah," in a monotone, as they swayed their bodies to the right and to the left, forward and backward.

10

To me it seemed as if they had lost consciousness. They were in a trance and I was imitating them, swaying with them and repeating, "Allah, Allah," for I too was being carried away with the occasion. I do not know how long things went on like this. The beat of the drum gradually became fainter and fainter until it faded away altogether. Then the movements wound down, the voices fell quiet and silence reigned.

The men all sat down and wiped away their sweat and got their breath back. It was as if they had been running away from something. Then we suddenly heard the melodious sound of a flute, soothing and sweet. A magical air of poetry returned to the house. I now knew that it was the turn of the Mevlevi. I left my cubbyhole and ran up the stairs to the roof so I could see the whole courtyard as the dervishes danced. The women had all gone up there and stood at the parapet, looking down at what was going on below.

I found Auntie standing by herself, apart from the others. I went and stood at her side, watching with great attention and amazement what was going on below us in the courtyard. One of the dervishes got up from his place and stood before the shaykh of the Mevlevi. The dervish bowed to the shaykh with hands across the chest, displaying the utmost respect. The shaykh responded with a slight inclining of the head. They exchanged not a single word.

I asked Auntie the meaning of it all.

"That dervish there came — as is the custom — to ask the shaykh's permission to start the dancing."

The venerable shaykh stood up. He proceeded to recite in a subdued tone a prayer in Persian of which we understood nothing at all. The dervishes interrupted him every now and then, shouting with one voice, "Him . . . m . . . m . . . m." The shout had an echo that was like the roar of the sea or the crying of the wind.

When the shaykh had finished the prayer he stepped forward alone, placed his right hand on his chest and raised the fringe of his cloak with his left. Then he spun round the pool with regular steps, bowing his head in humility and submission. After this he went back to his place and intoned another prayer in Persian. Again the dervishes interrupted him with shouts of "Him . . . m . . . m."

The shaykh returned and sat in his place. The dervishes then all

11

started up in a single movement. They turned, spinning, several times around the pool as the shaykh had done. They then took off their black cloaks. Their bodies seemed sleek and slender in their sweeping white smocks, bound very tightly round their waists. They started their dance with slow spins, their hands crossed over their chests, their heads inclined forward slightly, their eyes cast down with expressions of supplication and self-abasement. Next they placed their hands down around their waists and their movements steadily became faster. They placed their right hands on their chests and raised their left hands over their heads. The pace of their whirling quickened and their smocks spread out into wide circles from the center of which rose the trunks of their bodies, firm, erect, and unbending. Their hands were raised in entreaty to the heavens, as if that was the object of their prayer. Their heads inclined a little to the right, their eyes gazing vacantly into space, a sign of ecstasy, the stage of release and the reverence of mankind toward his holy self. All this was expressed in their dance with a clarity that defies words.

"I never realized that the Mevlevi dances were so beautiful and so accomplished," I told Auntie. "It's the first time in my life that I've ever seen them. Who was it, I wonder, who devised this dance?"

"Haven't you heard of Jalal al-Din al-Rumi? He was the greatest of the Persian Sufi poets, the finest poet of divine love. He it was who set up the ritual of the Mevlevi and inaugurated this religious dance."

"What a great artist he was," I said. "Goodness, look at this young dervish with the slim waist and pale face. How rapid his whirling is. How refined his movements are."

"But the most amazing one," replied Auntie, "is that short, middle-aged, plump dervish with the long gray beard. He is just as rapid and refined as his slim young colleague."

I stood astounded at this fabulous spectacle which my mind had never for a day been able to imagine: ten dervishes dancing round the pool in the light of the moon, among the trees and flowers, to the melodies of flute and lute. Looking at the rapid spinning of these dervishes, it seemed to me as if I was seeing everything around me turn and turn, the dervishes, the trees, people — all became the spinning of our eternal existence. If I had not gripped the railing I'm sure I would have fallen to the ground.

The melody of the flute became quieter and quieter and then fell silent. The dervishes stopped dancing. Noiselessly they withdrew from the center of the courtyard, put on their black cloaks, their exhaustion apparent. The women returned to their reception room. Auntie sat down in her place, silent and self-absorbed. I went back to the window of my cubbyhole halfway up the stairs and saw Abu'l 'Izz facing the reception hall. He opened the hall door wide and inside could be seen a huge table on which all kinds of Damascus sweetmeats were arrayed. In the middle of the table was a pyramid of sweet balls decorated with pistachio nuts and cream. People poured into the hall at Abu'l 'Izz's invitation and started to gorge themselves ravenously. My uncle signaled to Father to follow him, which he did. They both went upstairs and I was surprised when they came into my cubbyhole. My uncle closed the door behind him. His face looked grim. Suddenly he shouted in Father's face, pointing to himself, "Am I not your elder brother? Am I not the eldest son of the deceased?"

Father nodded in agreement, at the same time amazed at the question.

"How can this fine party marking forty days after our father's death," my uncle went on, "have been set up without my being consulted? Have I simply been invited along with the other guests as if I am a stranger to you and your sister? What made you do what you have done today?" he said in a voice that rose in intensity. "Have you taken leave of your senses, Mahmud? I never thought you were quite so stupid. You, the only educated one among us, with your degree in law. Allah help us! I was embarrassed at meeting people. What is all this I've seen today? Pernicious customs, worn-out and long-forgotten traditions, a drum, a lute, singing, dancing, shaykhs, the Mevlevi, food, drink? And all this set up on the occasion of sadness."

He spoke without giving Father the chance to get a word in. Father stood there dumbfounded, listening in the greatest confusion as my uncle went on without a pause.

"Tell me, in the name of Allah, who are we to set up such a huge party to mark the fortieth day after our father's death? Was our father, with all due respect, 'Izzat Pasha al-'Abid, or As'ad Pasha al-'Azm? Everybody knows that our father was a small merchant who died bankrupt after being paralyzed for ten years. People must be falling about laughing at us. By Allah, I shall not contribute a penny of my own money to the expenses of this party. You and your sister can bear the cost. Do you think you two are in charge with your silly ideas?"

He seemed to have reached his conclusion. He stopped talking and got out a packet of cigarettes from his pocket; he selected one, lit it, and put it in the corner of his mouth. He then took out a handkerchief and mopped the sweat from his face, sitting on a chair quite close to me. Father now found the chance to say something.

"Steady on, steady on," he said in an unusually high tone. "Heavens above, I'm in the same position as yourself. I too was invited to this party just like any other guest. Allah, I thought you were the one who had set it all up. I was surprised, and I was cross with you for not having consulted me."

My uncle stood up suddenly, jabbed his finger at Father and said in amazement, "So you too had no idea about this ridiculous festivity? Is that really so? Then all this has been arranged by our virtuous sister, Sabriya! What a cheek! The girl's gone mad. Why has she done this? It's enough to drive you out of your wits."

"At the end of the afternoon," said Father, "I received a note from Sabriya via somebody who works for the oil-seller, inviting me and my family to come round this evening and stay up to hear recitations from the Qur'an to mark the fortieth day after the death of our father."

"She sent me a note just like that too," said my uncle.

"To tell you the truth," resumed Father, "I'd forgotten that today was the fortieth day after his death. When I received the note I thought it would be simply a matter of a couple of shaykhs reciting the Qur'an in his memory, then Sabriya would offer us a bit of food and we would have dinner with the shaykhs. We would then pay them their wage and each of us would make his way home. I'm totally taken aback by this enormous party."

"We had to do something, but how could Sabriya do it all by herself?"

"Thank Allah for Abu'l 'Izz," replied Father. "Did you not see him taking everything on his shoulders? But, I wonder, how could Abu'l 'Izz agree to do it all without consulting us?"

"Abu'l 'Izz! Huh, Abu'l 'Izz!" he laughed scornfully. "You want him to ask our consent? Why? So we can say no? He jumps at such an opportunity. Do you remember the day our mother died? I gave him a large sum of money and asked him to do the necessary, as he knows more than any of us about these matters. And what did he do? After it was all over, in addition to the large sum he took from me, he presented me with a list of charges that went on forever. I didn't think he'd go so far. I was taken in by his appearance of piety. But in dealing with him his true nature becomes clear and the truth comes out. Allah knows how much Sabriya has paid him and how much he will take for himself. And all this is going to come out of your pocket and mine. You know that ten gold Ottoman coins are today not enough for the Mevlevi alone? I always suspected that Sabriya had some money tucked away. Perhaps she took some from our mother or our father without our knowing anything about it. Come to think of it, I'm sure. Didn't you notice how our parents always favored our sister over us two?"

"My dear brother, don't be so suspicious," Father sighed. "Where can Sabriya have got such money? You know best about our parents' affairs, Raghib. Our mother sold all her jewelry before she died and spent what she got for it on medical expenses. And you also know she got nothing from that rich father of hers. He kept all his money for his sons. All he did was give some jewelry to our mother and her sister. And our father died bankrupt. Fortunately he had the bright idea, just as his affairs were collapsing, to transfer the house, the warehouse, and the furniture to our mother's name. Otherwise the creditors would have had the whole lot. And when he became paralyzed, the rent from the warehouse went to Sabriya. She used to collect it each month and spend it on herself and Father. It wasn't much, certainly not enough to save. And, heavens above, I really don't know how she managed things. I can't remember her asking you or me for a single piaster. We mustn't forget that caring for a paralyzed man for ten whole years is terribly hard work. Nonetheless, she never thought for a moment of getting help from a servant. Sabriya was of heroic stature. We must never forget how tired she got and how she did more for our father than we did."

"I know that, old chap. But you're straying from the point as usual. Just tell me, where did she get the money for such a party when she was in the financial state she was in?"

"I'm baffled," said Father, twisting his lip. "She must have borrowed it."

"Allah Almighty!" said my uncle. "She borrowed to set up this ridiculous business? And who's going to pay that money back? Her share of the proceeds of the house may not cover the expenses of the evening. I'm going to find out and call her to account and put a stop to her provocations. I'm going to make her sorry for what she has done."

Father looked out of the window. "Some people have finished eating and are starting to leave," he said. "We ought to go down and stand at the door to receive condolences."

"I'm not going down," my uncle objected. "Let them know that I'm not at all pleased with this nonsense. I don't know why Sabriya has invited my friends, for I was always a bit embarrassed with the neighbors."

"Let's at least be charitable this evening. Let's not cause a scandal."

"I refuse to go down. Go by yourself."

"We are all creatures of Allah, to whom we ultimately return," answered Father patiently. "Whatever has happened has happened, Raghib. What's the point of letting people know about our problems and private affairs? In only an hour's time people will be on their way. We can then sort out our affairs as we like. We've got all night." He took his brother's hand and dragged him along. My uncle paused but went with him as if persuaded.

They left my cubbyhole without having taken any notice of me or addressing a single word to me from the time they came in to the time they left. It was as if I was not there or was part of the furniture.

I turned my back to the window, amazed at what I had heard. I was surprised at what Auntie had done and felt my uncle was right to blame her, for there was no justification for laying on such a party.

What had compelled her to do what she had done, I wondered. There must be some reason behind it all. What was that reason? Why was it that my uncle was always critical of his sister, whereas Father tried to mitigate her offenses and take her side? He sometimes recognized her merits.

I felt as if I was suffocating. I wanted to run away from the house before the guests had all left, but at the same time I was extremely curious to know what was going to happen between my uncle and his brother. I really disliked rows in the family.

The door suddenly opened and Mother appeared.

"Heavens above," she said angrily and critically. "Here you are, hidden

16

away, while I've been looking for you everywhere. The grownups are handing coffee out and lighting cigarettes for the guests and all you're doing is sitting here comfortably."

I made no reply and said nothing about what had passed between Father and my uncle. She noticed my confusion.

"What's the matter with you, girl?" she said. "Get up, get a move on. Go and take the sweets from Abu'l 'Izz. He's waiting for you at the bottom of the stairs."

I did as I was told and raced down the stairs. When Abu'l 'Izz saw me, he came up a few steps and handed me two large plates full of twisted *kunafa*, and I carried them to the reception room, where the female guests were sitting. Mother took them and put them on the table in the middle of the hall. I got ready to get some more plates of *'awwamat* and baklava and other sweetmeats.

Mother invited the guests to eat. They came round the table and I noticed that they would eat only if Auntie ate first. This was the custom.

Auntie's face was pale. Her mind seemed to be wandering. She was sad and exhausted. In spite of all this she took a piece of *kunafa* out of consideration for her guests and to avoid drawing attention to herself. She went off quietly and nibbled at it slowly, forcing herself to swallow it. The guests, meanwhile, wolfed things down at amazing speed, until they had finished everything. When the eating was over, they got up to say goodbye to Auntie and to offer her their condolences. Each chose some words that they thought appropriate and different from what the person before them had said.

"May you and your brothers live song," said one. "We thank Allah that he died in honor."

"We thank Allah that he died while his children were still living," said another. "He who leaves children never dies."

"If Allah wills," said a third, "this will be the last time you will be mourning. From now on when we come to eat it will be to celebrate."

Another whispered into her ear, "This is the way of the world. From distress comes only illness and pain. I ask myself, what is the fruit of grief?"

She answered each of them with a fitting remark.

The guests all left, men and women. Father and my uncle both came to the upstairs reception room, where I was sitting with Auntie. As they came in, I noticed for the first time the enormous difference between the two men.

Anybody who did not know them would never have guessed that they were brothers. They were poles apart in stature and temperament. Father was pale in complexion, tall and slim, measured in his movements. He spoke seldom, and then only quietly. His eyes showed his modesty and kindness. His brother, on the other hand, was swarthy, stout, short-necked, and broad-shouldered. His voice was loud and his look was brazen.

As soon as my uncle sat down, he gave Auntie a harsh, passionate, angry look. Auntie sat silently, totally unfussed. She was relaxed, her elbows on the side of the chair, one leg over the other, not at all agitated. Indeed, she was defiant, prepared for any assault. Her long black dress, her black head-covering that fell to her shoulders, her pale face — all gave her an awesome dignity.

For a short while there was an artificial silence, during which each was examining the movements of the others. Then my uncle spoke in strangled tones, full of contempt and violence.

"What's all this you've been up to today, my lady Sabriya?"

"What have I done?" she replied calmly and quietly.

"Are you pretending not to know? What's the meaning of this ridiculous party which you have arranged this evening without consulting us at all? As if you are the only child of the deceased and we men are of no account whatsoever?"

She replied coldly, without moving a muscle, "I remained his only daughter all the time he was ill. Ten whole years, when I hardly ever saw you. It was as if you were guests, strangers. I was left looking after everything by myself, as if he had no other children but me. I have every right to continue to be his only daughter after his death."

"There's not much point getting into a futile argument with you," he said aggressively. "Where did you get the money for this party?"

"Have no fear. I'm not going to charge anything to you."

My uncle stood up. He tried to crush her with his look and shouted in her face, "Are you mocking us? Answer my question, girl, in one word. I don't want any nonsense. Where did you get the money from?"

Without a trace of anxiety on her face, she said calmly, "You don't scare me with your shouting. Calm down, take a seat and I will tell you where the money's come from."

He sat down as she asked him to. It seemed as if, by her composure and quiet words, she was taking control of the situation. She looked at each of them in turn, staring at them whenever they moved. She then gave a smile of triumph. She said, slowly emphasizing each word, "I sold the carpet."

Everybody stared at her and shouted at once.

"You sold the carpet?"

"Yes, I sold the carpet. I sold it to some foreigner. He's now left and gone back to his own country."

She turned to Mother and my uncle's wife.

"The day my father died," she said, "I was looking at you both. In the middle of mourning you were measuring the carpet with your eyes wide open. You both wanted it for your houses. I've saved you the trouble of having a row about it."

My uncle's wife tried to control her emotions as much as possible.

"I'm not concerned about whether I have the carpet in my home or anywhere else," she said with her foreign inflection. "But to sell it is a great crime because it's a rare antique. It's hard to say how much it's worth."

Auntie silenced her with a couple of remarks uttered in a dramatic and contemptuous way: "What's it got to do with you? Did the carpet belong to your father, Christo?" She used this expression because my uncle's wife was supposed to be of Greek origin.

After that my uncle's wife said not another word.

Auntie carried on.

"You all know that the carpet belonged to Mother. It had been given to her by her father as a wedding present. She told you all many times, 'This carpet is for Sabriya. I'm going to give it to her on the day she gets married.'"

Mother broke in.

"But you never got married," she said, "so you can't take the carpet as a wedding present."

Emotion showed on Auntie's face. Her voice shook as she replied, "In that case, dear lady, let us consider that today is my wedding day. All my life I've wanted to do something just for myself. To invite people just once, to host a party or banquet, and to upset those who have upset me —" and here she looked directly at my uncle and his wife — "and today I've done that, and as for you, you can do what you like . . ."

Father kept quiet, his hand on his cheek. He listened to all that was being said but did not add a single word. It was as if he was completely uninvolved. But my uncle's face became so tense that it turned blue.

"Shut up," he said aggressively. "What does all this nonsense mean? I know how to get even with you. We'll sell the house tomorrow and take the price of the carpet from your share."

Auntie stood up and pointed her finger at him, so close that it almost poked his eye out.

"You get even with me, you criminal?" she said. "It's me who's going to get even with you. You were the death of me as I was growing up. And now you want to get even with the dead!"

My uncle showed his big yellow teeth, as if he was laughing, and said, "What? What is this lunatic going on about?"

Auntie counted on her fingers.

"You denied me my rights to live. You were the death of me on two occasions. First, when you spread all sorts of lies about me to Father and persuaded him to take me out of college a year before I should have taken my certificate. You did this because you were jealous of me. I was doing well in my studies and you were a good for nothing."

Her voice rose above his. The words poured out of her mouth as if she had been rehearsing them so many times she knew them by heart.

"You were a failure," she shouted. "I was the successful one. And the second time you were the death of me was when you prevented me from marrying the man I loved. Do you think I don't know that it was you who arranged for somebody to kill him? I was in agony over him. I swore never to marry anybody else. I have lived the life of an old maid in the midst of my sorrows. And after all this you want to get even with me!"

There was shock at the revelation of this great family secret, the secret of an awful crime my uncle had committed.

Father got up to mitigate the effect of what had been said in front of his daughter, his wife, and his brother's wife. He came between my uncle and Auntie and guided her gently to her seat, saying, "Calm down, Sabriya. What on earth are you saying? Have you lost your wits tonight?"

"You can hold your tongue," she chided him. "You might as well not have existed. If you had stood up for me you might have saved me. You think only of yourself. You don't care. I never once got your help when I asked for it. I know you know I'm right, but what's the use of you being convinced so long as it causes you any embarrassment? If you saw somebody on fire you wouldn't try to put the fire out. Education never did you any good. If I had been able to complete my studies as you were able to, I'd have been a thousand times better than you and that braggart of a brother of yours. And when I need you, you only want to shut me up in a small room with one of the neighbors, as that fine lady put it," she said, pointing at my uncle's wife. "Most of my contemporaries have become school principals or senior officials. I've passed my life servicing a paralyzed invalid."

Father swallowed the rebuke without comment. But my uncle appeared to me in his true light, submissive before the strong but a braggart before the weak. After Auntie's outburst at him, he became very quiet. When she turned her wrath on Father he found it a suitable opportunity to withdraw. I saw him make a sign to his wife to follow. They left the room and quietly went downstairs. I heard the sound of a door being slammed. After a moment of silence, Auntie said, "It's time for you to go home as well."

"Allah," said Mother, "we'd like to spend the night here with you, but . . ."

"You go," I interrupted, "and I'll stay here with Auntie."

"No, in the name of Allah, no," Auntie quickly replied. "Nobody's going to stay the night with me here. You must go with your parents. I want to be by myself. I don't want anybody at all with me."

"You mustn't tire yourself out, Auntie," I said. "I'm not going to go even if you try to drive me away. I'll be absolutely no trouble to you. I'll go straight to my room."

There was this room I used to have in Grandfather's house. Auntie had prepared a desk and a comfortable bed for me. I would escape to this room at exam times and study all by myself, and get away from Mother's nonstop chatter.

I really did want to have a talk with Auntie after my parents had left. I wanted to give her my sympathy and to offer her comfort after this nightmarish evening. As soon as I started to speak to her, she put her finger to her mouth, signaling me to be quiet. She gave me a look to remind me of my promise not to be any trouble to her. I did as she wanted. There was no alternative but to submit after I looked at her face, which had turned from the color of ivory to a grayish blue. Her looks wandered all over the place. It seemed to me as I saw her trembling hands that her nerves were at breaking point. She was like a hand grenade with the safety pin removed. She would explode if she was touched. She frightened me and I preferred to play safe. I kept my mouth shut.

There was a moment of silence, and then she drily commanded, "Go and sleep in your room. We'll leave everything as it is until the morning." She then added, shaking her head, "Tomorrow is another day."

It was uttered in a menacing, drawn-out way. In spite of a sense of foreboding about the words, I felt reassured.

What I was afraid of was that she would ask me to clean the house up. It was in a terrible mess, with dirty things all over the place. There were chairs everywhere. Remains of food after Abu'l 'Izz had taken all he could. Cigarette ends. All this was scattered throughout the reception area and also on the upper floor — indeed, in virtually every room of the house. Of course, I would have worked alongside her, but it would have taken till morning, for it was already quarter past midnight. I went up at once to my room, near the one we were in. Meanwhile, Auntie went up to a room that gave on to the roof which they used to call the Eyrie. I knew that Auntie loved this room more than any other place in the house. She put her own cupboard there, her desk and her trunk that always remained locked. She used to say whenever I called on her, "I do love to sleep in this Eyrie. There's nowhere better. It's warm in the winter and on a clear day the sun never leaves it from morning to night. And it's cool in the summer. When I open the windows a playful breeze brings in the scent of roses and jasmine, of citron and *zilif*. There's no lovelier place in the morning. When you are in bed, you can look out on the whole of Damascus, its huge domes, its slender minarets, its roofs that join up with each other, the sky, clear blue or studded with clouds, or a flight of pigeons released by breeders in the area. But what's the use when I can't be far from your grandfather for a single moment. I can't move him from the ground floor up to this Eyrie, far from the kitchen and the bathroom. As you know, he never wearies of calling out, 'Sabriya, Sabriya!' It was preordained that I be incarcerated in this house. I have to put up with the cold and the damp in the winter and the humidity in the summer, all for his sake. If only he was aware of what I have done for him."

Poor dear Auntie! She was denied even this simple wish.

My mind and body were utterly worn out. The awful events of the evening, with their painful surprises, had marked me for life.

I had become aware of things that had taken place in the family and did not feel at all comfortable about them. I had come up against the male's self-centeredness and cruelty towards even his close relations. I lacked the capacity to assess all I had seen and heard, to weigh it up and work out the truth of the matter for myself.

As soon as my head hit the pillow I fell into a deep sleep. Only a person of my tender years could be so blessed after that traumatic evening.

I woke up to the persistent and uninterrupted ringing of the doorbell. I was alarmed. I shook my head and rubbed my eyes to get rid of the effects of sleep. It seemed that I had overslept. The sun was already up and had flooded the room. I rose from the bed. My attention was attracted by a thick book in blue binding that had been placed by my pillow. I noticed on the cover a piece of paper on which was written in large, clear letters: "To my niece, Salma."

Many years have passed since that night and I still wonder what secret impulse inspired me to conceal the book under the bedclothes, even though I was in a great hurry. A stirring in my subconscious must have made me sense that something had happened.

Had Auntie fled from the house and left me the book?

The bell went on ringing. Somebody was also knocking loudly at the front door. I put on a dressing gown and raced downstairs. Was Auntie not up yet? Had she left the house? Had the din of the bell not reached the Eyrie, where she was sleeping?

Before I reached the ground floor I turned to the courtyard outside and my eye fell on her. I uttered a terrible scream of terror at what I saw.

She had hanged herself.

I saw her tall body, hanging from the lemon tree, in her black dress and black shawl. Her head was leaning slightly forward, her face, framed in a black surround, was pale and white.

I was out of breath and I do not know how I reached the front door or how I opened it.

I was met by the faces of my uncle and Father. Behind them was a stranger whom I learned later was the house agent. They had come to look at the house.

I cried out at my uncle, so out of breath that my heart almost stopped, "Come in. You can be happy now. Your sister has hanged herself."

I threw myself on to Father's chest and lost consciousness.

I do not know how long I was unconscious. When I finally came round, I was stretched out on a sofa in the *liwan*. Father was leaning over me, wringing trembling hands. He sprinkled cold water on my face. His face was paler than before. My uncle was sitting on a chair in front of me, leaning his head on his hand, concealing part of his face that had gone blue. The third person, the agent, had hidden himself, avoiding matters that did not concern him.

"When did you see her?" Father asked in a gentle, trembling voice.

I made no reply. He repeated the question.

"When? Was it when you came downstairs from your room to open the door?"

I nodded and said nothing.

"Did she say anything after we left?" he asked.

I raised my eyebrows, meaning no.

Father realized that I was unable to say anything.

"Try and pluck up some courage and help us," he said. "Get up and get dressed as quickly as you can. Then go home before the police get here. It's best that we say you weren't here so you don't have to be questioned by the police. Things are not easy for you. You're not strong enough to cope. And you may get us into trouble."

I looked at him blankly, saying nothing and not moving. I was overwhelmed with nervous anxiety. I felt like a piece of damp old cloth tossed away on to the sofa.

Father took my shoulders and pulled me into a sitting position. He then shook me with some force in order to restore me fully to consciousness.

24

"Make haste and get up," he said loudly. "We don't have a lot of time. Get your clothes on and go home. Tell your mother what has happened and ask her to come here at once."

I did as I was told, as if I was a clockwork toy without any will of my own. I got up and shuffled along, leaning on the chairs that were scattered about the room. I made my way to the stairs and started to go up them. It was very hard. I thought the staircase would never end. My knees almost snapped. I had to support myself by holding on to the balustrade so as not to fall. I got to my room and dressed myself as if I were an automaton. In spite of my state, I took the blue book from under the bedclothes and hid it in my bag.

When I came downstairs again, I did my best not to look at her. But it was impossible. I could not prevent myself; it was one last glance of farewell. She was still hanging from the lemon tree, like a black flag at half-mast, protesting loudly at oppression and injustice. Her eyes were closed and her face seemed to me to hold an angelic innocence and the simplicity of a sleeping infant.

It was my fate to see death for the first time in my life in the grimmest and most horrific of circumstances.

I then noticed that the birdcages — of the goldfinches, the canary, and the blackbird — had been opened. My aunt had released them all from captivity before her own tormented soul found release from its long bondage.

I chanced to turn round and saw my uncle walking among the chairs in the courtyard. He was beating his own forehead with one hand and dabbing his tears with a handkerchief with the other. He went up to the body of my hanged aunt, embraced the feet that were swinging in the wind, buried his face in them and sobbed aloud.

Was my uncle now aware of the consequences of his treatment of his sister? Was he filled with remorse now that such remorse was useless? Or did the mist in his mind lift? Did he now realize all at once what was right and what was wrong — but after it was too late?

It was an unusual sight, totally unexpected. I felt a certain sense of satisfaction when I saw him in anguish. Father, gentler-hearted, warmer-spirited, was more restrained.

I went towards the front door without saying a word to them. Father followed me.

"Just a moment," he said. "Nobody must see you leaving the house." He took out some coins from his pocket and gave them to me, saying, "Take a taxi home."

He opened the door, looked to the right and then to the left, surveying the whole quarter, and said, "Off you go. Be quick. Don't look at anybody. Make sure you don't talk to anyone about what has happened — except your mother."

I set off and he gently closed the door behind me.

I decided not to take a taxi. I preferred to walk, however long it might take. I wanted to be alone for a little while. I pulled myself together, got my equilibrium back and mumbled to myself, "Poor, poor, dear Auntie."

Was this the vengeance she had spoken to me about? You did not get even with anybody. You were in despair and you went under. You could not stand it any longer.

How frightful to think of ending your miserable life by committing suicide without having had a moment's happiness.

Cold tears welled up in my eyes. I wiped them away with my handkerchief and hurried on unconsciously until I was standing before the front door. I do not know how I got there, how I had gone from Suq Saruja to the middle of Salihiya, where our house was, in one of the quarters branching off the Salihiya road. I was like one of those animals that return to places driven simply by instinct.

I put my hand up to the doorbell and pressed it. I hardly moved. Mother opened the door.

"Gracious me!" she cried. "What is the matter?"

I stood before her, rooted to the ground.

She fell silent as she looked at my pale, drained face and bloodshot eyes. I also looked at her fiercely, without saying a word.

"In heaven's name," she shouted, "what's happened to you?"

She pulled me in by the hand. I pushed her away and went in, loudly saying in a tone that was unintentionally melodramatic, "You're all criminals . . . All of you are criminals."

She gasped in amazement.

"Criminals?" she said. "In Allah's name, what's happened to your mind? Have you gone mad? Allah! Allah!"

I went up to her and spoke into her face, loudly emphasizing every word, "Sabriya hanged herself, because you lot all ganged up against her. You can relax now and be happy."

Mother looked hard at me. She then clasped her breast and cried out, "She hanged herself? Allah help us in this bad luck that's befallen us."

"There, you see," I said. "You aren't thinking of the person who's hanged herself. You're thinking of the bad luck that's befallen you, of the scandal it will cause as it goes its way from mouth to mouth."

She did not show any interest in what I was saying and, still in a state of shock, started to shower me with questions.

"When did she hang herself? Have you been frightened? Where did she hang herself?"

"I know nothing about it," I screamed. "I was woken up by the front doorbell. When I went down to open the door for Father and my uncle, I saw her hanging from the lemon tree. She preferred to die rather than live, after what she went through at your hands yesterday. Don't ask me anything about it. Let me go to my room and shut the door. Take care you don't tell anyone that I was there. Father wants you to go there now. At once."

She listened to me and gazed at my face. I do not know how I looked. She let me go to my room and troubled me no further with questions and comments, perhaps out of concern for me being ill or crazy, or perhaps because she was frightened of me after she had seen what she had seen.

I threw myself on to my bed, still in my clothes and shoes. I closed my eyes. I saw her there right in front of me, tall, suspended from the lemon tree in her black clothes, her head leaning forward on her breast. How would I ever be able to get rid of this image printed indelibly on my mind? Never had I felt such love for Auntie as I felt now. Never had I felt such loathing for my family as I felt now. I saw them as a band of conspirators, plotting against one defenseless female. My uncle, his wife, and then my mother. As for Father, I was vexed by his spinelessness, but I was aware of his basic decency and nobility of spirit. He was weak-willed and was dominated by his wife and his brother. Did Auntie not say of him only yesterday, "I never once got your help when I asked for it." She also said to my uncle, "You were the death of me on two occasions, the day you prevented me from continuing my studies and the day you prevented me from marrying the man I loved. Do you think I don't know that it was you who arranged for somebody to kill him?"

Why had she not asked for Father's help? How was my uncle the cause of the death of the one she loved? There were some fearful secrets in our family I knew nothing about. This is what the little blue book Auntie left behind would make clear.

I reached out to get the book from my bag. I do not know why I withdrew my hand as if I had been stung, or as if I was frightened or in awe of it. Certainly I was apprehensive about reading in it things that would make me sadder or angrier. So I put off reading it until another time.

Or perhaps I felt I was unable to take in what I read now, while I was in such a distressed emotional state. I took my hand away and stretched out on my bed.

A measure of peace began to take over. I could hear the sound of Mother's footsteps as she came to the door of my room, hovered outside for a moment, and then went away again. She was, of course, listening out for me, fearful of some further mishap befalling me after the terrible shock that made me lose my self-control.

Oh dear! I was embarrassed by their excessive concern. I sometimes felt stifled by it. It was quite suffocating. Why did they not just leave me alone? It is very difficult being an only child, one born after a long marriage. I came on the scene after a period of childlessness that had lasted over five years. My arrival was a miracle, for Mother was over forty years old and had never had a child before. My mother's pregnancy and confinement were occasions for such eagerness and excitement. And my father was no less delighted. They saw the whole world, with its ups and downs, through me. They were interested in nothing but me. Their whole existence revolved around me. They watched over my eating and drinking, my hours of waking and my four hours of sleep, my moments of sadness, my moments of joy. I had now reached the age of fifteen, but in their view I was still a toddler needing help and supervision. It was intolerable. When would I be free of this burden that weighed down on my chest, this burden of their solicitude? It was sometimes most irritating. At other times I was sorry for them and went along with them as much as I could. Here I was now, pitying my mother. I had been cruel to her almost as if it had been she who had hanged Auntie.

I heard her tapping on the door. I got up at once and opened it for her. She was wearing a housecoat and had a cup of milk in her hand. She came over to me, looked at me with anxious searching eyes, and said, "Oh dear! Oh dear! How can I go out and leave you all by yourself?"

"It's all right," I said. "You'll find me as you left me."

She gave me the glass of milk and said, "Drink this. I won't go until you have."

Actually I needed the milk desperately. My mouth was very dry because of the many tears I had shed and I could move my tongue around only with difficulty. My whole body was also damp with sweat.

She handed me the cup and I took it without saying anything. I sipped at it as if it was some vile medicine.

"You'll become ill if you stay like this. All things are in the hands of Allah and we must act in accordance with His wisdom. What has happened was decreed for your aunt from the day she was born. Ask Allah above to pardon her for the sin she has committed. He is forgiving and merciful."

I looked hard at her, concentrating my hostile gaze on her eyes.

"Allah forgive her?" I cried. "Wasn't it He who decreed the end for her from the day she was born? What is the crime she has committed for which she has to be forgiven then?"

"Don't be blasphemous," she said. "Ask Allah above for His forgiveness. Good things come from Allah and evil comes from within yourself."

I gnashed my teeth in anger. "What's the use of arguing with you?" I shouted.

"I'm going out now," she said. "I don't know how we're going to cope with all this. Your poor father. He has a gentle heart and his nerves are frail. I pray to Allah to keep him from falling sick. We must both — you and I — do what we can to lighten his burden."

I remained silent and she left the house.

Ah me! How I envy my Mother for this simple faith of hers. She attributed everything to Fate and to what was already ordained in heaven. She then rejoiced in comfort, humility, and content. I went back to bed, quite unable to do anything at all. I could not even change my clothes or wash my face. I started to feel furious and also scared. I would see this woman hanging in front of me wherever I turned. The utter silence irked me, a silence full of whispers and fantasies, a silence that made the senses alert to any movement or noise.

Death! How awful it is! And how frightful it is to contemplate. But it is the inescapable fate of us all. I do not know how we can ever remove it from our minds, how we pretend to forget about it. Even if we reach a great age, or suffer from the most awful diseases, we put our trust in miracles or fantasies that might enable us to elude it as far as possible. How can people strive to commit suicide when they are at the peak of their vitality and in the best of health?

Is suicide an act of courage or cowardice?

I have no doubt that it is an act of cowardice and courage at the same time. This is unreservedly the case with Sabriya. She was cowardly when she confronted an ugly face she was unable to change, after finding herself a worn-out, middle-aged woman. She was not qualified for any work and had no certificate. It had been decided for her that she live dependent on her brothers, who were now complaining about her. She preferred death to this humiliating life of drudgery. She was indeed courageous when she showed herself capable of carrying out this act of suicide. Without doubt she had planned it from the time she heard that her brothers were going to sell the house and rent a room for her in the humble house of some neighbor.

Did she not tell me herself that she would not leave that house except as a corpse? And she did indeed leave that house as a corpse. She had from that moment reached a stage of such despair that she sentenced herself to death, and then lived with the specter of her own death for a whole month. What staunch courage that was. She never complained of her lot to anybody. Whenever I analyzed her complex personality my regard for her increased, and also my sympathy for her anguish. What was her sin when circumstances were stacked against her? She killed herself when all roads were blocked in her face. Her suicide was one great protest against all the oppression that fenced her in.

But what really puzzled me was the motive for laying on that extraordinary party to mark forty days after the death of her father. What did this mean in the context of her intelligence and understanding?

Was it in order to sell the valuable carpet and so annoy her brothers? This did not make sense. She could have contributed the value of it to the poor, or given it to one of the mosques. She could have arranged a party for herself rather than one for her father. In fact, she held her own memorial service while she was still living, because she was quite sure her brothers would not give her a suitable memorial. Did she not say to Mother that fateful evening, "Dear lady, let us consider that today is my wedding day."

Perhaps she intended it to be the night of her death and had planned to kill herself. Or is it that people who commit suicide have some flukish flaw in their minds? What is the relevance of a memorial for some poor wretch who has said no to life, has preferred death, and who has indeed striven for death?

These questions and ideas continued to haunt me, while the swinging corpse was there before me, whether my eyes were open or shut. The hours passed slowly, very slowly. I was depressed, my heart was beating rapidly, my body was worn out. I felt as if I was being strangled. I was possessed by fear and apprehension. I was afraid I was going to die. I got up from my bed, left my room, and went to the small landing in the middle of the house. Mother had turned this landing into a dining room. We ate there only on special occasions, such as when we had dinner parties. On the landing was a big table, always covered with a yellow embroidered cloth. I got fed up with looking at it as I passed it so often. Round the table were chairs, some placed right next to each other. There was not much space on the landing between the chairs and the walls. I would go round this confined area as if I was some caged beast.

Our house was so depressing. Never until this day did I feel quite how depressing it was. It was one of those houses packed tightly together in the narrow quarters where often it was hard to breathe. We occupied the third floor. Many times both Father and I tried to change the arrangement or the function of the rooms, but we always met with resistance from Mother and we never succeeded in persuading her.

Mother was one of those people who live only for others, to satisfy them or to serve them. She did not live to satisfy herself or to provide comfort for herself. It pains me to think that most of the women of our country are like this. Mother had turned the best room of the house into a reception room and had put the best furniture in it. She would receive our guests there once a month: on the fifteenth of the

31

month or whenever we had unexpected guests, and that was not often. Father and I liked to sit there, especially in the winter, because that room, unlike any other room in the house, was warmed by the sun's rays. We liked to go there in the summer too, for a moist breeze would play in it when we opened the broad windows overlooking an open space at the end of the street that was planted with green grass and oleander bushes with red flowers. But Mother would get very upset, fearing that the furniture would be damaged by our sitting there, or that the white curtains would get dirty from Father's chain-smoking. In the end Mother locked the door and hid the key from us.

Of the other rooms a small one was allocated to me, and my parents slept in one slightly bigger. Then there was a room next to the kitchen which Mother turned into a combined reception and dining area, after she had opened up a small window that looked on to the front door. We used to squeeze in and spend most of the time there. These rooms all resembled prison cells packed with austere, antique furniture. As a result of all this, Father did not spend much time in the house, apart from meals and sleeping there. At other times he would go off to the coffee-house and play board games with his friends and not get home till midnight.

The only two things Mother was unable to keep Father away from were smoking and the coffee-house.

Can you wonder that he sought solace in these two things in order to put up with her?

I often wondered how my parents had married, for they had absolutely nothing in common. Father was as modest and placid as Mother was quarrelsome and domineering. She was ten years older than Father and was fat and far from beautiful.

On the other hand, Father kept his youthful elegance. His one defect was his indifference to all that was going on around him. I wondered how otherwise he was able to live with Mother, who used to busy herself with everything and loved to impose herself on all that was around her. What made Mother's behavior acceptable was her enormous tenderness and her exemplary self-sacrifice for the sake of her small family, and consequently her ability to take all the responsibility on her shoulders alone.

Whenever one of us was ill she would stay up all night at our bedside until we were better. She took on all the chores of the house without a murmur of complaint and put us before herself in everything. She readily bought luxuries for us but she would never get anything but essentials for herself.

I will never forget the row that flared up between my parents about my father spending all his evenings out of the house. I left them arguing and went off to spend the night at Grandfather's house, where I concentrated on my studies.

I felt that Auntie — may Allah have mercy on her soul — was pleased to see me and make a fuss over me. I have a lump in my throat when I say, "May Allah have mercy on her soul." The phrase will remain forever fixed to her memory. Or do you imagine we cast aside our memories of her and make only occasional references to her? But I feel as if I can see her in front of me now, her tall, slim figure, her long, wheat-colored face, her deep, dark eyes and her sharp glance, passing to and from Grandfather's bed, giving him food and drink with her own hands. She would then get him ready for bed. When she had done everything for him, she would bring dinner to the *liwan* and invite me to eat with her. I told her as we ate some stuffed *kubba*, which she cooked superbly, "Auntie, I'd like to ask you a question and I want you to answer completely frankly."

"Ask whatever you like, my love," she said. "Rest assured, I'll hide nothing from you."

"How was it Father married Mother?" I asked. "Who got her engaged to him?"

She laughed and laughed until there were tears running down her cheeks. It was as if I had told a good joke. I was amazed.

"Why has this question occurred to you now?" she asked. "I can assure you that we didn't find her for him." She then added, "You're as old as you are and you don't yet know how your parents got married or, to be more accurate, how your mother ensnared your father?"

"How on earth am I to know if you don't tell me their story?"

"I'll tell you if you promise not to let your mother know what I'm about to tell you. It'll be all the worse for me if she hears about it."

"I promise."

"Your father," she went on to say, "was twenty-three years old when he got his law diploma. He was a shy introvert. He wasn't like any of

33

the rest of us. He was quite different. After he graduated he tried to get a job like any other fresh graduate. Unfortunately he succeeded only in getting a minor post in the Department of Finance at Homs. He was led to understand that he would be transferred to Damascus after two years. He went to Homs to take up his work. I remember how my mother — peace be upon her — saw that day he set off as ill-omened. She implored Allah to preserve her son from the influence of ill-natured people.

"Your father stayed in a hotel for a few days. Then he started looking for a room to live in. His meager salary was not enough to let him live indefinitely at a hotel. He came across a small room in the house of an old widow who had one unmarried daughter.

"We heard afterwards that this old widow, who was your grandmother, was really a wily old girl. There was nobody in all Homs like her. As soon as your father came into the house, it seems that she and her daughter began preparing their trap. They found him a valuable catch, an ideal husband for the spinster daughter who had missed her bus. They took a lot of trouble to make a fuss over him and to give him every luxury. They put on an appearance of piety, pride, and ample means. The old woman led him to think that she did not really need the rent for the room, but did it only to oblige him — for she had heard something of him, his good reputation, his decency and his piety. And that was why she preferred not to insist on more than a token rent from him so he would not feel under any obligation.

"It seems that your father believed everything he was told. He found their hospitality — and remember, he was a stranger there — most welcome. It was not long before he fell into the trap! The wily old lady managed to marry him off to her daughter before you could snap your fingers and before he could come to Damascus to seek the advice of his family. She was afraid we would talk him out of the marriage. After he was married, your father discovered that his bride was more than ten years older than him and was far from being a beauty, for he saw her for the first time only on the day of the marriage. He was astonished by how big she was and at her soft hands, which were the only fair things about her.

"As for the ample means, these were limited to the modest house that the old woman and her daughter were living in and a small shop at the side of the house. The humble old widow soon turned into a cantankerous old mother-in-law. Your father had to put up with her for three long years. When she died, he decided to move back to Damascus. Your mother sold the house and shop and with the money bought the house you are now living in. Your mother refused to live in this big house, despite your father's love for it. She taught him after they got married not to disagree with her.

"This upset my mother a lot. She wanted her children to live with her, as was the custom in those days. And then your mother didn't produce any children for five years. During this time there wasn't a doctor, a midwife, or a shaykh in all Damascus whom she did not consult. But all in vain. She got depressed about it all and submitted to the fate that Allah had decreed for her. Then, shortly after this despair, she conceived you. She did not believe it at first. She thought there was something wrong with her. When the doctors confirmed that she was indeed pregnant, she was beside herself with joy. Your arrival in this world was a miracle, and my mother — may Allah bless her — named you Fruit of a Barren Womb."

"It seems to me," I said, "that Grandmother died without forgiving my mother for marrying her son."

I said this because I was beginning to feel annoyed at this prejudice against Mother, even though I accepted Auntie's story. It had the ring of truth, but what we reveal to ourselves we do not reveal to others, especially things about those we are closely connected to.

"I don't believe my mother is as awful as you have painted her," I said.

She had noticed my irritation and wanted to soothe me.

"I will not deny," she said, "that your mother has many excellent qualities. She looks after the house admirably. She's a splendid manager and is kind to her family. She has a good heart, but do you really think your father has been happy with her?"

"But he's not as miserable as you suppose."

How naïve I was. How foolish my feelings! How trifling these things seem when there is something far more important to think about. At times of great distress how the mind strays to insignificant and irrelevant matters to allow it to escape from the present and to give rest to the body that is physically drained to the point of utter exhaustion!

Did they bury her after she hanged herself? The day passed and a gloomy darkness descended on the house. It did not occur to me to put a light on. But it did occur to me to go and join them there. There was no point in my staying at home by myself.

As soon as I had made up my mind to go I heard the sound of a key turning in the lock. It was my parents. Mother's eyes were all swollen and red, her face puffed up. She had been crying a lot. Father was as haggard as a corpse, his eyes cast down. When they saw me he tried to say something but his lips trembled and his eyes were filled with tears. He caught his breath as if he was choking on something in his throat. I rushed to hug him and we wept together. Mother tried to part us.

"Isn't one disaster enough for today?" she said.

She then took me by the hand to the kitchen.

"Why are you so late?" I asked her. "I was very worried and was about to come and join you."

"Dear me," she said. "In all my life I've never had such an awful day. Had your uncle not had such excellent relations with senior officials, Allah alone knows what the complications would have been. The investigation would have included the neighbors and some of the people who call on us. We would never have been able to get her into the grave. We almost died of despair and exhaustion. Dear me, I've wept gallons for her. I feel as if my heart is split with grief. May Allah have mercy on her for the deed she has committed."

I nodded and said nothing.

"Your father hasn't eaten anything all day," she said. "You know how much he suffers from stomach ache whenever his meals are late. Come and let's get dinner ready. If I tell him you won't eat anything as long as he doesn't eat, then he's got to eat something for your sake. He's very worried about you after this calamity."

Mother was very clever. She succeeded in killing two birds with one stone, for she obliged both Father and me to eat something, each for the sake of the other, even though neither of us had any appetite.

She made some tea and I took a large tray, putting tea things on it, along with some bread, jam, stuffed eggplant, cheese, and olives. I took them to Father in the sitting room. I spoke to him as Mother had told me and he responded without a moment's hesitation.

We gathered round the tray and ate with no great enthusiasm at first. We needed sips of tea to help us swallow the food and avoid choking on it. Then we found ourselves pouncing on the food unconsciously, chewing it, swallowing it and drinking the tea until we had finished it all off. Then we both got up, washed our hands, and changed for bed. We went off to our rooms, carrying our grief with us, shunning conversation so as to avoid weeping and rekindling the distress that was beginning to subside. Perhaps from that moment it began to pass away gradually, leaving behind the odd word of regret or the occasional gasp of pain.

In this way a painful and distressing life was concluded. Oblivion began to consume her only a matter of hours after she had committed suicide.

F or three days I did not go to school. I was unable to face people or to talk to them or to answer the questions that my schoolmates would inevitably throw at me about Auntie's suicide, which had become the talk of the town. I chose to stay at home. My parents would go out early in the morning, Father to his work and Mother to Grandfather's house, where it had been agreed that she and my uncle's wife would receive visits of condolence.

But I was not alone. No. I was with the woman who had hanged herself. I was living with her through the blue book which she had left for me. I was able to follow her life from her adolescence to the day she left the world with no regrets.

I started to read, carefully, attentively.

Some sections shook me up and made me so sad that I wept. Some made me recoil wih horror. Others made me so angry that I almost tore the book to shreds.

I felt for the degradation of womankind when I read this passage:

SABRIYA

Sometimes I feel I am like a high-spirited dog tethered by a strong chain to a stake fixed to this old house. Whenever it tries to slip its lead the chain is made tighter and tighter until it bites into the flesh. When it moves, the blood flows and the pain intensifies. My mind rejects this form of bondage but I cannot free myself of it. I am helpless, helpless. There are generations behind the way I have been brought up. Over the ages religion, customs, and tradition have imposed taboos with roots so strong in our hearts that they are venerated. Can one feeble individual like myself throw them off by herself? I cannot understand how my tongue freezes when I am with Father. Or how I am struck dumb in the presence of my brother Raghib, however much he is in the wrong and I am right. Why am I unable to express to Mother the emotional turmoil that rages in my bosom even though I know she loves me dearly and has enormous sympathy for me? Perhaps it is because she will never understand me, no matter how much I try to bring my ideas closer to hers.

Elsewhere I read the following:

I have suffered the greatest defeat when I have defeated myself . . .

I have recently managed to put an end to the violent turmoil that has been eternally raging in my innermost being and has been like a kettle that is constantly on the boil. I have stilled it by constant self-restraint, by training the spirit to be patient and content with the state of things as they are, however bitter. It is as if my circumstances have all conspired to be against me. For most people there is a limit to self-sacrifice, but for me there have been no limits . . .

I now find I am paying a high price. This has been my biggest mistake. So long as that mistake is my own, then I have to bear it to the end . . .

I once intended to elope with the man I loved. I was sure he understood me and was in harmony with me and that he alone could rescue me from this prison-house, from this awful incarceration.

The tragedy is that they are not aware that they are imprisoning me or that they are being tyrannical. If only I could live my life as I please, and not as others decide.

But the looks of my sick mother, looks so full of love for me . . . I am paralyzed by her submissiveness and silent pleading. They bind my rebellious spirit with cords. The weaker these cords, the more I cannot resist them and I find I am unable to escape.

Mother has recently managed to check this rebellious spirit, which will remain imprisoned within me until I am buried. This she was able to do when I decided with all my heart to forget about myself and to remain at her side until the end. Mother, who had been grief-stricken when my dear brother Sami was killed in the revolt. I shared the grief with her. How could I abandon her in her final days?

I was certain that if I ran away from home there would be absolutely no return. If I had been the cause of Mother's death I would have lived ever afterwards consumed with remorse, kept awake by a gnawing conscience. Mother went down with bronchitis in the prime of life and her illness dragged on. I had scarcely buried her when Father had his stroke. I live now only to serve him, however long his illness lasts. This is my fate. When Father dies there will no longer be any reason for me to live in this world, for I will have lost everything! I've grown old before my time and am cut off from all the good things in life.

All my ambitions have died. I feel full of remorse but it is too late now.

I put the book aside and thought about it. Did the poor woman live only to be a servant to her parents?

I went back to the book and was saddened to read the passage that she had written right at the end:

It is now spring and blossoms have started to push out and stretch upwards.

The ancient lemon tree is proud of what it produces. It still bears fruit in spite of its age. Why doesn't it boast about it? A pair of butterflies flit about in the air, dancing, one fluttering around the other. If one succeeds in touching the other, it turns back in flight, intoxicated. The other comes to catch it up and circles around it and they carry on their dance together.

40

The thrush repeats its song, introducing a new melody.

His mate lends an ear. I see her stretching her head out of the nest at the top of an orange tree. She watches him, rejoicing in what he says to her.

A blue feather has sprouted in the goldfinch's wing. He has stretched his wings out in front of the female to allure her with his blue feather, chirping all the time, and hopping from branch to branch with excitement.

The tomcat is full of spirit with its compelling mewing.

His talk today has a mixture of moods — flirtatiousness, reproof, sympathy, and menace. The female sweetly displays her charms, seductively and coquettishly. She stretches out before him, feigning indifference to attract him all the more.

All living things around me are throbbing with vitality. They are exercising their rights joyously and spontaneously. All except me! I am denied what is not denied to the smallest insects or the meanest worms!

My femininity wails in its cage like a wounded beast.

I feel that I am becoming more and more desiccated every minute I am trapped behind the high walls of this old house with this sick old man.

Auntie seems to have written up these memories in the last years of her life. This would explain why the first pages have no dates. She went back to her memory and concentrated on the things that had had a large influence on the course of her life and then recorded them in great detail. I was convinced of that as I read the first pages about her childhood. There was a judicious analysis of the events that persuaded me she had written them up long after they had taken place and that she had emancipated herself from the emotions of the time. Her comments made sense and seemed the result of reflection.

This is what came on the first page:

I was ten years old, but I looked older than those of similar age. When I went to school I would wear a black tunic with a white collar. I would put on a flimsy white headscarf and tie it round my neck.

I was irritated by this headscarf. It held back two long plaits which

I was very proud of and it prevented them swinging onto my back.

Mother had made me wear this headscarf ever since I was seven years old. She impressed on me that I had to take care that it never slipped from my head. I was a young girl and men were not permitted to see my head uncovered. Otherwise Allah would punish me with hellfire on the Day of Judgment. I used to like going to school with Sami and his friend, Adil. They would accompany me first to my school and then go on to theirs.

I would walk between them, not saying a word. I would listen very carefully to what they said, which was usually about the books they read which they had borrowed from libraries and then swapped.

Every now and then Adil would take me in with a glance and sometimes he would address remarks to me. I became aware of new limitless horizons opening up before me. I wanted the way to school to be longer so I could enjoy more of Adil's enchanting talk.

I also started reading the books Sami borrowed from Adil.

I would be delighted when I found I could understand some of the things I read about. I was younger than my three brothers, but Father used to say that I was more conscientious and more intelligent than the others.

I will never forget the day I finished one school year and passed into the fourth grade. I went back home that day, carrying the report with grades showing that I had passed with flying colors. I had a certificate of appreciation as well, commending my brightness and diligence. The family were all gathered together in the *liwan* for lunch. I rushed up to Father and gave him the report card and the certificate, feeling very pleased with myself. He read them aloud, kissed me and said, "I've got a precious present for you."

"It's a gold bracelet, like the one last year, isn't it, Abu Raghib?" said Mother.

Father nodded his head.

"If Allah wills it, if Allah wills it," he said. "By Allah, she deserves it."

Father then turned to Raghib, my eldest brother, who had failed in his grades that year.

"You're a fool," he said. "In my opinion, this girl, who is six years younger than you, is worth ten of you. Aren't you utterly ashamed in her presence? She has succeeded in her grade and you have failed in yours. You spend all your time fooling about and dreaming, while she has been at her books studying, and what is the point of her studying? She'll be getting married soon and will be devoting all her time to her home and her children. But as for you, what is a man's value in this day and age unless he has some education and qualifications?"

Raghib hung his head in shame, blushed, and said nothing.

"If I had been luckier," Father went on, "you'd have been born a girl and she a boy."

I found myself laughing at this, in spite of myself. It was hard to imagine Raghib as a girl. His voice was broken and he was sprouting a moustache.

When Father left and my brothers, Mahmud and Sami, after him, Raghib took the opportunity to vent his wrath on me. He hit me and punched me, saying, "How dare you laugh at me, damn you. You will not laugh at me from now on."

I cried out and called for Mother's help. My nose was bleeding and I almost fainted. She came quickly and cursed at him and said she would complain to Father. He was insolent and provocative in his answer.

"Do as you like. If you feel you can do without a daughter I shall carry on hitting her until she stops laughing in my face."

Father never realized, perhaps out of ignorance of child psychology, that what he did planted seeds of hatred in the hearts of two of his children.

I don't know why, when he was criticizing Raghib before us all for neglecting his studies — and this happened more and more — it never occurred to him to compare him with one of his brothers, who were also doing well. He seemed only to compare him with me, in order to humiliate him, because I was a girl and the youngest.

This hatred grew and became embedded in both of us. Today I have no doubt that this hatred had a great influence on the course of events throughout my life, and throughout Raghib's life as well.

I did not realize I had fallen in love until the school vacations, when I was cooped up in the house, only able to go out if Mother escorted me. I had an intense wish to see Adil, this swarthy young man with a sympathetic voice. His father was a baker who used to provide bread for the whole of our part of Damascus. Adil used to deliver bread each morning to the houses of the quarter before he went to school. The last call was at our house and from there we would all go off to school together. When the summer vacation came I would wait for him to come each morning so I could open the door and take the bread from him. We would gaze at each other for a few moments. Our eyes would declare what we did not dare to admit, or what we did not know how to acknowledge.

One morning Adil spoke to me as he was handing over the bread. It did not seem fair to him that I was confined to the house while he was completely free to play in the quarter with Sami and other friends.

"How do you pass the time all day?" he asked.

The blood rose to my cheeks.

"I help Mother with the housework," I said quietly. "Then I read some of Sami's books when he goes off to play with you."

"Do you like reading novels?"

I nodded.

"I'll give Sami a lovely novel which I've just finished reading," he said. "It's called *Virtue*. It's translated from the French by a famous Egyptian writer called al-Manfaluti. Have you heard of him?"

I shook my head.

"You'll love it," he said.

I heard Mother call from the kitchen.

"Who are you talking to, Sabriya?"

I shut the door hastily in Adil's face and hurried back to the kitchen with the bread.

"That was Adil with the bread. He asked after Sami. He wanted some books from him."

"Put it in the breadbox and let's get breakfast ready. Your father and brothers will be waking up soon."

Mother used to wake me up every morning before dawn so I could help her clean the house and get breakfast ready. In our country they train a girl, as soon as she is aware of herself, to serve the men, be it brother, husband, or son. So when she has grown up she feels that such servitude is part of nature. I resented my brothers being able to enjoy more sleep than I did, especially during the school holidays.

It took me two days to read *Virtue* and I understood it completely. I wept a lot over the young hero and heroine who were in love and who drained the cup of bitterness when they became disappointed in their love.

When he was delivering bread, Adil asked me, "Have you read the story?"

I nodded and tears came to my eyes and I was almost crying.

"No, no, no," Adil smiled. "I don't want ever to see you cry. From now on I'm not going to choose sad stories for you. You seem to be very sensitive. Yesterday I gave Sami a copy of the novel *Magdalene*, which was also translated by al-Manfaluti. If you read it you will cry because it's a very sad story. Even I wept over it when I read it. I'm very cross with myself if I am the cause of making you cry or feel pain."

I took the bread and looked at him, feeling flustered. He gave me a look full of gentleness and longing. I slowly closed the door, savoring the image of his lovely face.

I put the bread away, and went and sat under the jasmine tree and started to think.

Why is Adil cross with himself when I cry? Could he be in love with me? . . . Ah, how beautiful that word is.

My heart danced for joy.

That day I felt that the house, with the trees and the fountain, were all dancing with me. I cut some jasmine blossom and sang to myself. I sat on the rim of the pool and joined the flowers together in a long chain and made a garland. I put the garland around my neck and stood in front of the mirror, gazing at my own beauty. How I wished I was the prettiest girl in the world!

Father and my brothers came down for their breakfast. I did not join them.

When Mother asked me why not, I said I had already had some breakfast.

I went up to Sami's room. I looked for the novel and found it on his pillow. I browsed through it and was entranced from the first page.

Father and my brothers went out. Mother wanted me to go with her on a visit to her brother's. I refused, saying the school vacation was almost over and I had some vacation tasks to finish off.

She despaired of me and went out, leaving me to myself.

It was the first time I had been left alone in the house. I was so happy to feel I was free to do whatever I liked, with nobody to supervise me. I could do just as I pleased.

I threw myself into the novel, devouring it as if I was starving. I was thrilled by the letters the heroine, Magdalene, wrote to her lover, Stephen, and to her girlfriend, Susan, to whom she described her lover. I wished I had a friend with whom I could exchange such letters. I would be able to write to her about Adil and my feelings for him. I loved the style of the letters and copied extracts into the little notebook which I then hid among my books.

I was distressed by the story, which actually made me cry — as Adil had predicted. I was very cross with the heroine for betraying her lover and marrying his friend. And then I felt sorry for her, forgiving her when she suffered intense remorse, a remorse which drove her to suicide.

The school vacation was almost over and we three friends — Sami, Adil, and myself — would once again be going to school together each morning.

I was so looking forward to this. I would listen to what Sami and Adil were saying and understand it all. I would even join in the conversation. Was I not, like them, a serious reader?

I did not anticipate the disappointment that was in store.

Raghib saw me coming home from the tailor's with Mother one day and said to Father, "Look, Father, in the whole of our neighborhood is there a single girl as tall as Sabriya who goes out of the house unveiled?"

Father became aware of an issue that should not have passed him by. He said severely to Mother, "This is your fault. Shouldn't you have bought her a veil that covers her face, as I suggested, rather than that coat which you got from the tailor's?"

"But, Father," broke in Sami, "Sabriya is still young. She's only ten years old. It's not her fault if she was made tall, is it?"

"Be quiet, you," Father snapped. "People who see her would suppose she was twelve or thirteen years old. Try and be like your elder brother, concerned with the honor and dignity of your sister."

Sami held his tongue but looked annoyed.

"I'll buy her a shawl," said Mother. "She can wear that over her coat and I'll get her a black veil which she can wear over her face. That's how young girls like her cover themselves up nowadays. The headscarf is no longer fashionable among girls of her age."

"Whether it's fashionable or not, the important thing is that Sabriya does not go out from now on with her face uncovered."

"As you wish, sir," said Mother with her customary submissiveness.

Raghib gave a smile of triumph and I felt perplexed. I was listening to things being said by my family that concerned me, but I didn't dare say anything myself.

From that moment I realized I was much weaker than all the forces that were ranged against me. I was being fettered by heavy chains.

One week later I found I was going to school alone. A heavy black veil had descended over my face. I could see the way ahead through it only with great difficulty. My eyes had to get used to it. I almost stumbled as I went along.

My biggest disappointment was not going to school in the way I had been looking forward to for three whole months. It was totally unacceptable for a young veiled girl to walk out with young men even when they were close relations. I felt a sense of oppression. I had been defeated. This humiliation made me introspective even at that tender age. I no longer joined in the games I used to play and enjoy with my schoolmates.

I was not interested in anything except reading the books Sami brought home and throwing myself into my studies. I was best in the class and this consoled me from that day that I had to wear the veil, when I could no longer see Adil or listen to his wonderful talk. I would look forward to those fleeting moments when I took the bread from him each morning. He began to bring the bread to us early and then come back to meet up with Sami and go with him to school. He seemed to realize that I could stay longer with him when Father and my brothers were still asleep and when Mother was busy with the housework. I used to get up very early, get dressed, take a book, and appear to be going over my homework while hovering in the corridor, my ears alert to every movement. When I heard a light tap at the front door I would hasten to it and open it slowly. We lingered for a few moments discussing and commenting on the stories and novels we had been reading. I became obsessed by Adil. I became more and more devoted to him every day. Awake or asleep, I dreamt of him. I preferred to be by myself so I could pretend I was whispering to him, recalling one of his remarks or one of his gestures.

One day he brought me a spring flower. The previous day he brought me the story of Qais and Laila. He had marked some of the verses that described the anguish of ecstasy and the agonies of love. I learned these lines by heart and constantly repeated them to myself.

As a result of all this I appeared to be solemn and preoccupied all the time.

Once I ventured to underline some lines Laila delivered to Qais and returned the book via Sami, who was quite unaware of anything.

Days, months, years went by in a routine way. We were unaware of the passing of time. Nothing changed except the kind of books Adil and Sami exchanged. They became more serious — discussions of literature, ideas, and politics. There were magazines from Egypt with poetry, criticism, and short stories. I read them all, understanding some, while others made no impression.

We grew bigger and Raghib grew a black moustache. He enjoyed twisting it with his fingers and massaging it in front of us all. He would lord it over us whenever Father was absent, especially over me. He liked to order me about, to humiliate me, to take me away from my studies, to make me feel that I was of no value. Whenever he saw me writing or reading, he would ask me to do something — "Get up and fetch me some water." Or, "Make me a cup of coffee." Or, "Iron this shirt for me." Or, "Sew this button on for me."

I would put up with it patiently but with an internal bitterness. I was afraid that those eyes would see into my small head and discover my love for Adil.

And so I kept out of his way and avoided eye contact with him as much as possible.

The even tenor of family life ceased when Raghib abandoned his studies after a long run of failure. He stayed at home picking quarrels and finding fault with anyone he chose. He then asked Father to lend him some money so he could go into partnership with a friend, a merchant's son. Father refused and there were daily rows between the two of them. Then Mother, with all the art she could summon up, wheedled Father into granting what her eldest son wanted.

One day I heard my parents talking. They were sitting in the central courtyard beneath the jasmine and did not realize I was in the room we called the cubbyhole and could hear everything they said. I left the homework I was doing and recorded in my notebook the following unexpected conversation.

"Give me a rest, woman . . . In the name of Allah, you've become unbearable. Day and night, you talk only of that son of yours, Raghib. I've told you a hundred times, do not mention his name to me."

"What do you want, then? Do we abandon this son of ours who is now a young man? Is he to hang idly around the place, wandering around the streets all day? . . ."

"And why don't you say, half the night as well? Do you think I don't know what time he gets home at night? I pretend not to notice for fear of him being offensive to me. He has become the size of a mule. When has sound counsel ever done any good to him? I've washed my hands of him. I've done for him what is required of me. A son like him returning home every night after midnight! You keep quiet, overlook it, and think I don't know . . . It's not something we've been used to, nor our parents or our grandparents before us. Do you remember my father, may he rest in peace? We went out with him — my brothers and I — every night to the mosque for evening prayers. We would then come back home — we were married and fathers then — and he would usher us in before him and then lock the door and put the key in his belt. The door would not be opened again till the call to dawn prayer."

"Yes, and do you remember how you all used to complain and

resent his authority? But you never dared go against him."

"Go against Father? Allah forbid! We were dutiful sons, not like this wretched son of yours."

"Heavens above! . . . Why is it that when one of our sons is in trouble he is my son, but when he does well he is your son?"

"Because you spoil and mollycoddle him. If you'd left him to me I'd have brought him up as I wanted to and he would not have reached the state he's in now."

"Why is it my fault when he has not been endowed with learning? There are plenty of others like him. That's the way they're made. He is, praise be to Allah, able to read and to write and to add up. Don't you see him every day reading the newspaper from cover to cover? . . . That's enough. Goodness, did you have a string of diplomas and certificates? But, praise Allah, things have gone well enough for you."

"But my days were not the same as these days."

"This kind of talk is not much use. Whatever has happened has happened. We've got to find a solution. He is our son and we are responsible for him. So long as you are unwilling to advance him anything, why don't you take him with you to the store so he can be trained in buying and selling, and practice commerce, just as you did with your father?"

"Allah help me. I've got to rely on Allah. You're crazy, woman! Don't you know your own son? . . . A worthless liar. He'll bankrupt the business in two weeks and drive me to a bed of sickness. I cannot abide the thought of dealing with him. I tried once during his summer break. You remember that. What happened? He took advantage of my absence from the store and sold some cloth without my knowledge and put the money in his pocket. And after that you tell me to take him with me to the store . . ."

"That mistake will not be repeated. It was a childish prank and he knew that you would be indulgent. He wouldn't have done it to anyone else."

"Play some other tune. I've promised myself that he will never enter my store again after what he did."

"In that case, you must give him some money so he can try his own luck. Let him, sir, rely on himself. Who knows, perhaps Allah will make him prosper."

"We are from Allah and to Allah we will return. When he told me that he wanted to go into business with one of his friends and open a store in Suq al-Hamidiya to sell perfumes, face powders, and rouge for women, I realized what they were up to. They were going to make their store a place to ensnare young girls. I'm a son of the suq" — he struck himself on the chest — "and I know what goes on in these stores. If your son was serious, he would consider trading in, say, consumer goods or soap or wood. All these bring in good profits, much more than face powder and rouge, which attract only chattering, empty-headed women. Mark my word, they will go bankrupt within a few months. Am I a bank to advance them cash whenever they go bankrupt?"

"Abu Raghib, do you want me to talk, or shall I remain silent?"

"Say whatever you want to say."

"Didn't you once ensnare me in the store when I came with Mother to buy some cloth? I was fourteen years old at the time and, young though I was, I was not blind to the way you stole a glance whenever I let slip my veil just a little so I could inspect the cloth you were laying out before me. Why do you not allow others to behave as you allowed yourself to behave?"

"Since you've brought the subject up, Umm Raghib, shall I tell you something I have concealed for many years, or shall I keep quiet?"

"Speak, my good man. You're not doing me a favor."

"Your mother — may she rest in peace — was a smart lady. It was she who arranged my engagement to you. Your mother was a regular customer at the store, and had been ever since it was opened by my father. She knew me extremely well. She used to come and visit my family and got to know everything about us. When she was satisfied with us she used to bring you to the store and set you before me as a tempting morsel. How could I fail to gobble you up with all your beauty and perfection? Now, be honest, didn't your mother suggest that you lift your veil up deliberately just a little bit so I could set eyes on that lovely face of yours?"

Mother did not reply to this question. Instead she burst into laughter and said, "You mean, you weren't content with what fate had brought you. Are you suggesting that Mother hoodwinked you?"

"No, by Allah. I don't mean that. I'm perfectly happy, and that

51

is why I call the blessings of Allah on your mother's memory whenever I think of her."

Mother then said with a flirtatiousness that astonished me, "Light of my heart! . . . How can I know what goes on in your store every day while you are also dealing with women? What you have said has alerted me to things I was unaware of. By Allah, I think I'll send a few of my women friends along to you to spy on you and tempt you, so I can know what is going on."

"Don't do that, Umm Raghib! I'm a man of emotion and cannot resist beauty, especially when it is associated with coquetry. Please don't bring this upon yourself. Maybe one of your dear, dear friends will act the traitress to you. How often this has happened in the world. Satan lives still, woman! Sister can betray sister!"

"Abu Raghib! . . . What are you saying? You who keep the fast and pray at the prescribed hours and who performed the Pilgrimage to the two Holy Places. You are unable to resist the come-hither of a young girl? The young men are not at fault, then? I'm disappointed in you. Oh, you men! As the proverb says, 'She who trusts a man is like one carrying water in a sieve.'"

Then Father said in a soft voice, but with a great deal of feeling, "Did you really believe what I was saying, Umm Raghib? I was teasing you. By Allah, I wouldn't exchange you for the most beautiful women of Paradise."

I then, between the branches of the jasmine, saw Father pull her to him and kiss her passionately on the lips and neck as she tried to pull herself away from him. He clung on to her all the more and I heard her to say to him, "You don't love me. If you really love me, you'd do what I asked you. You don't consider what I think at all."

A tremor passed through my whole body and the blood burned in my cheeks. This was the first time I had seen my parents showing overt affection for each other. I dropped the pen and it made a noise. I was afraid they would become aware of my presence and I withdrew from the cubbyhole on tiptoe and went up to my room and hid myself under the bedclothes.

Mother has succeeded. With a dalliance that Father has found irresistible she has got what she wanted. Much against his better judgment, Father has paid money over to Raghib. A few days ago Raghib opened up a store in Suq al-Hamidiya with his friend. Soon after the store opened, we became aware of a change in Raghib's behavior and in his attitude towards us. Things are no longer as they had been. He has become jolly and wakes up very early. With one of us he is playful, with another he jokes. He goes off to work and does not come back until the evening, at the same time as Father. Raghib sometimes brings back fresh fruit of the season or some cakes. Mother is delighted with this and with maternal pride offers Father what Raghib has brought.

"This is what Raghib has brought us today," she would say.

"Allah does not forbid such luxuries," Father would mumble sardonically.

He would then shake his head, full of misgivings about what the future would bring.

I cannot deny that Raghib has become extremely generous whenever there is money in his hands. Yesterday he gave me a bottle of expensive perfume, saying, "This is my first present for you from the store."

I was delighted with the perfume. It was the first perfume I had in my life. That day I felt something like sympathy for Raghib after the wrangles of childhood and his bullying of me during his adolescence. Perhaps because I was the most vulnerable member of the family, he used to satisfy himself by taking it out on me.

One week later. He has given Mother a lovely shawl. With enormous pride, she has shown it to everybody who has come to the house as the first gift she has received from her firstborn.

He has also given me a box of makeup. Teasing me, he said, "You've turned into a young lady. You should put some of this powder on your pale face when you are meeting guests. That's what other girls of your age do. It'll make the marriage-makers take heed. Otherwise how are we going to get you out of the house?"

We laughed at his words. But Sami took note. And when Raghib left the room, he said to Mother in my hearing, "Please take note of what I am about to say and be persuaded. Do not, I beg you, give in to the idea of Sabriya getting married too soon — even to the best of men — before she has got her school-leaving certificate."

"What's the use of a school-leaving certificate," said Mother, "if your Father won't agree to her going out to work? We won't necessarily find the ideal husband at a time that suits us, my son."

"A school-leaving certificate, Mother, is security for the future. Women work when they need work. Perhaps her husband will go bankrupt, or become incapable of working. Or he may die and leave children for her to care for. Why should they be denied this security? A word from you can settle matters. Say to the marriage-makers, 'We have no girls ready for marriage, and that's that.'"

He then turned to me.

"Take care you are not near any marriage-makers. If you have to, you must know how to keep them at a distance. Otherwise they will marry you off to whomever they want to in spite of what you think and without even asking your opinion."

I shook my head.

"Do you think I'm dumb enough to need your advice?" I said.

"You're both talking nonsense," Mother said as she left the room. "Marriages are made in heaven."

"Sami," I said, "you disappoint me. According to what you say, the only reason for studying is to get a school-leaving certificate for the sake of security for the future. But learning and the cultural education of the woman, finding out and getting to know about things, and matters you can philosophize about are, according to you, of no practical importance."

"Oh, you silly girl," he said. "Why are you saying these things to me? I said all that because it's the only logic that will persuade Mother."

Two months later. Father was quite right in not wanting to open up the store to Raghib. Raghib started staying out at night more and more. He would come back in the early hours drunk. I have noticed Mother looking preoccupied and concerned until he got back. She is also very critical of him, blaming him completely. Sometimes she weeps in his presence, bemoaning her misfortune. He listens to her with scorn and indifference. He then tries to reassure her. She does all this without Father knowing, so as to avoid bringing any criticism upon herself. After all, it was she who had persuaded him to advance the capital.

Now he has started going off to Beirut, saying he has to get some new merchandise for the store.

He cannot hide all this from Father. I have heard him say to Mother, "In the name of Allah, your son's business seems to be thriving. Each month he needs to go to Beirut to stock up with new merchandise. It's amazing, by Allah. The profits of the store in a month cannot be enough to allow him the expense of traveling and staying for a whole week in the expensive hotels of Lebanon. Is this what serious-minded traders do?"

A few months later. The anxieties of Father — himself an experienced merchant — turned out to be absolutely right. Six months did not elapse after the opening of their store before Raghib and his partner went bankrupt. There were more rows in the house than ever before and it was Mother who was the wretched victim. She took all the blame from Father. She felt she was being gnawed away by a beaver because she had persuaded Father to advance money to Raghib which he then frittered away so irresponsibly.

But with his other children he seemed quite content. I heard him sharing his anxieties with Mother's sister, Umm Rashid, whom he greatly respected. He used to say that she was more like a man than a woman.

"Raghib's business, Umm Rashid, is sure to send me to the grave. And it is your sister who has been the cause of it all. She's the one who has brought this disaster upon me."

"Be patient, old friend," said my aunt. "Allah will bring compensation."

"But as for the other children, with all my heart I am quite satisfied with them. May Allah grant Mahmud prosperity; he gives me no trouble at all. He's loyal. He has entered the law college this year and in three years' time he will, if Allah wills, be either an officer of law or an advocate. And Sami, in spite of his mischief and impulsiveness, will do well in a tough examination and enrol in the medical school. As for Sabriya, she's a bright, hard-working girl. I'll leave her at school until she gets married."

55

"If Allah wills, you'll get them all married in your own lifetime. You'll see your grandchildren and your great-grandchildren. Let us trust in the Providence of Allah and hope that one becomes a lawyer and the second a doctor. As for Raghib, I hope he won't cause you too much distress. It's a phase he's going through, like most young men. How often have I heard of successful men who have reached positions of importance but yet in their youths went through the kinds of difficulties Raghib is going through."

"But Raghib is not like that. I'm afraid I know him only too well."

"Look on the bright side and hope for the best, Abu Raghib. You're a good, intelligent man. You mustn't abandon hope in Allah. Do you know why I've come all the way from the far end of Midan to see you today? I've come to reconcile you to Raghib."

"Umm Rashid, you know how important you are to me. I'll agree to anything but this."

"But you will not let me go away disappointed. Otherwise I'll never enter your house again for as long as I live. I'll take responsibility for Raghib and never let him ask anything of you again. He'll look for some other work for himself. There's plenty of work outside trade, sir, that does not require capital."

Father was silenced. Then Aunt called out, "Raghib, come in and kiss your father's hand in front of me. Make him a happy man. Allah is satisfied when parents are satisfied, my son."

Raghib came in, head bowed, and kissed Father's hand.

"But for your aunt and my esteem for her," Father said, "I would never have spoken to you again in all my life."

"You won't see me do anything you disapprove of, Father," said Raghib. "By Allah, the only thing I'm concerned with is pleasing you."

Joy spread over Mother's face. She had been as silent as a naughty little child.

Several months later. It has been a particularly severe winter. At the end of October we moved to the upper floor, abandoning the *liwan*, the downstairs reception room, and the small rooms on the first floor. Winter is very tough in our Damascus houses, for the kitchen, bathroom, and toilets are all on the first floor. We find ourselves forever going up and downstairs, clumping about in our wooden clogs. Mother suffered more than the rest of us because Father would not excuse her from making the *kubba* or the white vermicelli cakes, those winter dishes that we really cannot do without. How could we do without such winter dishes for we live in order to eat! . . . The first pleasure in our life is eating! . . . So Mother spent most of the time in the kitchen or, you might say, in an ice-box.

Mother used to hate winter, though she loved to see the snow falling. The view of the courtyard became splendid when the trellises were covered in snow, when the citron and the orange trees bore white mantles and when the fruit appeared amidst the snow like colored stars. Mother used to worry about our slipping over whenever there was a film of ice on the marble floor. She would boil up some water and pour it over the ice to melt it from the passageway to the foot of the stairs and as far as the kitchen door and the toilet.

"I've made a safe passage for you," she would tell us. "Keep to it and don't spoil the beautiful snow with your footsteps. It's like newly carded cotton."

With spring came the rosebuds. Violets opened up, then the jasmine, the *banafsha*, the citron flowers, the orange and the lemon blossom. Happiness is restored to the house with all this refreshing fragrance. At the end of the spring vacation we took our food into the courtyard again as usual.

The school year was almost over. One evening after dinner Sami said to Father, "There're only three weeks left to the exams. It's been a lot of hard work this year, Father. There's a huge amount of stuff to learn. Adil and I have agreed to work together and stop going to school so as to prepare for the exams. May I invite him here so we can revise together in the Eyrie? It's cut off from the rest of the house and we won't get in the way."

"I've no objection if you find that useful."

"Yes, it'll be very useful for us both. Adil's better than me in science and I'm better than him in Arabic and French. We'll work together on all these subjects."

"The only condition is that we don't see either of you at all, from the front door to the Eyrie and from the Eyrie to the front door. Your mother and sister must not be disturbed by the presence of a strange man in the house."

"We won't disturb them. They won't see us at all."

"May Allah give you success and make you prosper."

There was a look of irritation on Raghib's face, but he said nothing. Since his bankruptcy he had become less arrogant and interfered less in our affairs.

But for me, the blood rose to my cheeks as I heard all this and my heart beat all the more. I was afraid I might be noticed so I busied myself adjusting my plaits, as if I had no interest in what I heard.

What a magnificent thing to happen!... Adil coming into the house and being with us all day for three whole weeks!... I was so looking forward to seeing him. Ever since his father had stopped him delivering bread to the house because he was too old for it, I hardly ever saw him. Only when he called at the front door to ask for Sami or to return a book and I happened to open the door were we able to snatch a few words together; these occasions were not enough to satisfy.

That night I dreamt sweet dreams. I saw Adil and myself in our house sitting under the jasmine tree where I had once seen my parents flirting with each other. I saw him pulling me to him and hugging me violently. He would kiss me fervently on my mouth and my neck. I woke up, excited and happy. Then I closed my eyes again hoping that the dream would return. But I couldn't get to sleep. I stayed awake, drunk till dawn with my sweet dream. I went off to school before Adil came to the house. When I came home again in the afternoon I found Mother alone at home, sitting in the *liwan* ironing some freshly washed clothes that were piled up in front of her. I asked her about Sami and pretended not to realize that Adil was in the house.

"He's revising with his friend in the Eyrie."

"They'll be needing some coffee. I'll make some for them."

"Aren't you going to eat first?"

"I'm not hungry."

"That's strange. You always come home from school almost fainting with hunger."

I made no reply. I went into the kitchen, boiled up the coffee, put the coffee pot and two cups on a tray and went upstairs to the Eyrie. I knocked at the door and stepped to one side. Sami appeared.

"Ah, coffee," he said. "You're always excellent, Sabriya. That's exactly what we need now."

He then added with some surprise, "What's the matter? Are you hiding from Adil, your childhood friend? You *are* silly! . . ."

He pulled me by the sleeve into the room. Adil stood up and we shook hands. He looked moved.

"I hope I'm not taking you away from your studies," I said.

"You've come just in time," he answered. "We were getting tired and needed a break."

"Why don't you bring a cup for yourself and we can all have a drink together," said Sami. "Take my cup and I'll go down and get a cup for myself."

He left and started to run downstairs. Adil looked at me tenderly.

"I've missed you so much," he said.

He laughed, his bright teeth shining in the middle of his swarthy face.

"Father stopped me bringing the bread to you," he added, "because he says I've grown up. He's taken on someone else to deliver the bread. Allah knows, I'd love to deliver bread to you for the rest of my life."

I felt embarrassed and didn't know what to say. The dream I had came to mind. I'd love to have told it to him. We remained silent, exchanging glances that spoke more than words of passionate love. Sami came back in. I poured out the coffee and we drank it. It was the sweetest coffee I had tasted in all my life. I felt as if I was in a dream: Sami, Adil, and myself sipping coffee together in the Eyrie. It was unbelievable. I savored these moments and stored them up in my inner consciousness. It then suddenly occurred to me — what if somebody came upstairs to the Eyrie and found me sitting between the two of them, what would happen? There would be a scandal. I had not checked with Mother whether Raghib or Mahmud was at home or not. I got up and gathered the cups together.

"I'd better go now," I said. "I mustn't take your minds off your studies."

Three weeks later. The time has gone by amazingly quickly. Each day I have been taking coffee up and drinking it with Sami and Adil, after Father and my brothers had gone out and while Mother was so busy with her housework that she didn't notice.

Most of the time we talked about the books we planned to read during the summer vacation. I wrote a long list of titles Adil suggested of books he had either read or heard of.

There were of course the novels of George Zaydan; the books of Mai Ziyada; of Gibran Kahlil Gibran; *The Effects of Those with Bracelets* that talks of famous Arab women; the magazine *al-Hilal*; the series Ma'ruf al-Arna'ut had written in his newspaper, *Arab Youth*; the newspaper *al-Mizan* edited by Ahmad Shakir al-Karmi. All this was apart from the books that were easy enough to borrow — a wonderful treasure trove for the summer which I plan to devour ravenously.

I was feeling confident and triumphant. Life was opening up. I approached my studies with enthusiasm, hoping to pass with flying colors and go on to the secondary teachers' training college, the only one in the whole of Syria.

I was absolutely delighted at passing the exams, a delight shared by all. For all of us — Mahmud, Sami, myself, and also Adil — had passed with good grades.

Father hosted a splendid dinner to honor his sons' success. He invited my aunt, Umm Rashid, and her two sons, Rashid and Salim. I appeared before my cousins without a veil, for we had been suckled together and they were therefore foster brothers. My own mother had been ill when I was born and Aunt had breastfed me with her son Salim for a whole week. Salim is one year older than me. Rashid is a year older than Sami and they had also been breastfed at the same time.

Rashid is now about to enter his twenties. To me he seems a fully grown man, much older than his years. He is not handsome, for he has a huge nose, thick lips, and is very dark. But he is tall and dignified, with broad shoulders and a thick black moustache. I always appreciate his very Damascene dress: baggy trousers with violet embroidered pockets, a short, broad jacket with violet buttons that the tassel craftsmen are superb at making, a tall, wine-colored fez that tilts to the left with a black tassel that bobbed backward and forward, left and right, as if in constant motion. Rashid never says much and has a modest demeanor. He wants to appear grave so it can be said of him that he is a real man. He obviously considers himself as taking the place of his father, who was a famous leader of the Midan district. Abu Rashid had been shot dead by an unknown assassin when his eldest son was barely ten years old.

My aunt is a strong-willed woman who ignores conventions and traditions. She took over her husband's affairs to the extent that she used to disguise herself, dress up in men's clothes, put on a *kaffiya*, and ride a horse with her son Rashid behind her. She would be treated as a man, would go to the village, deal with the peasants, and supervise the threshing and weighing of corn. Sometimes she would go to the orchard they used to own in al-Qadam and oversee the sale of fruit and vegetables. Nobody gets the better of Umm Rashid or plays around with her. She has acquired such a reputation that they call her the Sister of Men. A forceful personality is able to stand out and overcome any difficulties and establish her own special way of life.

How I wish Umm Rashid was my own mother. My life would be completely different. Mother cannot be relied upon for anything. She rarely argues or makes any objection. She is always ready to carry out orders.

We sat at the table that had been set up in the courtyard under the trellis. Mother had cooked all kinds of things for us, *fetta makdus*, grilled meatballs cooked in yogurt, leg of lamb and rice and sausages, and vine leaves stuffed with meat. Mother has a great reputation for cooking this last dish. This was all accompanied by different kinds of salads and appetizers. Father had sent out for a plate of *namura*. When it was brought in, a tempting aroma rose from it, a smell of local fat that stimulated the appetite. All this would compare with the famed generosity of our Midan guests.

Father presided at the head of the table and served the food to his guests, filling their plates and urging them to eat all he had served out, refusing to take any excuses. He praised Mother's peerless cooking and declared his delight at the success of his children.

I was sorry to see some preoccupation, some gloominess on the face of Raghib, who was unusually silent. He seemed to be more than usually conscious of his own failure.

Later that year. One fine spring day Sami and I went up on to the roof to collect some fresh vine leaves hanging down from the trellis. Mother had asked us to do this so she could press the leaves in water and salt for the winter, when she could stuff them with meat. They would then taste as if they had been freshly cut off the vines. Sami stopped plucking them for a moment and said quietly, his eyes sparkling with a strange animation, "I'm going to tell you a very important secret, Sabriya — in all the family you're the only one who understands me."

"Go ahead," I said. "Don't worry. Your sister Sabriya is a bottomless well as far as secrets are concerned."

"Well, your brother Sami is in a state of utter bliss, for he is in love, up to his ears in love."

"That's tremendous news, really tremendous. Who's the lucky girl?"

"She's a marvelous young lady, she's unique. She's a student at the Franciscan school."

"How have you got to know her?"

"I got to know her in the bookstore. One day I went there to buy a French book. Then this medium-size girl with a slender waist came in. She dropped down a thin veil over her face which she soon raised to reveal a wheat-colored face with delicate features and two honey-colored eyes that gleamed with intelligence. She stole my heart away when her long black eyelashes fluttered. For one moment I was confused as I looked at her leafing through some books on display without paying me any notice at all. She then spoke to the bookseller in perfect French. I summoned up all my courage and spoke to her.

"'Would you do me the honor,' I said, 'of selecting a book for me as you select one for yourself? It mustn't be too difficult because my French isn't very good. I don't know anything about the contents of these books or their authors.'

"She looked at me searchingly, then took down a book, handed it to me and said, 'This is very good and quite easy. It's Alfred de Musset. I read it and loved it. Maybe you'll also like it.'

"'As you've suggested it to me,' I said, 'I'm sure I'll enjoy it.'

"She gave me a sweet smile and said, '*Merci.*' She then took the books she had selected for herself and went out, walking as if she was caressing the ground with her dainty footsteps. I went out and followed her with my eyes until she disappeared from sight. I almost melted with emotion."

"Patience, dear brother," I said. "All this is just at first sight."

"If you'd seen her you would understand."

"What next?" I asked.

"I read the book. I got through it in a couple of days and understood it perfectly well. On Sunday I was patiently anxious. I decided to go to the bookstore at the same time. She was already there. When she saw me she opened up the conversation.

"'Did you enjoy the book?' she asked.

"'Very much so,' I answered. 'That's why I'm here again so you can choose another book for me.'

"She took down a book and said, 'This is a novel by Anatole France called *Thais*. He's the best contemporary French writer. It's really good.'

"I then said in a low voice so the bookseller, busy with other customers, could not hear, 'Shall I find you here next Sunday so I can tell you what I think about the book?'

"She gave me an impudent smile, paused, and then said, 'Maybe.'

"The impudent smile of hers kept me awake for a whole week. I was afraid she would not turn up. I went at the agreed time on Sunday and she was not there. It was as I had expected and I felt very disappointed. I stood there flicking through books and reading titles without taking anything in. I had become obsessed by her. Would she turn up? Would she laugh at me?

"Fifteen minutes went by. I was about to leave the bookstore and wander off somewhere, when suddenly her gazelle-like form appeared at the door. She was wearing a brown coat that molded itself around her slender figure. She lowered a thin brown veil over her face."

I said to Sami, "Praise be to Allah. I was on tenterhooks. But Allah is great."

"Allah knows, I'm telling you the absolute truth."

"And then?"

"She asked me what I thought of the book.

"'I can't tell you,' I told her, 'because I haven't finished reading it yet.'

"'Idle boy,' she said. 'Why did you come here, then?'

"'To tell you that I hadn't finished it yet.'

"She smiled, innocently this time. Then she took down a book and left the bookstore. I followed her and walked by her. She showed no embarrassment. I said, 'I'm most impressed at your love of reading.'

"'It's what I like doing most. In addition to my schoolwork, I read one book a week.'

"I was then bold enough to ask her her name and she told me it was Nirmin.

"'That's a lovely name,' I said. It seemed to be a Turkish name and she told me her mother was Turkish and her father Syrian. Her father died two years ago and she had one brother, who was studying medicine in France."

"Didn't you tell her about our family, Sami?"

"Yes, of course. I spoke to her as she spoke to me. Then I took her to her home, which is at the far end of Salihiya in a quarter that branches off from al-Jisr al-Abyad. I said to her as we parted, 'I hope I shall find you at the bookstore at the same time next week.'

"'Maybe,' she said.

"'This "maybe" of yours I don't care for. It kept me awake at night all last week.'

"'I think you're laughing at me.'

"'I'm dead serious.'

"'So long as you're serious, you'll find me in the bookstore at the same time next week.'

"She then raised a finger and said, as she went into the house, 'Make sure next week you've finished reading the book.'

"I spent all week reading the novel. I had to keep looking things up in the dictionary until I understood it completely. And when Sunday came round again, I went off to the bookstore with a halo of happiness around my brow. She was on the sidewalk, waiting for me.

"'It's crowded in the bookstore,' she said. 'We won't be able to choose what we want. Let's go for a walk until there are fewer people there.'

"'Nothing could be nicer,' I said.

"She then took me along a path through the gardens. There was nobody about and she raised her veil and said, 'Tell me, have you finished reading the book?'

64

"'Of course,' I replied. 'Just as you told me to. Can I go against your bidding?'

"'You are an excellent pupil,' she said. 'What did you understand of it, you clever boy?'

"I outlined the plot and she listened. She seemed surprised until I said, 'I felt so sorry for Boniface, the monk who had been in love with the beautiful dancer, Thais, before he went into the monastery. He had seen her in Alexandria and could not receive her love because of his poverty. And Thais never had any feelings of love for him at all. Nirmin, isn't it the hardest kind of love, psychologically the most painful kind, when the loved one is unaware of the one who loves her?'

"Nirmin blushed and her sweet eyes sparkled. She looked at me playfully and said, as if she wanted to evade the issue, 'What you say does not come in the novel. You mustn't stray from the subject. Now tell me, what happened after Boniface took his vows?'

"'As you wish, my severe instructress. After Boniface became a monk, he went off to the desert of Thebes, living in a cell, but the memory of that dancer kept coming back to him. Her image would appear to him in his isolation. It would keep him awake and distract him from his devotions. He then forced himself to believe that a divine inspiration called on him to go to Thais and take her away from her life of sin and to lead her to the path of righteousness. He should bring her into the company of nuns. It was not for him to hesitate answering this call. He had to please the God whom he loved.'

"I then said to Nirmin, 'I have discovered, Nirmin, something I was unaware of before. What happened to that poor monk has happened to me in just the same way. I am fooling myself when, absorbed in my studies, I persuade myself that I must get up and go to the bookstore and get a book that will help me in my studies. Actually, things may not be like that at all. In fact, the only reason I come to the bookstore is to see you. You see what happens to those who delude themselves.'"

"What a devil you are," I said to Sami. "What did Nirmin say when you told her that?"

He laughed.

"She slapped my cheek gently and said, 'I don't know why you got yourself so involved in the story. I'm going to give you a poor grade for this summary, just as the Sister, teaching French literature, would give me if I strayed from the subject. But don't run away. I want to know whether you understand the story right to the end.'

"I then gave her a summary of the rest of the book."

"You've got to give me a summary of the book," I told him, "just as you did for Nirmin."

He grumbled a bit but then said, "OK, I'll let you have what you want. Boniface left his cell one night. He walked all the way to Alexandria, suffering a lot from the journey. There he saw Thais acting in a play. He remembered her as a glittering star in the world of art and beauty. But he pretended not to see this at all. He was certain that the strength of his faith and the robustness of his beliefs would not deflect him from his intention of leading Thais to virtue. He had not the slightest doubt that his honorable intentions were for her sake. When he went to the dancer's house he saw her enjoying luxuries that had been showered on her by her wealthy paramours. All this only strengthened his determination. He went up to the dancer and preached roughly to her, his voice aquiver, thereby revealing his burning passion for her. Thais was surprised by his incredible appearance, listened to him, and was captivated by the magic of his words, which partly frightened her, partly aroused her. For Thais was a good-hearted girl with a restless spirit and knew something of the teachings of Christianity. She had learned these from a black servant in her father's house before she ran away from home. So when the monk started to preach at her, she wearied of her tempestuous life, longing for a peaceful life in the shadow of a belief that would comfort her soul. It therefore did not take long for her to respond to his appeal and she was happy to take religious vows in spite of their austere asceticism. He would not let her leave the house until she had burnt her flimsy dress and her flamboyant feathers; she had to break all her links with her previous life. He took her away from Alexandria, to a nunnery, and left her there. He returned to his cell, satisfied. But the image of Thais did not go away. Indeed, it came to him all the more. He buried himself in prayer and entreaties that he might be rid of her tempting image, but it was no use. He managed to get her out of his mind for a while, but then images of dancers would haunt him, distracting him from his devotions, arousing him and making him think again of the dancer. When he could no longer put up with this state of affairs, he left his cell and built another on top of a column, so as to cut himself off from this world and its temptations. But the image of the dancer and the impudent small creatures came to him there on his column.

"Nirmin then interrupted me and asked me if I knew what the author was getting at in all this.

"'The author succeeded completely,' I said, 'when he was trying to tell us that human instincts are of the utmost priority, however much we may be concerned with piety and good works. For here we have Boniface the monk finally giving in to the ways of nature after having fiercely resisted them. He leaves his cell and comes to tell Thais that what he had told her was a load of rubbish! He told his love to come and enjoy the good things of this world before they died. The virtuous nun then threw him out and shortly after that God turned him into a bat.'

"Nirmin laughed. 'I think the author gave this frightful ending to the monk so the story would have a free passage without the men of religion objecting and getting the book banned.'"

I then told Sami that I thought it really was a good story. "I wish my French was good enough for me to read it easily. What was Nirmin's opinion of this summary of yours? Was she pleased?"

"She told me that it was very good," he said, "and that I had understood the story perfectly. I'd been able to sum it all up even though it wasn't easy and I had claimed not to be very good at French. I then took her hand in mine and pressed it gently. I raised her hand to my lips and planted a kiss on it, saying, 'I am very proud of this pledge, my dear instructress.' She didn't take her hand away. We stopped quietly for a moment and then carried on walking among the trees with the gentle breezes playing on our faces, as our hands did the talking. I had never realized that fingers could be so expressive of love or could be more eloquent than tongues. We reached the end of the path and Nirmin suddenly looked at her watch.

"'Time has flown by,' she said. 'I'm late. I can't go to the bookstore now.'

"'I would like time always to flow like this,' I said. 'I can think of nothing more lovely.'

"She laughed.

"'Why don't you come home with me,' she said, 'and I can show you my books. I can pick one out for you.'

"'That would be nice! But what will your mother say?'

"'She won't be surprised. I've spoken to her about you and told her I'd introduce you some time.'

"'It's wonderful that barriers between mother and daughter can be raised that they can live together as friends.'

"'Mother is educated and far-sighted. She has brought me up to be completely open ever since I was little.'"

I then interrupted him.

"Congratulations," I said. "Your friend seems to have a most understanding mother. What happened next?"

"'Well,' Nirmin said, 'I don't want you to think I'm in the habit of bringing young men home. You're the first one.'

"'I'm very happy you have such confidence in me. I'd love to know why. You don't know much about me.'

"'I think I can know somebody from his looks and behavior and whether he is good or not.'

"She opened the door and gave me a smile that was both innocent and complicit. She led me to a small reception room simply furnished, suggesting good taste. It was not like what we have in our house. There were pictures on the wall, a vase of flowers on the table with roses of matching colors. Then a very dignified, attractive, middle-aged lady came in. She greeted me with some reserve and sat opposite me. She started by asking me about my studies in an accent that was slighty Turkish. Meanwhile, Nirmin went off to get some coffee ready. I felt embarrassed by this sophisticated woman's penetrating gaze. It was as if I was taking a difficult exam from which I couldn't escape until Nirmin came back with the coffee.

"After we drank the coffee Nirmin suggested she show me her books. She opened a door that led on to a small room in which books were carefully arranged on the shelves. There was also a sofa and a writing desk. She brought down some books and put them on a table in front of me. She made various interesting comments about them and left it to me to make a choice.

"'I prefer you to choose for me,' I said. 'I've been very happy with your choice so far.'

"'In that case, take this collection of short stories by Maupassant. There are some lovely stories that are not as difficult as the story of Thais.'

"I felt it was time to go. I said goodbye to her mother, and as I left I whispered to Nirmin, 'I'll see you in the bookstore.'

"She nodded and winked."

I said I was really amazed that there were people like Nirmin and her mother in Damascus.

"You live in a very confined circle," Sami said. "You only know our relations and our neighbors. Ideas about things vary a great deal."

"I'm going to write up what you have told me in my diary as a contrast to the life we lead."

He then said, giving me a meaningful look, "I've told you my secret. You haven't told me yours."

"What secrets? I haven't got any secrets."

"Are you hiding something? Aren't you in love with Adil?"

I was taken aback and shocked. I looked at him in silence, feigning dumbness.

"Don't worry," he said. "Do you think I'm Raghib? You too have the right to be in love. And Adil has told me everything."

"Adil!" I cried out, staring at him in disbelief.

"Yes, Adil." He smiled and nodded and then added, "When I spoke to him about Nirmin — we never hide anything from each other — I asked him why he didn't look for a girlfriend who could give him happiness. He then told me there was one person whose fate he longed his to be linked to and that was my sister, Sabriya. He told me that you'd had a mutual understanding for a long, long time."

Sami shook his head and said with a grin, "You naughty couple! Has all this been going on without my knowing anything about it? I cannot deny that I'm delighted with your excellent choice. Adil is a man in a million, absolutely first-rate in all respects."

A feeling of great happiness spread through me. I wanted to hug and kiss Sami. But then Mother called up, "Haven't you finished picking vine leaves? I'm sure that's enough. Do come down now and have some lunch before it gets cold."

"What will Mother say?" I said to Sami. "We have been so absorbed in our conversation that we don't realize what we're doing. We've cut some withered leaves as well as fresh ones and also some bunches of grapes!"

An important event now distracted Auntie from affairs of love and study and problems of the family. This was the spread of the Syrian revolt in Jabal Druze. Auntie recorded in her diary whatever she read in the newspapers about the revolt and also the rumors she heard. She would make her own comments and from these it is clear that she was swept away by great enthusiasm for the revolt. In my turn, I will copy what Auntie recorded.

About her father she wrote:

I think Father is in a dilemma. On the one hand, his religious and national feelings push him in one direction and he gives his blessings to the revolt, which thrills him. But on the other hand, in his heart of hearts he wants it to stay away from Damascus so that it won't lead to any trouble, or to losses in his property or business. Sami is fired with enthusiasm, but Raghib is against the revolt and expects no good from it whatsoever. Mahmud, as usual, is not at all concerned. There have been frequent arguments between Sami and Raghib, who have even, unaccustomedly, raised their voices in Father's presence in the course of our evening discussions.

On one occasion this was the argument:

"Do you think, Sami," asked Raghib, "that the Druzes, with their antiquated rifles, are able to stand up against French airplanes and tanks?"

"Yes, sir," answered Sami. "They are capable of that. Isn't that exactly what happened to General Michaud? His force was completely wiped out and the news of it reverberated around the world. The Druzes brought down some planes and destroyed a lot of tanks. The French have themselves acknowledged that they have suffered severe losses. It's no longer a war of weapons, it's a war of men."

"Do you suppose," Raghib asked sarcastically, "that the French will accept this unexpected rout in silence? Mark my words, you're going to see them destroying the Jabal stone by stone."

"They won't be able to do that if the revolt spreads to all parts of Syria. And it's bound to spread. It's already started in Hama. It's going to force France into sending a huge army with all its armaments."

"Allah, what puerile ideas you have! France, which brought Germany to its knees, is to be defeated by Syria! It's ridiculous."

"I never said that we could defeat France. But we won't let her get what she wants here. Whenever she stamps out one revolt, we will launch another one, more ferocious. This is now the third since she came into the country. If it can be demonstrated that her losses here are greater than her gains, she is sure in the end to pull out. Guerrilla warfare is no small matter. It can go on for a long time."

"It's a long job, my dear friend . . ."

"Oh, yes, it's a long haul, very long. It's going to mean a lot of sacrifices on our part. Do you want to obtain your independence free of charge, without any sacrifice of blood?"

Father shouted, "Be quiet, you two boys. You're giving me a headache. What is politics to us? We are trading people and have nothing to do with politics or matters of state."

"This is not politics, Father," said Sami. "It's nationalism and that concerns every individual in the country. If not, he is a traitor."

"Shut up, you insolent boy," Father said testily, with a frown. "I tell you, politics is politics."

Raghib smirked in triumph. Sami concealed his annoyance and, with a grim face, left the *liwan*, where we had all been sitting, and went upstairs to his room. There was silence for a while. Then Father turned to Mother and said with some asperity, as if she had been the guilty one, "Go and slice us a watermelon so we can moisten our lips."

Mother got up and went to the kitchen. I joined her and put two slices of watermelon in a dish and took them up to Sami's room.

He was sitting on the edge of his bed, his head in his hands and a look of gloom on his face. I put the watermelon on the bedside table and said, "Why do you wear yourself out with useless argument, dear brother?"

71

"What upsets me is that our household represents elements in the whole of our society. Father represents the class of traders and property-owners who are concerned only with holding on to their properties and profits. They can see no further than the ends of their noses. They don't realize that imperialism has come to draw off these privileges until they are reduced to poverty. Raghib is self-centered and lives like a small child. He is attached to nothing and is happy only to prattle on, picking up something here, something there. That suits a nature that is always fearful that something will go wrong with him. He opposes the revolt simply because it upsets him. But worse than both of them is our brother Mahmud, who is unmoved by anything at all. They are absolutely typical of society as a whole. While I was arguing with Raghib, I saw Mahmud looking at us, not saying anything, as if he couldn't understand anything that was going on around him. I thought of grabbing his shoulders and giving him a good shake. I'd shake him with all my strength simply to try and wake him up from this profound indifference. I think one day I could persuade Raghib, but Mahmud . . . that's totally useless. You're shackled by these rotten old customs and traditions and woe on you if one day you flout them. Mother lives within the walls of this house as if it was a bubble. She hasn't a clue about what's going on outside."

There seemed to be only opportunists, charlatans, and traitors.

"God help us," I said sorrowfully. "Who will take up arms in the revolt and save the country then?"

"Fear not. There are educated people, people who understand and have faith in the cause, believing even that there have to be sacrifices. They can be found in all classes — government officials, students and merchants and property-owners as well. The most important are the workers and peasants. They are emerging with pride, with enthusiasm, and with a simple innocence. They don't complicate matters. The nation is in danger and must be saved. That is all that matters. Fortunately they make up the majority of our country."

"I feel much better," I said.

Why was Sami so much away from home? Sometimes he went off in the morning and was not back until the afternoon. He would come back exhausted. As soon as he had eaten, he would go up to his room, close the door, and sleep. And because he was a young *man* nobody would ask, Where have you been? Where have you come from? He was not reading so much as during the summer vacation. I was not allowed to talk to him about the books he had been reading. And he no longer spoke to me of Nirmin and his meetings with her.

I waited for him to come home. When he had finished eating, he went up to his room and found I was already there.

"Heavens above!" he said. "What's up with you? What do you want?"

"Didn't we agree not to conceal anything from each other? Why are you hiding something important from me?"

"What do you mean?"

"Where do you go every day? Why do you come home, exhausted, with dust all over your clothes? It doesn't look as if you've been with Nirmin."

"We agreed not to hide anything from each other about love and affairs of the heart," he said with a laugh. "We didn't agree to anything else."

"Are you afraid I can't keep a secret?"

"There are some things you can't be careless about."

"I used to think you trusted me. I was wrong."

"Don't worry. I still trust you completely. But I'm afraid you may say something to Mother and Father, or to Raghib, and then everything would be ruined."

"Have no fear on that score. I wouldn't ever make that mistake. Do you take me for a child? Or for being stupid?"

"Very well then, I'll tell you. But be careful. Adil and I have agreed to go every morning to Aunt Umm Rashid's orchard in al-Qadam. There we have target practice using Rashid's ammunition. Rashid is training us along with a whole lot of other young men from Midan. So when we join the revolt we will be trained and ready to mobilize."

"What are you saying? When you join the revolt?"

"What's the matter? You've gone pale. You who were so enthusiastic and so patriotic! What are the poor ignorant women doing then?"

73

"If I was able to go with you and take part in the revolt, I wouldn't be afraid of anything. But when you and Adil go off and join the revolt while I stay here, I burn with anger and am a prisoner of anxiety. That's unbearable."

"Be patient. That too is a great struggle. Be patient. This is a battle in which all are involved."

The revolt flared up in the Ghuta. Insurgents got as far as the suburbs of Damascus and one day fired on a police post in Midan and another in Shaghur. The French were baffled and went berserk. They fortified the police posts and sent out patrols day and night to all parts of the city. Firing on the police posts continued and the French imposed martial law and a dusk-to-dawn curfew.

We gathered together one evening. In tones of triumph, Sami said, "Didn't I tell you that the revolt would extend to the Ghuta?"

"But," said Raghib provocatively, "it will fail, just as the Hama revolt failed. What, apart from frightful losses, have we gained from the Hama revolt? The city has been destroyed and there have been countless innocent victims. They have imposed heavy fines on the people who have been reduced to poverty."

"The revolt in Jabul Druze is still aflame," answered Sami. "It will be reinforced all the more by the Ghuta uprising, for the French will be obliged to disperse their forces all over the place."

"But remember that the voluntary enlistment into the French army of Armenians, Circassians, and other minorities is in full swing. They all have more experience of actual warfare than the insurgents. They also are as numerous and as well armed as the French."

"Recruitment on the insurgent side is also going well. In this quarter alone dozens have joined up overnight."

"But what's the significance of those who join up?"

Raghib sneered. He counted on his fingers. "They're only a handful of politicians. Their objectives are well known. They want to create for themselves a popular base which the French will have to take account of when the revolt is over and the haggling starts. The most popular will get their hands on the best jobs. But the mercenaries are interested only in rape and pillage. Or they are out of work. Or simply stupid, like you."

Sami stood up.

"Are you crazy?" he said furiously. "What's all this you're saying? I bet even the French themselves don't see the insurgents the way you see them. They call them robbers and plunderers in their papers, but that's just propaganda. I believe in their hearts the French respect and appreciate them."

Sami turned to Father.

"Do you imagine, Father," he asked, "that Abu Sa'id the barber left his shop and family and joined the revolt simply for the sake of plunder? Or the imam of the mosque? Or the mathematics teacher? Or our neighbor, the retired officer? Or the seller of cakes, Abu Abdu al-Samkari? Are they all mercenaries?"

"I testify that there is no God but Allah," said Father. "They are all men of virtue and of honor. I know each and every one of them. They have joined up out of a sense of conviction. But the whole business is not without a mercenary aspect, as Raghib says. Anyway, the revolt has flared up. That's a fact, and we've got to support it as far as we can, whether it succeeds or fails. Are we not sons of a nation struggling to be free? Today I made a contribution of twenty-five gold pounds. By Allah, I paid it willingly for the sake of the revolt. There is no merchant in the suq who has not offered what Allah has inspired him to offer."

"That's a lot of money," said Raghib.

"Here we are, four men," said Sami. "If our country was independent and at war in a conventional way, it would be our duty to be involved whether we liked it or not. Or we would make a financial contribution much more than that Father has made."

"That's enough discussion," said Father. "Keep your views to yourselves, each of you. Why is it that whenever we get together we have to have this endless argument?"

"Have you put your name down for the medical school?" I asked Sami. "I've registered at the women's teachers' training college. I start in three days' time."

"Come up to my room," he whispered to me, "and I'll tell you something important."

We went upstairs to his room. He took out some warm clothes. "Is everything all right?" I asked. "Are you going on a journey?"

"Close the door and listen to me. Tomorrow we — Adil and I — are going to join the revolt."

"What are you saying?" I asked, catching my breath.

"Shh . . . not a word," he said, putting his finger on his lips. "Do you suppose the insurgents don't have mothers and sisters? And wives and children and loved ones? I hoped you would give me encouragement like those Arab women we read about in history. I don't expect you to pour cold water on my enthusiasm."

I made no reply and shook my head.

"Do what you can to keep Mother from knowing about this. Poor thing, I get cross with her excessive tenderness. Please make my excuses to Father and to my brothers, because I'm not going to say goodbye to them. They may create difficulties. They'll notice my absence tomorrow evening. Tell them I've joined the revolt. Don't let them know until after sunset. And I'd be grateful if you'd get this letter to Nirmin. Her address is on the envelope. You may be able to go and see her on Sunday, which is her day off from the Franciscan school. I've told her all about you. Please go and see her whenever you can, so we don't lose touch. I'll try and write to her as often as I can."

"And please don't forget about us either."

"As if I could," he said, patting my shoulder.

"Did you tell Nirmin what you are doing?"

"No, but I made a point of talking to her about the revolt so as to know what her views were. She was much more committed than I had expected. I even told her I was surprised at her national feeling. I said, 'You've been brought up in the bosom of the French since you were small.'

"'They teach us how to love our country without them realizing it,' she told me. 'We learn it when we study their history, which is full of sacrifice for freedom and independence.'"

"By Allah, then it's a huge sacrifice you're making. How can you leave Nirmin and join the revolt when you're up to your ears in love?"

"You won't believe me but my love for Nirmin grows stronger with my love for my country. I long for more freedom, for honor, and for a better life. We live in our own country, oppressed and despised. Just think of what we were talking about yesterday. Twenty young men — students and government officials — were arrested and charged with supporting the revolt. The Commissioner of Police interrogated them but got nowhere. He ordered his soldiers to take them to an orchard on the outskirts of Salihiya. He told them to dig a huge trench and then amused himself by shooting them with his own pistol, one by one. All this without a trial. Simply on suspicion. They were then buried in the trench that they had dug with their own hands. Adil and I may suffer the same fate. Who can say otherwise? I have too much respect for you and Nirmin to allow you to live oppressed and despised in a captive country."

Tears poured down my cheeks as I visualized the scene he had described. Sami seemed to me a hero, larger than life. I had never seen him so handsome as at that moment. I then thought of something.

"Have you enough cash on you?" I asked.

"Where can I get the money from? I've got a little bit and Adil and I can borrow some from Rashid to buy a couple of rifles with. But apart from that we don't need any."

"That doesn't make sense." I took off my two valuable gold bracelets and handed them to him.

"No. No. That's impossible. I can never accept those."

"I'm not allowed to join the struggle. Why do you also deny me the chance of giving to the revolt what belongs to me?"

"I'm afraid of Mother and Father, and Raghib as well, being cross with you."

"Let them be cross. Let them beat me if they want to. People are dying and suffering torment for the sake of the revolt. Am I not able to put up with blame, or a beating, if you wish? If you don't take them, I'll let everybody know what you're doing straightaway.

"All right then, give them to me and please be quiet." He paused and then added, "I'll take one for myself. Give me the other one for Adil if you like the idea."

"I like that idea a lot. Give him my best wishes when you hand it over to him."

"And your affection as well. We'll sell them tomorrow and give what we get to Rashid so he can get us the rifles."

He weighed them in his hand.

"They're heavy," he said. "Maybe we'll get more than we need for them. Sabriya, this is going to make Adil a very happy man and he won't ever forget you. What a splendid pledge of love you are giving him. Love of your country with Adil as the medium. Do go now and let me get my things together. Come and say goodbye. We may not have the chance tomorrow."

We embraced and I left his room, holding back the tears, for I didn't want anyone in the household to notice.

I did not sleep at all that night. I was in a state of acute anxiety and turmoil. I saw in my mind the atrocities the French had committed in Hama. My blood boiled at what we had to put up with. Had not Sami said that the road would be long, very long, and that many sacrifices would be required?

When I got up next morning, Sami was nowhere to be found in the house. It was his custom to go out early, so his absence aroused no comment. The day passed and I couldn't concentrate on anything. I wandered around the house from room to room. When Mother wanted me to do something, I obeyed as if I was a rusty old machine.

Father and my two brothers came home at sunset. The night curfew was still in force.

"Where's Sami?" asked Father. "Heavens above, that boy likes to get into trouble. If he is picked up by a patrol now, he'll be shot on the spot."

I swallowed hard.

"Sami won't be coming back, Father," I said in a shaky voice. "He's gone and joined the revolt."

The impact was as if I had tossed down a hand grenade. Mother struck her breast and shrieked, "Woe on me for this affliction. I have lost my boy."

Mahmud got up and slapped his hands together, saying dramatically, "Then he's gone and done it. I was afraid he would. What is he going to achieve? He's never handled a gun in his life."

Raghib turned to me.

"Why have you only now told us?" he asked. "I've been here all afternoon and you've kept this news to yourself. If I had been told, I'd have known how to dissuade him."

"He asked me not to tell you until the evening. He also told me to apologize to you for not saying goodbye."

"You realize," said Raghib, "you're putting your own brother in danger. Hundreds of insurgents are being killed every day."

Father then said, weighing his words carefully, "Nothing happens except by the will of Allah. Why are you grieving as if the boy has died? All that has happened is in accordance with what Allah has determined for us. He's in the same position as any other insurgent. There are plenty like him. Sami is grown up and is responsible for himself. Tell us, Sabriya, with whom has he gone and in what way?"

"He went with his friend Adil."

"All our troubles come from that son of a baker," said Raghib. "He reckons he is the philosopher of his time."

I said with emotion and without reflection, "But it was Sami who persuaded Adil to join the insurgents, not the other way round."

Raghib stared at me with wide-open eyes and said, "You seem to know a lot about it. Have you been attending their meetings?"

"How could I? I don't leave the house unless I am with Mother. In fact, Sami told me."

"Good heavens. Then you've been harboring Sami's secret."

"This is of no importance now," said Father. "Tell us, Sabriya. Whereabouts in the Ghuta is he heading for? Which group is he joining? Perhaps we can get in touch with him and get some money to him."

"He didn't tell me anything about that. It didn't occur to me to ask him. But he did tell me that he'd send us letters whenever he had the chance."

"I take refuge in Allah," said Raghib. "If one of his letters fell into the hands of the French, our house would be ruined. Allah Almighty, what trouble we're going to have as a result of him joining the revolt."

"Nothing matters," observed Mother, "so long as he comes home safe and sound. I pray that Allah keeps him from evil."

"I'm very concerned," said Father, "that he has set off without having enough money for his needs. The revolt is not being conducted by a regular army that provides its men with everything."

"Don't you worry, Father," I said. "I gave him my bracelets to sell." Raghib exploded.

"This crazy woman," he said, "is the one who has egged him on to join the revolt. She wants to model herself on what she has been reading in storybooks."

Father frowned and said, "How can you dispose of your bracelets without taking my advice? Did I give them to you so could sell them to whoever you liked?"

"Allah, what she has done is all right, Abu Raghib," Mother then said. "I'd have done the same thing if I'd been in her place." She then looked gravely at Raghib and added, "What is there between you and Sabriya? She has disposed of her own property. Has she taken anything from you?"

I felt as if I was being suffocated and burst into tears. I left them and went upstairs to my room.

Two days later Father sent for me when he got home from work. He put his hand in his pocket and brought out a blue velvet box. He opened it and said, "Just see how beautiful this bracelet is. It is more valuable than the pair of bracelets you gave to Sami. Make sure you don't give it to anybody. Otherwise I'll never buy anything for you again." He kissed me on the head and added, "May Allah be happy with you." His eyes were filled with tears.

I took the box from him and was almost in tears myself. I looked at the bracelet. It really was beautiful. There was a clasp in the form of two heads of intertwined snakes made out of small diamonds and rubies.

"May Allah never take you away from me, Father," I said, and ran off to show Mother the bracelet.

"That's really lovely," she said. "Congratulations, dear daughter. Your father is indebted to you because you gave the pair of bracelets to Sami. He said that day that he would buy you a better bracelet. He said you were a girl in a million, fashioned by compassion, goodness, and honor. And he has kept his promise. May Allah keep him with us forever."

What a gap Sami left behind him in the house. There was nobody in the house I could talk to as I had talked to Sami and I became introspective and suspicious. Two days passed very slowly.

But on the following Sunday I started the course at the training college. I got up early and took Sami's letter along to Nirmin. I took the tram from the Salihiya Gate to al-Jisr al-Abyad, which was not far from the training college. All the way I was wondering how this young lady would receive me. How closely would she fit the picture I had formed in my mind from Sami's description of her? I reached the house without any difficulty. It was at the beginning of a quarter that branched off from al-Jisr al-Abyad. I knocked at the door. After a moment it was opened by a tall, slim girl with ivory skin and black hair. She was wearing a house-dress. I glanced at her from head to foot. She was just as I had imagined her. I raised my veil and said, "I am Sabriya, Sami's sister."

Her pretty honey-colored eyes showed astonishment.

"You are most welcome," she said. "Do come in. Do come in."

"I'd love to but I've got to go on to my studies," I said, handing her Sami's letter. "Sami wrote this for you before joining the revolt."

Her eyes widened and she turned pale.

"The revolt?" she said. "I knew he was very committed to the revolt, but he never told me he was going to join up."

"Nor did he say anything to his parents or his brothers. He was afraid they'd get in the way. I do hope it will be possible for me to see you from time to time."

"I'd love to see you too. I want to hear news of Sami from you."

Her eyes filled with tears. We both stretched out our arms and
shook hands. I gripped hers hard. She smiled affectionately at me.

I walked down from al-Jisr al-Abyad to my college. I was filled
with all sorts of beautiful fantasies that were also tinged with something
like fear. Would the revolt succeed? Would Sami and Adil come back
safe and sound? Would I see Sami as bridegroom with Nirmin on his
arm, walking along in a flowing white dress looking like an angel?
Would Adil and I get married without any difficulty and live the life of
bliss we had dreamt of? What surprises did fate have in store?

I went into the college. The vast courtyard was like a beehive,
full of young girls who had come from all parts of Syria, for the
training college provided the only secondary education for girls in
the whole of the country. I joined some girls from my old school,
greeting them after the long separation of the summer break. Suddenly a bell was rung by the college superintendent.

The superintendent was a small red-headed woman with a freck-
led face who — I learned later — was Jewish and had very good
French. She was the sole link between the girls and the French
administration and the teachers. She stood in the middle of the
courtyard and called out, "Students of the seventh grade must stand
in a line and follow me."

We got behind her and followed her to the upper floor. She stood
at the door of the assembly hall and read out our names and took
us in one at a time. She pointed out our places until the hall was
full. She then came in after us.

"You are now going to have an Arabic lesson. Here is the time-
table," she said, pointing to a board on the wall. "You can copy it
down after the lesson," she added, and then left.

Shortly afterwards the Arabic teacher came in. He was a turbaned
shaykh with a white beard, of formidable appearance, dressed in a
dyed gown. He sat down on the platform and looked at us for a
moment without saying anything. There was a total silence. Some
girls lowered their veils over their faces and nothing at all could be
seen of them. Others fastened their headscarves under their chins,
concealing their hair. And others raised their veils without in any
way concealing their hair. I was among these.

He read out our names and became acquainted with us one by

one. He then called one girl out to the blackboard and dictated a line of poetry to her. He explained its meaning to us and then asked her to parse it. He talked about the words and showed us how to recite it. He told us to memorize what he said.

There was a big difference between the methods of our women teachers and the method of this teacher. I preferred the latter and I absorbed everything that the shaykh told us. Other lessons followed — history, chemistry, French. We got to know the teachers. In the middle of the chemistry lesson there was a tap at the door and the French principal came in with the superintendent. The principal was a tall lady with a ferocious look. She had come to inspect our class and made some remarks in a low voice to the superintendent. She then talked to the teacher in French.

I cannot explain why I had a feeling of revulsion from the moment I set eyes on her.

What would her attitude to me be, I wondered, if she knew that my brother was one of the insurgents in the Ghuta who was keeping the French on their toes night and day?

As time went on I derived a great deal of comfort from college, escaping from the oppressive atmosphere of the house, from Mother's sighs and from Raghib's remarks. I got to know my new fellow students. I sensed some of them had a great enthusiasm for the revolt, and I confided to them that my brother was an insurgent. In turn they brought me news they heard about the revolt.

The days went by and we adjusted to the new situation as the revolt spread like wildfire. The sound of gunfire all night became part of our lives. No sooner was there an attempt to crush them than the insurgents managed to reach the outskirts of Damascus and strike at one of the police posts. The French retaliated from behind their fortifications. We learned to distinguish the sound of French fire from that of the insurgents. The insurgents' ammunition was not of uniform size and kind, so every rifle shot was different. One would make a snoring sound. Another would make a whizzing noise or a sound like the chirping of birds. One could be German, another Ottoman or Austrian. When part of the night went by without the sound of gunfire, we would anxiously wonder what was happening.

Why were the insurgents not stirring things up? In the mornings the French would mobilize forays into the Ghuta, returning at nightfall, having accomplished nothing because news of the expedition reached the insurgents as soon as it left Damascus. Precautions would be taken and the expedition would be either attacked from the rear or ambushed. And so the French suffered more casualties than the insurgents. The French aircraft were unable to discover the massing of insurgents in the dense Ghuta woodlands and so could not guide the expeditions to them.

I shall never forget the songs we used to sing about the insurgents. We would sing them during the afternoon break when the superintendent was off-guard. One fellow student had a clear rhythmical voice. We would gather round her and ask her to sing. She quickly agreed and chanted to us:

"Arise and hearken, my darlings, to the sound of the bomb and the tank

For our men have arrived."

Then we would chant:

"The French have set off and have suffered great losses."

She would then chant with greater fervor:

"Arise and hearken, good neighbor, to the sound of cannon in our quarter

For our men have arrived."

And we would chorus:

"The French have set off and have suffered great losses."

One afternoon some girls who went out for lunch brought news of some heavy losses. A French force had set out for the Ghuta and had killed a large number of insurgents. The bodies were brought back on mules and displayed in Martyrs' Square as a warning to people.

I almost screamed when I heard this. My heart beat faster and faster. I felt I could not stay at the college in such a state of anxiety. The college gate was open and I went out, heading for Martyrs' Square. My hair stood on end; my heart beat furiously. I then stopped and retraced my steps, realizing that what I was doing was crazy. In such a state I would be unable to get all the way to Martyrs' Square. Would I be able to look at the mutilated bodies? And supposing among them I saw . . . Allah give me strength.

My knees gave way under me and I almost collapsed. I checked how much cash I had on me. It was enough for a carriage. I waited for one, which took me to our house in Suq Saruja. Mahmud had already come home. I was alarmed by his ashen face and wild eyes. He signaled to me to keep quiet and to follow him upstairs so that Mother, who was busy in the kitchen, would not hear us. He said in a voice that was much disturbed, "It's all right. I've seen all the bodies. I can assure you that they are not insurgents. They are peasants and ordinary workers. I can tell that from their clothes and from the way they look."

He collapsed on to his bed and started wailing to relieve his bottled-up feelings. He wept and wept and wept. I stood there embarrassed, not having a clue how to calm him down. I was even afraid that he'd have a heart attack and rushed off and got some rose-water. I sprinkled some on his face and gave him some to drink. He gradually calmed down.

"I heard the news at law school and my heart sank," he told me. "I was afraid Sami might have been among those killed. I raced from the school to Martyrs' Square without thinking of anything. Just imagine. I stood there and stared at those corpses, mutilated, bloodstained, and covered in mud. I didn't recognize any of the bodies. What kind of an outrage is this? Those swine can't kill the insurgents, so they slaughter defenseless civilians. They display the disfigured corpses and claim to be humane and civilized!" He started weeping again.

Mahmud was ill for three days after that, quite incapable of going to law school.

I realized that Sami had been unfair in blaming Mahmud. He was simply made that way. How could Sami want him to join the revolt and see dead people all the time or to practice killing people, however much he felt it was justified?

I passed an awful night after this. I felt I myself was at the battle-front. The insurgents were attacking all the police posts around the city of Damascus and were even reaching some of the city quarters and striking at city police posts.

The sound of artillery fire from the Damascus citadel directed at the Ghuta became merged with the zing of bullets and the droning of aircraft. I was unable to get any sleep until dawn. Nor, I think, did my parents either. Each of us kept what we were suffering to ourselves. I would visualize each bullet I heard striking the breast of either Sami or Adil. My heart plunged into a bottomless abyss.

May Allah pardon you, Sami, when you told me that my steadfastness was also part of the struggle and that I should have the courage of those who are fighting. Brother dear, this silent struggle is hard, very hard. It is unsung. It is heroism without the glory.

I woke up exhausted, my mind in confusion. I did not want to go to college and there was nobody who cared whether I went or not. When Father went out, I said to Mother, "Haven't you been worried about Sami? He has been gone a whole month and we've not had any news from him."

"You're asking *me* this question? Haven't I been on tenterhooks all this time?"

"But you've done nothing to find out about him."

"What can I do?"

"We could go to Aunt Umm Rashid and get news of the insurgents from her."

"Why should Umm Rashid have more news than us?"

"I didn't tell you, but Rashid has also joined the revolt. And Midan is nearer to the insurgents' bases. Aunt is sure to have plenty of news."

Mother thought for a moment.

"But we don't have permission from your father," she said.

"Sometimes I almost explode with anger at you, Mother. A woman of your age, old enough to be a grandmother, having to seek permission from her husband whenever she wants to leave the house!"

"Well, that's what I'm used to."

"Let's ignore this custom just for once, in order to get some reassurance about Sami. We can go there and get back without anybody knowing anything about it."

"Right, let's go then."

She would never have agreed if she had not been so acutely anxious about Sami after that terrible night.

Less than an hour later we were knocking at Umm Rashid's door. At first there was no answer and we were almost in despair, ready to go back home. Then Aunt's voice reached us, soft and anxious, "Who is it?"

She was reassured by our voices and opened the door.

"May Allah reward you. What has brought you here so early in the morning? I almost died of fright."

"Why, Aunt?"

She made no reply but led us into the kitchen.

"You see what I've been doing?" she said.

There was a pile of rifle ammunition on the kitchen floor.

"Rashid — may Allah keep him — placed all these bullets in kerosene containers," she explained, "and then buried them at the time the French were starting to round up arms in Midan. It seemed to us, light of my life, that the insurgents did not have enough ammunition. Rashid sent me a message, asking for this ammunition, come what may. I dug it up, but it was covered with dirt and rust. I've been able to clean half of it and take it to him. And this is what's left. When you called I was sitting polishing each bullet so that it shone like gold."

As Aunt was talking, Mother looked at her, eyes wide with amazement.

"How did you get it to the Ghuta?" I asked. "There are French police posts everywhere. In the name of Allah, Aunt, you're a heroine."

"The credit is not due to me, by Allah. It is due to a neighbor who is not well-off. He's got a cart which he uses. I went to him and told him the story.

"'Upon my soul, dear lady,' he said, 'your wish is my command.' He would take no payment for what he did, I swear to Allah, even though he is poor and has a family. He explained to me, 'I want to do something for the revolt. I want to get my own back on them. I can't join up because of my family. So, Allah forgive you, how can you want me to take a payment?' We put the bullets in the donkey's nose-bag and covered them with straw. I dressed up as a peasant woman and we rode together on the cart. At the police checkpoints they inspected us but couldn't find anything. One checkpoint, then another, then another, until we reached the Ghuta."

"I thank Allah that you are safe, Aunt. Can you give us good news about how Sami and Rashid are?"

"Praise be to Allah, they're both as fit as lions. I sat with them and they told me how they attacked police posts and French forces were sent out after them. And also how they set up ambushes. They introduced me to their comrades and to somebody called Adil, who's from your part of the city. He's a friend of Sami, Allah bless them. The day before yesterday this friend shot at an airplane with his antiquated firepiece. The plane was flying low, so as to show the French infantry where the insurgents were gathered. A couple of his shots hit the fuel tank and the plane burst into flames. I saw the wreckage with my own eyes."

She raised her hands and went on, "May Allah preserve you, Adil, for your mother and for your country. May your hand be blessed, you splendid hero. Sabriya, do go and call on his mother and comfort her. Tell her what I've told you."

I found myself falling on my aunt, hugging and kissing her, the tears pouring down my cheeks. She didn't realize that it was because of my pride in Adil.

"I'll go today," I told her, "and see Umm Adil and tell her all about her brave son."

Aunt told us more about her adventures and Mother gazed on in silent wonder, seeming to contrast herself with her sister. Her self-esteem dropped as her respect for Aunt rose to an extent I could hardly believe. Aunt then said, "Winter has set in and some of the insurgents — poor things — don't have any warm clothing. An *abaya* is essential because they sometimes have to sleep in the open and need to wrap themselves up. I went round our quarter yesterday and collected thirty gold pounds in one day from neighbors and people we know. No household refused to pay as much as they could and I'm going to buy some *abayas* tomorrow. My friend with the cart is happy to get them to the insurgents in the Ghuta."

"Why don't we do that in our quarter?" I suggested to Mother.

"Allah, yes," she replied, "no reason why not, even if your father divorces me!"

We laughed at Mother's surprising zeal for the cause. I then said to Aunt, "You must take me to the Ghuta one day."

"This is just what we need," said Mother. "If you were kidnapped by some Senegalese or French soldier, what would we say to your father?"

"No, my dear, no," said Aunt. "I wouldn't be able to face your father."

"Please, when you next go to the Ghuta, do please give my greetings to Sami and Rashid and their comrades, and especially to Adil. Tell him that Sami's sister, Sabriya, sends him her congratulations."

We said our farewells and left Aunt, taking a tram. I talked to myself as we went back, keen, optimistic, and happy.

"If we can bring down airplanes, what more do we need? I'll tell my fellow students about Adil. I'll describe him to them without saying anything about our relationship."

We left the tram at Martyrs' Square and walked the rest of the way to Suq Saruja.

"I shall go and see Adil's mother," I said to Mother, "and put her mind at rest as Aunt wanted me to do."

"Don't be away for more than a few minutes."

Adil's house was only a short distance from our house. His mother was a bit anxious when she saw me.

"Everything's all right with Adil," I told her. "We've received news from the Ghuta and have heard that he and Sami are in good health." I then told her the story about the plane.

She hugged me and kissed me, saying, "It's good to hear your news, dear neighbor. The news is as welcome as your sweet face. Abu Adil will be delighted to hear it."

She invited me in for some coffee but I made my excuses and went back home.

No sooner had I taken my shawl off than Father came in. It was the hour of the midday prayer and he did not normally come home at this time.

"You and your mother must hide," he said, grim-faced. "I've some men with me."

"Why has he turned up now?" Mother said to me. "Make sure you don't mention our trip to Midan to see your aunt. He'd never forgive us."

I looked out of the window and saw two men bringing some chests into the central courtyard. Then Father came in to see us.

"The situation has become very critical," he said. "The insurgents are attacking the French patrols in broad daylight. There have been bullets flying about over our heads. All the stores have been closed. I've shut up our store and have brought whatever I could here. I've also brought some provisions which we might need. Allah knows what the next few days will bring."

Mother sighed silently. Each of us spoke to our own selves, concealing anxieties and forebodings.

This night was more disturbed than the previous one. In the morning Father said nobody was to leave the house.

"I'll not go out of the quarter, Father," said Raghib. "I'll just find out what's going on, nothing more."

Mahmud complied with Father's instruction. From the morning there was the unceasing sound of gunfire. Raghib was in and out of the house, bringing back news. It was the only time I ever heard Raghib say anything in praise of the insurgents.

"People are actually saying that the insurgents have been acting with the most amazing heroism. The High Commissioner is in Damascus visiting the Azem Palace. The insurgents have attacked the palace and the surrounding quarters. They've charged at tanks and hurled hand grenades. They say the High Commissioner has left the palace surrounded by his guards. He went off in one tank escorted by others. He has gone straight to Lebanon. I was told this by someone who saw it with his own eyes from a minaret overlooking the courtyard of the palace."

"Too bad," said Father. "If only they had been able to kill the High Commissioner or to kidnap him. He's a madman. He's got us and his country into this mess. If he had treated the Druzes with more forbearance, there would not have been a general revolt. Indeed, those victims who have fallen are all a charge to him."

Mother did no cooking that day. We did not sit around the table to eat. If one of us felt hungry, we could go to the kitchen and help ourselves to a snack.

Planes came and circled above. There followed the sound of cannon and explosives. It became almost dark. Raghib went up to the roof and came back immediately.

"You'll hardly believe this," he said. "Shells are coming from al-Mazza and from the citadel of Damascus. They are coming down in the heart of the city, quite near here. I saw it all with my own eyes."

"Our beloved Damascus, what an outrage," said Mahmud. "These dogs are destroying you over the heads of your citizens."

Just as he spoke we heard a crash in the central courtyard. Raghib looked down from the window.

"I can see fragments of shells and bullets," he said.

"It's mad for us to be here. We should all go down to the cellar," suggested Mahmud.

"You're right, my son," Father agreed. "Let's go down."

We all went down to the cellar, each carrying a blanket or an overcoat. We rolled a carpet out and sat on it in silence. Our faces seemed to be different. They were lined by panic and distress.

Mother wept.

"Oh dear, oh dear," she wailed. "My mind has gone out of my head." She recited the Throne Verse from the Qur'an and then added the prayer taking refuge in the Lord Allah of creation. "Oh my dear, dear Sami, where are you now, my boy? Killed? Or maimed? And nobody to look after you."

"Shut up, woman," snapped Father. "Allah will recompense good for evil. We can do without your moaning. All of us are exposed to the same danger."

"Allah," reflected Mahmud aloud. "If the house collapsed and we were all to be buried alive in this cellar and nobody knew anything about it, that would really be a horrible way to go. Sami is in a far better situation than we are. He would die an honorable death. He would be dying for a cause."

Father grumbled at this talk of death.

"Stop talking about it, Mahmud. May Allah be pleased with you."

As for myself, I had no sense of fear at all. My mind was seething and I felt heartbroken.

"What cowards we are," I observed to Mahmud. "Our country is being burnt and destroyed and we are like rats who have slunk into their holes."

"What do you want us to do?" he asked with some asperity. "Scratch at the skies? It's you who wanted the revolt. And this is what revolts mean. The only thing we get is ruin and destruction. Just wait and see."

"But it cannot build until it has first destroyed. If all the men and women of Damascus stormed the citadel, they would be able to take it over and silence the cannons."

Father checked me and said firmly, "I don't want to hear another word. Say rather, 'Allah, deliver us from evil.' Say that in your hearts, I beg of you."

There was an electric power failure and we were plunged into utter darkness. The din of the explosions became louder. I huddled closer to Mother. I could hear the muttering of her prayers and the regular beat of her heart. We stayed like this until the next dawn. I have never known a night so long.

We were heedless of the damp in the cellar. We neither ate nor drank. We did not go to the toilet. We did not doze. We were, each one of us, a bundle of nerves, tense and self-absorbed, expecting an awful death at any moment.

We opened the cellar door to let in the pale yellowish beams of dawn. Raghib went up a few steps to survey the central courtyard.

"Praise be to Allah," he said. "The house is still there, but there doesn't seem to be a single pane of unbroken glass."

The sound of cannon, shells, and rifle-fire could still be heard coming from all around. The din was louder with the cellar door open. I looked at Mother's face. It seemed as if she was about to faint. Her face had the wan coloring of death, her eyes were unfocused, and her lips and turned white. Raghib went up the steps and I followed.

"Come back, girl," Father shouted. "If you're hit by a bullet or a shell, you'll be killed instantly."

"Just a second, Baba," I said. "I'm only going to the kitchen next door."

I found Raghib leaning on the wall. He said to me, "Don't tell them that I'm going out. I'm going to take a walk round the quarter to get news. I'll soon be back."

I went into the kitchen and made a pot of tea and took it down on a tray with a large piece of cheese and some cake.

"May Allah reward you, my girl," said Father. "You've exposed yourself to danger for the sake of poisoning us with tea and cake. Is this the best time?"

"We're all very thirsty and can't put up with it much longer."

I poured out a cup for Mother and helped her drink it. She rallied somewhat.

"Get your strength back, Umm Raghib," Father said. "Leave it to Allah, old lady. You believe in Him. We will not be afflicted except as Allah decides for us."

He then turned round and said, "Where's Raghib? Where's that idiot gone?"

"I expect he went to the toilet," I suggested.

We ate the cake and the cheese, and drank the tea to the din of the cannon and shells and the whiz of the bullets.

Raghib came back, his face pale. All his blood seemed to have drained away. He was shaking as he spoke.

"The swine . . . they've destroyed Damascus. It's become a ruin. The casualties must be tens of thousands. Most of the houses of the quarter have been deserted and are protected only by a handful of the local street-gang leaders. We have no idea when it'll be our turn. Everybody has fled to the Muhajirin quarter, leaving behind the bodies of their children, their possessions and their money under the rubble, fuel for the fire. What do you think of the idea of going up to Muhajirin ourselves before this part of the city is bombed? They say the French will never bomb the Muhajirin quarter because they have suggested that the foreign missions go there for safety. The people of Muhajirin have opened their houses for refugees from the rest of the city and are feeding them as much as they can."

"No, my son," answered Father. "In circumstances like these, we are each of us responsible for our own selves. You and your brother can go up if you wish. I am responsible for myself and these two women —" and he pointed to Mother and myself. "We shall not leave here. Let what will happen. If it is our destiny to die, then what can be sweeter than to die and to be buried in our own house?"

"I'm not going to leave here either," asserted Mahmud.

"I can't leave you here and go by myself, even if I wanted to," said Raghib. "Either we all live or we all die."

He came back to his place in the cellar and had some cake, nibbling at it nervously in silence.

The bombardment went on all day. We did not close the cellar door. We felt bitter and resigned rather than terrified. We kept our own peace and a flame was kindled in our hearts. Every now and then one of us would say a few words about the situation we were in, wondering how long it would go on. Or one of us would go up to the kitchen and bring some food for the others, some bread and olives, or some purified buttermilk. We would then return to our solemn silence, to our humiliating surrender to events.

The day went by very slowly. Night fell — another night like the previous ones? Intolerable. We were at the end of our tether. But in spite of the incessant noise of cannon and shells, we were able from time to time to snatch some sleep after our wakeful rigors. We would then wake up, even more tense and anxious than before.

The explosions did not let up for a moment. We no longer felt any fear. We seemed no longer to care. We fell into a terrible state of apathy. We would come out of the cellar and go to the bathroom or the kitchen. Shrapnel would fall nearby and we would step coolly over the pieces on our way to brew some tea.

There was a pause in the bombardment during the afternoon. It then resumed and then stopped again, and we had no idea what was going on around us.

During one lull in the bombardment Raghib went out, ignoring both Father's instructions and Mother's pleadings. He was away for a long time and we became worried. When he came back, he told us that he had heard that the headmen of the various quarters of Damascus were parleying with the French. The French were ready to cease the bombardment if the insurgents withdrew from all parts of the city, and if the citizens paid the fines in cash and in weaponry that the French would impose. The headmen went themselves to the insurgents and confronted them with the order and they agreed to withdraw.

"Our insurgents have not been routed then," I said. "They have retreated so as to preserve this precious city from devastation and out of consideration for its inhabitants."

Damascenes started returning to the ruins of their houses as soon as the bombardment stopped. They dug out the bodies of their loved one from the ashes and rubble and buried them in silent grief. They returned to their houses to sort out and inspect what was left of their valuables that had been buried.

Saidi Amud Street, which included the oldest and most prosperous houses, was totally gutted. In due course, that area and adjacent quarters became known as Hariqa, or Conflagration. Objects of value in Damascus — expensive trifles, evidence of successive ancient civilizations in our land which had been cherished with the utmost care for generation after generation — all were destroyed, fuel for the flames of destruction.

After this calamity Damascus became like a humble dove that folds its wings over a fracture and remains silent in steadfast defiance. Damascus, a smile of sorrow, harboring tragedy.

The secret of your eternal survival, dear Damascus, is that silence in the face of disaster. You have suffered so much. Through raids and plunder you remain forever.

In spite of the enemy's ferocious tyranny in his treatment of the old city and of its defenseless, innocent citizens, the revolt was still raging. Heads were held high and determination did not falter. People were more ready to join the revolt after the bombardment than before. Dear land, what you offered was your spirit, your sons, and your wealth.

In the midst of these anxious times, Abu Adil the baker continued to bring us bread with comforting regularity. He had received a letter from his son with the news that both Adil and Sami had come out of a bloody battle in good shape. Some insurgents from our quarter had lost their lives, but the quarter did not mourn for any of them as much as they mourned for the upright Abu Abdu al-Samkari who, it was said, had been killed in front of the Azem Palace after having thrown a hand grenade and destroyed a tank and its crew.

Abu Abdu was both courageous and astute. Nothing got in his way. Whenever anyone from the quarter came to him with a request, he would respond immediately. He would close his store and do what was asked of him. He would stipulate no wage, but would put what was given to him in his pocket without a glance. You

could always find him laughing cheerily as if the younger generation of the quarter were his children and the older ones his family
and friends. He was a poor man, with a wife and four children to
look after. His wife worked as a washerwoman for the quarter. Every
Thursday she came to do our washing and then helped Mother
clean the house.

On that Thursday morning there was a knock at the front door.
I was surprised to see Umm Abdu there, only two days after her
husband had been killed. I gave her a hug and cried when I saw
how thin and pale she was.

"You must be in mourning and very tired, Umm Abdu," I said.
"We won't do any washing today. Here's what we normally pay
you. Do go home to your children."

"No, by Allah," she insisted. "I shall not go home. I've got your
washing to do. Today is the day I always do it. You are overwhelming
me with your kindness, but work takes my mind off things, my dear."
And she wiped away the tears with her sleeve as she began to weep.

In her whole life Umm Abdu had never enjoyed any luxuries.
How now could she afford the luxury of grief? The breadwinner
had gone and she shared the hunger of her four children. She had
no time to allow herself any rest, and she nursed her grief until the
wound was almost healed.

She sat down in front of the washing bowl and rolled the sleeves
up her tawny arms. Thick blue veins quivered, witness to what she
had had to put up with throughout her life. She went to work with
her usual thoroughness. From time to time tears poured down her
cheeks. She wiped them away automatically and went on with her
work.

"I'll hang out the washing today," I said.

"May Allah increase your goodness. By Allah, if I had the strength
to go up to the roof, I'd go and hang it out myself."

As I took the washing from her, she was looking upwards out of
the corner of her eye, saying, "May Allah not reward him."

"Who are you beseeching Allah not to reward, Umm Abdu?" I
asked.

She stopped wringing the clothes, looked at me and shook her
head.

"Shaykh Abdul Ghani . . . He went on grumbling to my husband until the joined the revolt. He would say to him, 'The French are going to violate the honor of our womenfolk. The French are going to destroy our mosques. The French . . . the French . . . He who meets his death in the course of the struggle will have a palace in heaven as lofty as this, and as wide as this.' Tell me, Sabriya, why didn't the shaykh and his sons join the revolt? Each of them has the strength of an ass.

"This is what makes my blood boil. My poor husband went off — the father of a family. He was a man of honor. He used to say to me, 'Do you want me to be an honorable man, Umm Abdu? All my comrades have joined the revolt to defend their honor and their country. Am I to lie hidden in my store like a woman in her house?'

"One day he went out, saying to me, 'I have commended you and the children to Allah' . . . And he never came back."

She then looked hard at me and said from her heart, "We're a poor lot, a wretched lot. We chase after our bread from morn to night. What does the revolt, what do politics mean to us? It will be all the same to us whether it is the French or a national government that rules us. Or whether we are ruled by blue monkeys."

I looked at her for a long time, taking in the words that impressed me. I then said, "No, no, Umm Abdu, what kind of talk is this? You're a sensible woman. The nation is for everybody, for poor and rich alike. The French are intruders here. They have come to seize our resources and to grind us down so the rich become poor and the poor die of hunger. But a national government would concern itself with every individual. It would build schools and hospitals. It would help the poor and find work for them. It would help them build homes. Charity and justice would be available to all."

Umm Abdu thought for a while.

"Don't blame me, my girl," she said. "By Allah, from the day I suffered this tragedy my mind has not been the same. I'm saying all sorts of things so as to get it all out of my system. Allah gives us the good things and may He give victory to the insurgents and may He preserve Sami for you and look after all the other insurgents."

She went back to her scouring and washing with more energy than ever. The simple woman seemed to be persuaded by a few words. In turn she persuaded me of her point of view without her realizing it. The reference to Sami reminded me of the anxiety in my own heart. I recalled his long talk about social justice and the struggle against poverty, sickness, and ignorance. I shall never forget something he said: "When we have achieved our independence we shall embark on a battle among ourselves fiercer than the one we are waging with the imperialists."

I thought of the costly bracelet Father had given me. Do I possess this precious trinket to wear only on a few occasions? There are children who are in agonies of hunger because their providers have died for their country. I looked at Umm Abdu and at her body drained with grief and exhaustion, driving itself on to work. I ran up to my room, with the image of your precious eyes before me, dear brother. I went to the drawer of my cupboard and took out the bracelet. It was still in its box, for I have not worn it. I hid the box in my pocket and went off to the kitchen. Mother was absorbed in getting a meal ready. I returned to Umm Abdu, who was still at work near the pool in the central courtyard.

"Did anyone in the quarter make a contribution to you, Umm Abdu?" I asked.

"Yes. May Allah reward those who do good. Your father was the most generous of those who made a donation. May he long be with us. He gave me three gold pounds. The headman of the quarter — he's an excellent man as you know — advised me not to touch the money he had collected for us, so he could buy a room for my children and me to live in. I can then feed them as a result of my own efforts, my girl, and they're still flesh and blood, my heart's delight, and they need a crust of bread, but can I pay the rent for a room? We're at the end of the month."

"Is the money that's been collected enough to buy the room?"

"If only it were! . . . It's not enough to buy half a room. People have become tight with their money, putting pennies aside for a rainy day. They're right. We are at war, rainy days. But the headman consoled me by saying, 'Things will get better, Umm Abdu. Allah knows what we know not. Be patient.'"

I took out the box and opened it. The bracelet sparkled in the sunlight.

"Do take this, Umm Abdu," I said. "Sell it and add what it gets to what you have."

She looked at the bracelet in astonishment.

"No, no, my lady," she said. "What a loss it would be. Allah bless you for it. If Allah wills, you must wear it on your wedding day."

"Keep your voice down. This is something between ourselves. I don't want anybody else to know."

"In the name of Allah," she whispered, "I can't take it from you. Your father has paid enough and more."

"This is my personal property. If you don't take it, I'll offer it to somebody else who has lost someone in their family in the struggle."

"I'm more entitled to it than others. I'm a widow, the mother of orphans, without any property. But I'm afraid that I'd be suspected of having stolen it. Where would someone like me lay hands on something like that?"

"If you get into any problem like that, then come to me and don't let it bother you. But take care not to be cheated by anybody."

"I'll take my cousin with me. He's familiar with the suq and understands such matters."

I handed the box over and she hid it in her bosom, mumbling to me a prayer.

I said, "Allah, look after Adil and Sami." I then laughed at myself and thought, "What a cheap bribe! . . . But it is all I hope for you. I ask Allah for His pardon. It is not a bribe. It is a sacrificial offering. Did You not accept the ram of Ibrahim instead of his son, Ismail? Or is it necessary to shed blood for You to receive sacrifices?"

Nobody asked any questions about the bracelet. The memory of it was lost in the flood of terrible events that we went through afterwards. Damascus's disaster awakened pride and aroused rage in the minds of many from all parts of Syria who went off in large numbers to join the insurgents, in angry defiance of the imperialists. Jabal Druze sent men to the Ghuta and provided weapons that had been taken from the enemy. The French felt hopeless, sending one expedition after another, returning outwitted, after suffering terrible losses.

The months went by. The insurgents held their own. The soil of the land was daily soaked with the blood of martyrs. The French started to recruit new battalions of mercenaries who lived off the land. They turned their backs on their own people. These mercenaries had no mercy when the French let them loose on the villages of the Ghuta. They would plunder what there was and then burn the place down and torture the inhabitants.

Early one morning there was a knock at the door. I went to open it, filled with sudden panic. Who could it be so early in the morning?

Aunt Umm Rashid stood there with a flushed face and bloodshot eyes popping out of her head.

"Speak, Aunt," I said, my heart beating wildly. "What's happened to you? Has something happened to Sami?"

She embraced me.

"Yesterday. Yesterday, how my heart grieves for him, he fell in battle."

She then cried out, in her clear loud voice, "Heaven help you, Sami, you hero, you patriot. You are one of the best."

At the sound of her loud voice, everybody came running to the door.

I slipped away from her embrace and leant against the wall without saying anything. I was dazed. My aunt took me by the hand and I went with her to the inner courtyard as if I had no will of my own. My mind refused to accept what I had heard her say.

I did not recover from my state of shock until I heard Mother wailing. I stood in front of her and shouted at her, "No! Do not wail like that, Mother. Sami has died for the sake of his country. We should cry out for martyrs in the way we do for bridegrooms." I then proceeded to ululate for joy. I had never ululated before in my life, and it came out as if from no human throat. It was like the howling of a mad dog.

I was unable to stop myself shrieking out. The noise I was making was unlike any normal wailing, either for a wedding or for a funeral. Nor was it weeping. I went on making this crazy noise until I was exhausted. When I finally recovered, I found myself surrounded by women who were looking after me.

Our house filled up with people, those we knew and those we knew not. Somehow the news got to everybody in the quarter, and to people and friends further afield. They came to us in tears as if they had themselves lost a dear one.

Oh, my dear Sami, how precious you were to all who knew you or who knew you qualities.

Adil came to my mind and my heart sank into an abyss of despair. I dried my eyes and held my tongue. Words were incapable of expressing an iota of this agony that was silently devouring me like a cancer.

Among the people in the house my eye lighted on Umm Adil, and I realized that Adil was still alive. I burst into tears and Umm Adil took me to her bosom and sobbed with me.

This awful day was very long, very long, and seemed to have no end. The women sat in the reception room and the men in the central courtyard. Our front door stayed wide open and people came along and shared in our loss, regardless of the authorities or the spies that were all over the place.

Night fell and people started to trickle away. Only close relations remained. Then they too started to steal away from the house, leaving only Umm Rashid and her son Salim.

My parents aged overnight. Raghib and Mahmud held back their tears like little children. Umm Rashid was in no less an agony of grief, but she had a certain amount of self-control and she did what she could to console us. She made us each drink a glass of milk to keep us going and finally persuaded us that we should all go to bed.

I went through moments when I just could not believe that Sami was really dead. I thought I was having a nightmare like one of those dreams I had when I slept to the sound of gunfire and the whistling of bullets.

O my dear Adil, how I feared that you had met the same fate as Sami.

How much I need you now. I want to put my head on your shoulder so we can weep together over our friend, Sami.

It seems as if I dozed off a little and then I woke up as if stung by a snake. Did any sleep steal over me on the day of your death, dear brother? . . . I could no longer bear stretching out on my bed . . . I now knew the meaning of the phrases "sleeping on hot coals" and "lying on a bed of nails." I jumped up and went downstairs. I paused a second before the door of the cubbyhole, where I could hear Raghib talking quietly. I could not make out what was being said, but I heard the name Rashid being repeated. I pushed the door open and went in. The small room was full of cigarette smoke. Raghib and Mahmud were sitting in front of Salim, who was smoking nervously, his face flushed.

"What's happened to Rashid?" I asked. "Tell me . . . what are you hiding? Has he been killed as well?"

"I take refuge in Allah," said Salim. "Can these matters be hidden? Rashid has been wounded. He was wounded a few days before Sami died. Comrades carried him to Amman and it seems he is seriously wounded. They've asked me to go to him in Amman as soon as possible, because he is in great need of funds. He asked me in a letter not to tell our mother, because she would be sure to go and see him, and he doesn't want to give her any trouble. With Sami's death she's got enough to distress her. He wanted her to stay with you. I really don't know what to do. How can I go to Amman without Mother knowing?"

I said to myself, "Anything is easy except death. If only Sami had been badly wounded and was still alive."

I said to Salim, "Perhaps you should tell your mother that you will stay in your house in Midan to guard it against looters. Ask her to come and stay with us and look after us. To reassure her further, tell her that Raghib will stay with you in Midan. You can then go to Amman and come back without her knowing about it."

"This is what I suggested," said Raghib. "In my view, it's the best solution. And I'll go with you to Amman. Don't say anything to your mother. We'll take any cash we need from Father."

Aunt Umm Rashid used to carry all her cash with her wherever she went. She would buy up old gold coins, sew them into a belt, and wrap that around her. She would put the ends of the belt into a pocket which she tied to her waist and then let her outer clothes hang over it. Whenever she or one of her sons wanted some cash, she would lift up her clothes and fumble around to get whatever was required.

Two days after they set out for Amman, Aunt started to get anxious. She wanted to go to the house and check on them, for there had been more explosions in the Midan quarter than in any other part of Damascus.

I clung to her and wept.

"How can you leave us alone," I said, "even for a few hours? But for you, Mother would have died of grief and depression. The house, as you see, is never free of visitors. What will people say about you when they no longer find you with us?"

"I'm afraid those two headstrong lads will not be careful after this tragedy. Isn't one disaster enough for a family?"

I realized she was afraid that Raghib and Salim might join up with the insurgents. I pretended not to know this and said, "They are sure to come back today or tomorrow. It's not far from our house to yours, is it?"

Aunt accepted what I said, although she was concerned and preoccupied with the grief that was almost killing us.

That dark period passed.

How long are nights of grief, how cruel is their torment.

The next morning we — Mahmud and I — waited impatiently. In the afternoon Raghib returned alone. His face showed signs of anguish. I asked him about Rashid.

"He's in a very bad way," he said. "He's out of danger but only because his right leg was amputated above the knee."

"His leg has been amputated?" I sobbed. I closed my eyes and buried my head in my hands, visualizing Rashid, with his strong body, stumbling around on one leg. I almost fainted. We were still in the corridor and Raghib went on, "He was hit by shrapnel, which shattered the bones in his leg. The doctors in the Ghuta tried to deal with him, but their basic medical equipment wasn't sufficient. They had to carry him from place to place whenever the French attacked. On one occasion he was carried by cart, on another by donkey. He was getting worse all the time. At last they got him to a hospital in Amman. The wound was septic and his whole body was infected. They had to amputate his leg as soon as they got him to the hospital to save his life. He has suffered the most intense pain. Well, you know Rashid and how he can put up with things. He's now in a poor psychological state. Aunt will have to go to Amman because he can't stay by himself at the hospital, which is very bad and expensive. We can't bring him to Damascus. He'll get arrested even if he is ill and has had one leg cut off. And Aunt doesn't have a lot of cash left because Rashid spent most of it on the revolt.

"Salim told me," he went on, "that it's been a bad season. They've taken the grain from the threshing areas. Livestock has been stolen. Orchards have been burnt and there's nobody to look after the fields or to plant seeds. I discussed it all with Salim and we thought it best to rent a small house in Amman where Rashid can go as soon as the wound has healed."

"Aunt will have to go to Amman tomorrow," I said. "We'll conceal things from her and tell her that Rashid wants to see her in Amman because it's too difficult to move around in the Ghuta. She can then receive the awful news when she is by herself."

"Damn these revolts," he cursed, giving me a reproachful look. I made no reply.

They say that everything starts small and then gets bigger and bigger. Everything, that is, except grief, which starts big and then gets smaller and smaller.

But my grief for Sami grows and grows day after day. Since Aunt went to Amman, I've got worse. I want to sob my eyes out. There may be some consolation in tears. But my tears froze or flowed back into my head. All the time I feel that my eyes are staring at nothing, and I find myself gnashing my teeth until it hurts. When grief is linked to depression and bitterness, then it seems to become something else, something with a dash of savagery in it. It loses that open vulnerability and tenderness that mark those who mourn for their children.

I wept only when Nirmin came to see me. She was swathed in black. I don't know how she heard the news or how she found her way to the house. We gave each other a hug and wept in silence.

Nirmin had become very dear to me after I became aware of her great devotion to Sami. When she left, I urged her not to lose touch. My fellow students also came to call on me. They did what they could to lighten my burden.

After the forty-day mourning period, they asked me to go back to college. The teachers asked about me. It seemed that I had become a special student. It was even said that the Arabic teacher had asked after me in one lesson. Mother noticed that the girls were conspiring to get me back to school. She was afraid I might fall ill, for I had lost a lot of weight and was barely recognizable.

I was persuaded.

"But I'll need a doctor's certificate after this long absence," I said.

"I'll bring you one," said one schoolfriend. "My dad's a doctor and he won't hesitate to write a report when I explain the situation to him. I'll bring it by tomorrow morning and we can go on to college together."

The sympathy I received from everyone was comforting. The fact that I was the sister of one of the martyred insurgents was enough to elicit help and concern both from people I knew and from total strangers.

In the Arabic class the teacher looked at me with kindness. He shook his head, expressing deep condolence. It seems that he had known Sami. Perhaps he had taught him at some stage. He called me to the blackboard. I sensed that my fellow students disapproved. How could I answer questions when I was in such a state of grief and had missed so much after my long absence? He asked me to write on the board that uplifting verse from the Qur'an "Think not of those who are slain in the way of Allah as dead. Nay, they are living. With their Lord they have provision."

"Do you understand this verse?" he asked me.

My eyes filled with tears and my voice choked as I nodded.

"If you understand it completely, you will be convinced by it. You will stop weeping and all this gloom will disperse."

He then explained the verse to us all, telling us in great clarity and detail how it came about. His words consoled me. When he had finished, he sent me back to my place and called another student up to explain the verse.

I shall never forget the way our teachers kindled the spirit of our national feeling without worrying about the French or their spies.

There was, for example, the history teacher, a retired army officer. He came into our class one day looking very gloomy. He sat down at his desk and said nothing for a while, but examined our faces one by one.

"Listen to me, girls," he finally said. "Take note of what I am about to say. What I'm about to tell you today is more important than study by far. There is a rumor going round the city that the French have decided to issue a decree about the teaching of some subjects in French. If we accept that, it won't be long before they issue another decree making the teaching of all subjects in French compulsory.

"You must be on your guard and refuse to accept this. Boycott the school until, with the will of Allah, the decree is withdrawn. Otherwise we will become like our Algerian brothers, who excel in French but do not know the language of their parents and grandparents. Imperialism aims at severing the links with our heritage and our glorious past."

He said all that without worrying whether what he said would reach the French or what the French might do as a result.

When the math teacher gave us a problem, he would present it as being about famous people in our history, especially the women.

For example, he would say, "Khawla bint al-Azwar buys such and such and sells such and such. Do you know who this Khawla bint al-Azwar was?" He would then proceed to tell us about the heroic deeds of Khawla.

Or he would say, "Nusaiba bint Ka'ab took her share of fodder on the day of the battle of Uhud. She distributed one-third to the families of those who had died in the battle, one-quarter to the poor of the city of Madina, and one-fifth to those who were being protected. How much did she have left? Do you know who Nusaiba bint Ka'ab was?" And he would then tell us, adding, "It's not my job, as I understand it, just to teach you mathematics. It's my job to give you a nationalist education, and to make each one of you an advocate for your country and for the Arab nation. It's women, my girls, who fashion men."

I received a letter from Adil, brought to me by his sister. She was lingering at the front door one morning and followed me on the way to college. When we left the quarter, she stopped me and handed over an envelope, saying, "This is from Adil. He's sent it from the Ghuta."

I was numb with shock. I took the letter and put it in among my books without saying anything. I went on my way, full of confused feelings. Was I overjoyed to receive the letter or did I feel oppressed? I was shaking all over. What words would Adil employ to express the shock that had afflicted us both.

I was dying to read it . . . But I would not have the chance until the mid-morning break. I attended the classes but understood nothing the teachers said. I hid among my fellow students and opened a book from time to time to glance at the letter and to finger it. A quiver ran through me as if I was touching Adil's hand. At the break I went off to a quiet spot by myself and opened the letter. I began to weep as soon as I saw the first word. It was fated that the first letter from my lover was a letter of condolence.

He wrote in the letter, "The image of your grief-stricken eyes never leaves me. At every moment I am in agony. Your image drives me to fight the enemy with a ferocity and an abandon that annoy my comrades. I want to average our precious martyr. I want to heal your wounded soul. I suffer, my darling. I feel that I am responsible for you before Sami. I wonder how I can wipe away the distress from your eyes and restore to them their sparkle of intelligence. I am kept awake all night. How can I do that when all the pores of my body breathe grief? I leave my bed and wander about the orchards of the Ghuta. The specter of Sami appears angrily before me. He chides me, saying, 'Have you forgotten? On the day we joined the revolt we made a declaration to each other. What is the meaning of grief now? Why this self-abasement? Whence this weakness?'

"At this point I realize that Sami has not died and will never die. He remains alive in our hearts and in the recesses of our minds. And whenever we repeat his words about humiliation and sacrifice we will find comfort and solace."

I folded the letter and hid it in my breast. I had not had my fill of reading it even though I had memorized every word.

Some lines of Shawqi came to me, and also of Khair al-Din al-Zirakli, about the revolt and the tragedy of Damascus. We had been reading them in class, memorizing them and chanting them. It was the custom in those days before printed textbooks for the teacher to dictate or write the lesson on the board. We would then learn the lesson by heart. But it was difficult to concentrate when all my thoughts were centered on Adil. No longer was there joy in my heart and nothing excited me. Even unexpected success in the examination made no impression on me.

The summer vacation started. I had been dreading it because I knew what a state of black depression I would be in. There was some consolation in the routine of going regularly to college, of talking to fellow students about study, teachers, and about the insurgents and the revolt. The only distraction I could look forward to were Nirmin's visits.

She was out of touch for a long time. I don't know why. I didn't want to take the initiative and call on her for fear of adding to her troubles. But one day she turned up unexpectedly. Mother had some visitors and I didn't want to sit with them. So I took Nirmin to my room and we sat on the edge of the bed. It seemed that Nirmin wanted to tell me something but she hesitated.

"What's the matter, Nirmin?" I asked. "I feel that you're not quite yourself."

She put her hand to her face and burst into tears. I tried to comfort her until she calmed down a bit.

"Did you know that I didn't enter for the exam," she said. "I've now lost a year and I've given up studying."

"Why?" I asked in astonishment.

"During the bombing of Damascus all our property was burnt. We used to live off the proceeds and send money to my brother in France so he could finish his studies. We haven't saved any money at all. We've spent all our income and have even been obliged to sell off our jewelry, Mother and I, to pay the rent for the house we're living in. Our school rules do not permit students who have not paid their fees to enter for an exam.

"I went to the principal on the actual day of the exam to explain the circumstances and ask her to give me some time to sort things out so I could pay the fees. She answered me with a face so immobile, it seemed as if it had been carved from wood. She was unable to deviate from the school regulations.

"I left her, weeping tears of despair, my pride hurt. I have resolved never to look again at that school where I had spent ten years and where I had been one of their star pupils."

"Oh, you stupid fool," I said. "Have you lost a whole year for the sake of a school fee? Why didn't you come to me? I'd have paid it."

"It all happened on the very day of the examination. I could have borrowed from the other students, but I was so upset and felt miserable. Even if I can manage to pay this year, I thought, how can I manage to do it next year?"

"Next year Allah will arrange things in a way you do not know."

"But I'm not sorry, as you may think, believe me. Since Sami's death, nothing matters any more. I no longer regret anything."

Nirmin left and I felt a great sorrow in my heart.

What a searing pain there was in my soul. Whichever way I turned, I found myself face to face with tragedy or frustration.

One day Father was warming his hands at the stove.

"The news today is good," he said. "The battle of Midan has been most remarkable. They say the French lost fifty men, killed, but only a few of the insurgents have died."

"Three only," said Mahmud, "but including one of the leaders."

"We would never have dreamt of it. Who would have believed Syria capable of standing up to France for more than a year, and to have imposed such losses, both human and material?"

"The battle of Midan cannot compare with the battle of Yalda or the battle of Babila. Or the battle of Jawbar or the other battles in the Ghuta. The losses of the French in those battles were numbered in hundreds."

Father sighed from the bottom of his heart. Sorrow flashed across his forehead as he fiddled with a pair of tongs, shifting the coals round. I knew exactly what was going on in his mind. He was suddenly remembering Sami. He was wishing that his son had lived to witness this battle which he had hoped for for so long. I glanced at Mother as, without saying a word, she brushed away a tear. Then Raghib joined in the conversation.

"But in the battle of Jabata al-Khashab we lost the best of the insurgents. Most of them were well-educated young men. The French did not hesitate to display the body of our commander, a splendid young man, in Martyrs' Square."

"Such provocation will rebound on them," said Father. "Anybody who hitherto has declined or has hesitated to enlist in the revolt will do so now. I am very pleased when the French make such fools of themselves."

"What's the use, Father," asked Raghib, "when the French are not giving away anything regardless of the losses they sustain? They will not agree to any negotiations until the insurgents surrender unconditionally."

"They won't give up," said Father with some irritation. "It's going to be too much for the French. If they don't keep their word, will the blood of our martyrs have been shed in vain?"

"What is to be done?" said Raghib. "The moderate nationalists have appointed delegations both inside and outside Syria. These delegations have gone to the High Commissioner in Beirut, and also to Paris and to the League of Nations at Geneva. They've presented their grievances and have made proposals. They've offered reasonable solutions, but nobody has listened or understood them.

"The upshot of it all," Raghib went on, "is that whenever things get bad, the French change their High Commissioner and bring in someone else who studies the situation anew. They withdrew their military High Commissioner, who had bombed Damascus, creating an international embarrassment for France. Even people in France protested. They brought us a civilian, a political sophisticate, skilled in making tours and assessing the situation. I remember you used to say of him. 'There's nobody smarter than him at issuing statements and clarifications full of misleading promises. They all used to end up in a dead end, unconditional surrender, war for those who want a fight, peace for those who want peace.'"

"Well," said Father, "they've failed abysmally. For all its political talent, the French Republic has gained nothing."

"The failure was inevitable, for the revolt was at its peak. The insurgents took no notice of threats. The French government recalled that man and sent us another civilian High Commissioner, the exact opposite of his predecessor. He listened to everybody but said nothing. He issued no statements, made no clarifications. Several months have passed and he is still studying the situation without saying anything at all."

"At our college," said Mahmud, "we call him the Dumb One."

"He's smart though," said Raghib. "He's worse than his predecessor. He wants to gain time. He wants to turn time into a sharp weapon which he can use to stamp out the revolt."

"With the help of Allah," observed Father, "we can be steadfast until we achieve what is our due."

"I wish that we could," said Raghib. "You yourself, Father, are you able to contribute to the revolt this year the amount you contributed last year?"

Father thought for a while in silence, rubbing his head with his hand.

"No, by Allah, no, my son, I can't," he said. "For one week, for two weeks, I have earned nothing at all. If the situation goes on like this for another year, I'll go bankrupt, for sure."

"There are plenty of people in the same situation as yourself, Father. And there are also the farmers who took up the revolt and showered it with their produce, as well as with money and men. They can't go on like that. Their savings have run out. Who can plant and sow when under fire? Is it not nobler for us to accept voluntarily the situation, however bitter it is, than to put up with it in spite of ourselves?"

I felt acutely upset and left the *liwan*, while Raghib went on talking about the meaninglessness of the blood spilt. I went up to my room and stretched out on my bed in the darkness. Through the window I could see a dark cloud hiding the stars above. It was dark everywhere.

Where are you, Adil? For a whole week I have not seen your sister and I know nothing about you. I long so much for you, so as to know what you think about what Raghib has been saying. Do you still say that the wish to sacrifice grows with danger?

113

What makes me almost explode with anger is that Raghib seems to be right! If the economic situation gets worse, it will not be in the interests of the revolt, which has not received any support from outside. It has survived on contributions from our own people. I have never before seen poverty in the faces of people in our streets and quarters as I do now.

I was unaware of the famine of the Great War, the horrors of which people still talk about. I can only remember the recovery that took place immediately after the war.

Consequently I am not familiar with the sight of poverty. It has been a painful shock. A couple of days ago I saw in Salihiya Street something I will never forget. A middle-aged man was leading two skinny little girls by the hand and whenever he saw a woman who was obviously well-to-do he would stop her and say, "Are you in need of a maid, Sister? Then take this girl. All you have to do is feed her. Allah is your Protector. I want nothing from you. The reward is with Allah."

The woman would push him to one side and carry on her way. Who knows, she too may one day be in desperate circumstances. There was a hopelessness in the father's eyes, and fear and anxiety in the eyes of the little girls as they followed him, saying nothing, fearful of the unknown fate in store.

Poverty is indeed an obscenity. Often when I went to school I was upset by the sight of huge numbers of unemployed workers standing in groups near Martyrs' Square and the Arnus quarter. Their faces were marked by signs of depression and despair. Each one of them was ready to take on any job at any rate of pay simply to keep body and soul together.

I had no doubt that these strong men would have been ready to join the revolt so long as there was somebody to look after their family and somebody who could have provided them with weapons. But where are the arms?

It was said that the price of one cartridge clip had risen to half a *majidi*. In such straits people were no longer making contributions with the same open-handedness that they had shown in the past. In response to this, the insurgents specified amounts that had to be paid by the wealthy. They would sometimes kidnap a member of a family that had been a bit slack in paying and hold him hostage until they had laid hands on the amount designated.

And today from my window I saw a peasant leading a donkey carrying a small amount of firewood on its back. Two huge men followed the donkey, each carrying an axe over his shoulder. Each hoped that the peasant would sell his wood and that they would be employed to chop it up.

A passer-by stopped the peasant.

"How much is this small load?" he asked.

"One pound, sir."

"A whole pound," haggled the man. "Is it sandalwood? How expensive life has become."

"No, my friend. It is dry wood from olive trees. It lights from one match. Sandalwood is no good for fires."

The man laughed.

"What do you know about sandalwood?" he asked.

"This tiny load isn't worth more than half a pound."

"No, by Allah."

"I offer you sixty piasters then."

"Heavens, no. Not a piaster less than seventy-five. Otherwise I don't sell."

"I'm only buying it for your sake and for the sake of that poor broken-down donkey of yours."

One of the huge men was following the haggling, mechanically looking first at one man and then the other, backward and forward, to and fro. I was most anxious lest a deal not be struck. The poor man might lose his patience and bring the axe down on the neck of the other. In conditions such as these how could the revolt continue?

My heart bleeds as I write this.

We no longer hear the sound of gunfire except from afar. Expeditions are continuing to go out to the Ghuta. The French have brought in fresh troops, whom they have withdrawn from Morocco, where they have crushed the revolt of Abdul Karim al-Khattabi. We almost died of anger and despair as we saw these soldiers invading our land.

Spring has arrived. It seems to be quite dull. I no longer enjoy the sight of violet blossom tumbling down in cascades on the walls of our house. I am no longer stirred by the tender melodies that come from our neighbor's gramophone. Happiness shatters within our selves and this colors everything.

Our spirits are low, in spite of the verdant Damascus springtime.

It has become extremely difficult for the insurgents to launch an attack on the police posts in and around Damascus because of the heavy fortifications erected around them.

The last Ghuta battles to take place have been at Ain al-Suyais in the village of Ain Farma. On the day of this battle Raghib said to Father, "Today the insurgents have satisfactorily avenged the battle of Jabata al-Khashab in spite of the heavy casualties. Already countless French soldiers have been killed, as well as mercenaries. It's even rumored that some officers, both senior and junior, have been killed."

Father raised his hands.

"May Allah give strength to our insurgents," he said. "May they be granted victory over their enemies. Allah hears all and responds."

After this ferocious battle more insurgents fled to Transjordan, or to the countryside, or concealed themselves in remote corners of the Ghuta, fearful of savage reprisals from the French expeditions, something that always happened when the insurgents won a victory.

One day Salim suddenly turned up after a long absence in Transjordan.

We gathered round him, breathlessly asking for news of our aunt and of Rashid's health. He gave brief answers, for he seemed tired and depressed. He then said, "I've got a difficult task to discharge."

He was silent and then added hesistantly, "We have at last been able to persuade Rashid to surrender. I'm here to carry out the necessary procedures, because Rashid was sentenced to death *in absentia*. His surrender needs a special amnesty from the military tribunal before he returns."

There was a very grim look on Father's face.

"Nothing can be done except through the will of Allah, the Sublime, the Great," he said. "Rashid's surrender is necessary, my son, after what he has suffered. What is the point of you being in Amman, so far from Damascus? You have left your business behind all this time."

"Is Rashid the only one to surrender?" asked Raghib. "Each day there are lots of insurgents who are surrendering now the revolt has collapsed."

Salim shook his head and looked angrily at Raghib.

"No, Raghib," he said. "If the revolt has not achieved the success we hoped for in relation to the casualties we have suffered, neither has it failed. The French realize that we are a nation that does not bow down to servitude. We shall never submit to indignities. If the French fail to honor their promises, we shall resume the revolt once more.

"I have been present at meetings of our leaders. Many took place at our house in Amman for Rashid's sake. Most refuse to surrender and will become refugees in neighboring Arab countries until such time as the intentions of the French are clear. They all agree that the revolt should be resumed if necessary.

"The leader of the Druze revolt has refused to give up. He decided to fortify himself with a band of men in a desert village on the frontier. Those who surrender will carry on a peaceful struggle — strikes and demonstrations — if the French don't keep their promises.

"So, you see, the revolt has not been such a flop as you may suppose."

Raghib fell silent. His expression showed that he was not convinced, but he didn't want to argue about something that was so sensitive to all present.

I was much comforted by what Salim said and hope revived. I began to wish for Adil to surrender as soon as possible once I was persuaded that in surrender there was no dishonor.

A few days after Salim's visit we all went to Midan to welcome Rashid home. I was surprised and delighted when I saw all the people of the Midan quarter come out to greet him. The whole area was decorated with carpets and with sprigs from trees and verses from the Qur'an in praise of struggle. The people made a great show of welcoming him, carrying him shoulder-high right into the house, where they sat him down in the center of the *liwan*.

Young men chanted, "Rashid, our squire, you are our glory. We're going to cook our rice with our swords."

Then another group chanted, "The men of Midan and the men of Shaghur are brothers against injustice and aggression."

People kept coming to the house to greet Rashid until the last call to prayer of the day.

Each quarter greeted their returning warriors with similar demonstrations and songs. This showed how people refused to acknowledge that the revolt had failed. The French disregarded such provocation during this tense period, this time of surrender.

When men from outside had left, women from the family and neighborhood went in to give their greetings to Rashid. He embraced Mother, with tears in his eyes. Then he patted me on the shoulder with affection and mumbled some words that were the most consoling that I had ever heard.

"I am happy for Sami," he said. "He died while the revolt was at its peak. He left us while we were all confident of victory. Not like me. I have had to surrender."

He gazed at the stump of his leg, bowed his head and bit his lip, trying not to cry. But the eyes of the rest of us were filled with tears. We wiped them away quickly, so as not to draw attention to ourselves.

Friday. This morning we were all having coffee as usual in the *liwan*.

"Abu Adil the baker is a man of moderation," observed Father. "He's a man of conscience, a man of decency. He knows what's what. I hear that his son, Adil, is surrendering today. The people of the quarter want to decorate the place in his honor and to welcome him with a demonstration, just as they do in other quarters. But Abu Adil has refused out of deference to our feelings. He told them that his son would not be happy with such a demonstration of joy when Sami, his friend, his contemporary, and his comrade in arms, had been killed."

Father then turned to Raghib and Mahmud.

"We must go and welcome him home this evening after sunset prayers."

As Father spoke I felt a rush of blood come to my head and cheeks. What pleasure it gave to my aching heart after the years of torment I had undergone, years of grief and anguish, hope and despair, fear and eagerness, raging anxiety and unceasing worry.

How am I going to get through the day, I ask myself. Shouldn't I be the first to go and greet him?

As the time for meeting him again approaches, I get restless and long more and more to see him. I feel disturbed and painted. How should I greet him?

Mother won't agree to our going to congratulate the family. We are still in mourning clothes, even though eighteen months have passed since Sami's death. I must see him tomorrow even if I die in the process.

I'll go and see him tomorrow before I go to college. His family know about us. He used to send me letters through them. His sister used to bring me news of him and pass on his good wishes. They will not be at all surprised at my calling.

Next day. I hardly slept at all last night. Adil was on my mind all this time. I kept thinking about how we would meet. What would I say to him? What would he say to me? When I finally got to sleep I dreamt dreams, some were beautiful, others were more alarming. Time passed very slowly. As soon as the sun rose I was up. I got dressed and waited, looking at my watch all the time.

"What's up with you today?" Mother asked. "Why are you going to college so early?"

"I left my French book behind. I'm going in early to study it. If I don't I'll be in trouble with the teacher of French. She's very strict and won't accept any excuses."

The ruse worked. I slipped out of the house before Father or my brothers emerged from their rooms. I realized that I was embarking on a perilous adventure but I would not retreat one step. As soon as I was heading for the house of Adil's family, I was so worked up that I could actually hear my heart beating. I sensed that Adil himself would open the door. It was as I expected.

Adil gasped when I raised my veil and our eyes met.

He led me in by the hand and closed the door. The long corridor was dark. He took me in his arms and pressed me to his chest with passion and longing. I buried my head in his neck. I savored his sweet smell. I trembled in his arms, feeling that all the blood in my body was at boiling point. I tottered as if drunk or fevered as a result of this encounter. We were like two small children, overwhelmed by a sudden happiness that was more than we could bear.

We drew apart from each other a little so I could look into his face and he could look into mine. Then we hugged each other again, saying nothing.

What an intensely sweet moment! How brief it was!

There was a knock at the door and we pulled apart in an instant, though at a peak of intoxication. Adil went to open the door. I put down my veil and went to the far end of the corridor, turning back before he actually opened the door to give the impression that I was coming from inside the house.

Adil opened the door. Some young men of the neighborhood, some of whom had been Sami's comrades, had come to congratulate Adil on his return before going off to work. They let me through, not one of them knowing who I was — sometimes there are advantages in wearing the veil!

I made my way slowly to college. What a wonderful start to the day!

The air was splendidly pure. The dark blue sky was flecked by thin clouds which I could see through the heavy veil. Moist breezes played with the veil and sometimes got through and caressed my face gently. Groups of swallows took flight and settled on the telegraph wires in a single row.

Where had all this beauty been hidden? Whenever I imagined myself in his arms, I could feel a tremor of delight. I wondered whether I was dreaming. How long would we be kept apart? We would have to steal moments which we had a right to enjoy. We would live in an atmosphere of fear. We would have to practice deception just to obtain fleeting encounters that were not enough to gratify our desire.

Why is it that the people of my country demand freedom and at the same time cannot grant it to each other? Half the nation was shackled in chains created by men. That is a wrong we refuse to acknowledge.

When I tear this suffocating veil away I shall be able to enjoy the light and the air. I shall go out of the house just as my brothers go out. Nobody will ask me where I am going, and I won't have to tell lies and fabricate ruses. The day will come when I tell them that I have got to know Adil, son of the baker. He fell in love with me and I fell in love with him. We will agree to get married when we have completed our studies. They will give me their blessing and congratulate me on the excellence of my choice.

When that happens we will really be in good shape, worthy of the freedom we vainly hymn today.

I was first to reach college. I smiled cordially at Abu Mazhar, the doorman, and gave him the small change that I had on me.

"May your morning be blessed with a thousand prayers from the Prophet," he laughed.

I was happy and wanted to share my happiness with the world. I wandered among the bright green bushes that formed corridors in the garden by the college entrance.

I had an overwhelming desire to talk about the sweetness of my meeting with Adil, about the intense feelings that possessed me when I was in his arms, but who could I talk to? I had many friends but there was really nobody to whom I was so attached that I could entrust my secret.

The best thing to do was to talk to myself.

The lessons passed by. I could not understand much of what the teachers were saying. My mind was all over the place. I went back home and up to my room and talked to myself as if I was crazy. One brief encounter was not enough.

If only I could sit quietly with Adil. We would talk to each other about what was in our hearts for years on end, but how do we achieve this? All ways seem to be blocked.

But when did lovers ever despair? They alone know how to devise ways of getting together, regardless of the obstacles and of the vigilance of others. Adil found a way.

One Thursday we were leaving college at midday for the weekend. I found him waiting for me on the sidewalk in front of the college. He gave me a sign to follow him. I slipped away from my fellow students. He went into a narrow street near the college and I followed. We went down a long street, a few feet only separating us. We had no wish to arouse any suspicion.

At the end of the street there was a garden enclosed by an earth wall. In the middle of the wall was a wooden gate. Adil brought out a piece of wood and opened the gate. I went in after him and closed the gate. I raised my veil and looked at him. He took me in his arms.

"At last we've been able to get together," he said. "I can gaze at those lovely eyes that have so tormented me."

He stole a kiss on my eyes.

I said nothing, but there must have been signs of anxiety on my face for he said, "Why are you so anxious? Don't be afraid. Nobody knows where we are."

"I'm afraid my family will find out what's going on between us and we will be kept apart forever."

"How will they know? This garden is walled and nobody but the owners ever comes here. I know the owner's son. He's an old friend and has given me the key so we can come here whenever we like."

I felt a bit better and looked at the key in amazement. I had never seen one like it before. It was made of planed wood and was at least one foot long. At its head were three nails in the form of a triangle. This piece of wood and its nails performed the function of a key. Adil saw the look of amazement on my face.

"I don't suppose you've ever seen a garden key before."

"I've hardly ever seen the gardens themselves, so how can I be acquainted with the keys?"

He laughed, his black eyes sparkling. The dimple in his right cheek deepened and his white teeth flashed in the middle of his swarthy face. How often had I longed to see this wonderful laugh of his. He pulled me to him.

"From now on," he said, "you're going to see it a lot, my love. Every Thursday when you leave college at midday, come here. I'll be here already. I'll have opened the gate and will be waiting for you behind it."

"But I cannot be more than half an hour late getting home. Otherwise they'll find out. My family are always on the watch."

He smiled.

"Let us at least be grateful for small mercies," he said. "It's better than not seeing each other at all, isn't it?"

"Don't ever mention the idea. I can't bear the thought of not seeing you after having tasted what I have tasted."

We sat on two stones that faced each other beneath the gnarled branches of an old willow tree. We talked and talked. We recalled the tragedy of Sami's untimely death. We reminisced about the cups of coffee we had drunk in the Eyrie and books we had read together, and the mutual longing we had for each other. We wept, and he wiped the tears away with his lips. It was balm. I had never known such a short half-hour. The time sped by. I left the garden before he did, went off quickly, and caught a tram to get home on time, for I usually walked home. Nobody noticed that I was a bit late.

Adil became a green oasis in the desert of my barren life. All the days of the week were concentrated on the day of our meeting, on that half-hour every Thursday. I dreamt of the next half-hour as soon as one was over. I would look forward to our rendezvous every second. We would sit on our stone seats in the shade of the old willow tree. We would concoct sweet fantasies. We were going to build a small house in a spacious garden where we would bring up our children. He would work as a lawyer so he could be involved in the national struggle. I would work as a teacher. I would bring my pupils up to love their country just as my own teachers had done. After these meetings I would go home feeling full of happiness and very pleased with myself. Adil would shower me with tender kisses and I would live on the memory of these for the rest of the week.

One day Adil brought me some good news. He had been accepted at the law school and had joined the National Bloc. Most members were older politicians, some of whom had been active in the revolt. There they had got to know Adil and had praised him to other members. He told me that he had plans to work as a part-time teacher in a private school.

On another occasion I said to Adil, "I have learned today the meaning of opportunism. I have witnessed it before me with my own eyes."

He showed surprise.

"How is that, my little philosopher?" he asked.

"I saw it the other day in my brother, Raghib. You know he was always against the revolt. He often used to argue with Sami about it whenever he could."

"Yes, I know. Sami was always telling me about it."

"Well, the other day he came home, puffed up like a turkey-cock, and announced, 'Give me your congratulations. I've just got a splendid job in the Department of the Interior.'

"Father asked him how he had got this job and he answered, 'I heard that one section head in the department had heard about my national feelings and that there was a vacancy in the section. I used to know one of his friends who had some influence with him, so I went to this friend and asked him to put in a word on my behalf and to tell him that I was the brother of the Martyr Sami al-Saruji, who had made the supreme sacrifice in the revolt and that my family had suffered terribly. The section head selected me for the post and vouched for me to the French adviser. So I got the job. There were other candidates with good qualifications who had a better claim to the post.'

"I could not bear this and said to him, 'It's just a fluke that you've benefited from the revolt when you were an out-and-out opponent of it.'

"He looked at me spitefully and said, 'I'm still against it. But it is enough that we lost Sami. That does not prevent me taking advantage of an opportunity.'

"Swear to Allah, Adil, is that not the uttermost opportunism?"

"We shall try to rid ourselves of this kind of thing when we have a truly national government."

"Raghib got what he wanted by the shortest possible route, but Mahmud spent a whole year after graduating from law school looking for a job in one of the government departments. At last he found a minor position in Homs, more junior than that of Raghib. He has taken it because Father's business has been deteriorating steadily. Where's the justice? Where's the fairness?"

"Why worry yourself about such individual cases? There are so many of them in our country. We are at a very difficult stage in our national struggle. We've got a lot to think about.

"The French are dragging their feet in keeping their promises. The first thing they~agreed to was that there should be free elections to choose the Constituent Assembly, who would draw up a constitution. Nothing has happened to implement this in spite of demonstrations demanding these elections. It's as if they suppose that by appointing a man of religion to head the government they've done enough to keep us happy, or rather to dope us. They still do not understand the nature of the people even now. And so we have decided to hold a huge demonstration throughout Syria. Everybody will take part and we will follow it with a general strike."

"Why aren't women taking part in the demonstration? Don't women have the right to defend their country? How long will half the nation remain paralyzed?"

"I made this suggestion at the last meeting of the Bloc. Many younger members backed me, but the proposal did not get the support of the majority, because of a fear that the French would exploit the issue and secretly stir up the men of religion. We are now at a critical stage when we need solidarity.

"Speaking of women," he went on, "did you read in the papers about the battle raging between those for the removal of the veil and those who want to retain it?"

"Yes, a fellow student brought in a paper and we read a splendid article about those who are for getting rid of the veil."

"This is not enough. You've got to carry on this important fight. It's a woman's fight as well. One of our writers has recently been so bold as to advocate the abandonment of the veil. I applaud his courage. It's no small thing in this prim society of ours. I meant to bring the papers with the articles for you to read, but I forgot them today. I promise to bring them next week."

The following week Adil was waiting for me as usual behind the garden gate with the articles as promised.

"I'm going to kiss you before you kiss me," I said at once, "because you've not forgotten them this time."

We exchanged kisses.

"Take care you are not like that poetess of Andalusia," he said, "who used to give kisses to anybody who wanted them."

I tapped him gently on the mouth.

"Naughty boy. How can you say such a thing? I who have bestowed my kisses on nobody but you and who will give them to nobody else as long as I live."

He took me tenderly in his arms and said, "I know that and believe it with all my heart."

We sat down on the two stones under the willow tree. Adil talked about the success of the great demonstration and of the general strike. He was full of optimism.

"I toured the old city with some friends. I wish you had been with us. I would not have believed that people everywhere could be so solid. All the stores were shut, even the small ones in the outlying quarters. If anybody had chanced to open up his store, the young men would have accused him of treachery and thrown stones at the store until he closed it. There have been plenty of demonstrations and strikes before this one, but none of them has had the same sense of purpose.

"The French don't know what to do, and they are aware of the impact the National Bloc has had on the whole nation. I wish you could have seen Martyrs' Square on the day of the demonstration. It surged with masses of people like a raging ocean. It was as if this great crowd of men, old and young, and children as well, were thinking with one mind and speaking with one voice. I was myself quivering with emotion. Never was I so moved in the fierce fighting as when I heard the crowds chant, 'We want elections. We want total independence. No Protectorate and no Mandate.'

"Then there was the slogan, 'Leave us alone, Frenchman. We, we are Arabs.'

"And then, 'May the Arab nation live forever. Muslim and Christian together.'

"Then they all chanted, 'The land of the Arabs is our homeland, from Damascus to Baghdad. France, don't go too far, don't praise your conquest.'

"When the police charged with their batons and their revolvers in order to disperse the crowd, the demonstrators were packed solid in front of them and started to pelt them with stones, without any fear of being hit or threatened. And when some were arrested, they sang, 'Oh, may the darkness of the prison prevail, we are in love with the dark.'

"It seems that the French sensed the danger of the situation and were afraid of the revolt flaring up again. They sent a message to members of the Bloc, asking them to settle the strike so that new negotiations could start for fixing a time for elections to the Constituent Assembly."

I listened to what Adil was saying with great excitement.

"We have begun to reap the fruit of the blood sown by our martyrs," I said.

"Yes, certainly."

Then he repeated the sentence that Sami used to repeat, "It's a long haul, very long, my dearest."

One Thursday I went into the garden. He looked at me crossly.

"Where were you last Thursday? I was waiting for you for ages. I was so worried about you that on Saturday I all but asked one of your fellow students why you had been absent."

"That would have been crazy," I said. "You would have caused a scandal to both of us. Mother was ill, Adil. She was suffering terribly from bronchitis. It's an awful business and I knew nothing of the symptoms. At first we thought she was dying. We brought some doctors to see her. They gave her medicine and injections until, after a few hours, her breathing became regular again. Before long she was back to normal and seemed only to be exhausted. But her spirits are very low. I can hardly believe that someone can almost die and then bounce back to health as if she had not been ill at all.

"I was terribly concerned about her. I am very worried when I leave the house and worry about her having a choking fit and dying while I am out of the house."

"I am so sorry," Adil said. "I'm very fond of your mother, even though I don't know her. Sami used to talk about her a lot."

"And if you did know her, you would realize that she was a paragon of virtue and modesty. The doctors have warned her about

127

physical and mental stress, but it's impossible for her to follow their advice. She doesn't let up all day long. Before Sami died she was the life and soul of the house. She'd always be laughing and smiling. She loved singing as she was doing the housework. She had a lovely voice which filled the house with happiness. But now she works away, struggling to hold back her tears. Every now and then she mumbles one song mournfully as if it were a funeral dirge: 'Oh, my sweetheart, how did they manage to take you away from us? I'm all in pieces and they've trained you to accept our being apart.'

"She would then dissolve into tears. How could she not have fallen ill? I think another factor in making her ill was Mahmud getting married."

"Mahmud married! When did that happen?"

"Yes, he's gotten married. May Allah not let you see such an abominable marriage."

"Why? And who has he married?"

"You know I told you that Mahmud had found a job in Homs. Some time after he went he sent us a brief letter saying he'd got married, because he was feeling very lonely. It seemed that he'd got to know a young girl of a good family and . . . married her! It was very difficult for my parents, and they were very cross with their fine quiet son because he hadn't sought their advice. Raghib and I tried to make it seem less important.

"'It may happen that ye hate a thing which is good for you,' we said, quoting the Qur'an.

"I then wrote to Mahmud, saying he should come and visit us with his bride and get his parents' approval. I wish I hadn't done that. Shortly afterwards he turned up with a tall, fat woman who seemed to be much older than him. If you saw them together you'd reckon she was his mother or his aunt. When Mother saw them, she asked, 'Where's the bride, my dear?'

"He pointed to the woman at his side. Mother choked in amazement and slapped her cheeks, unable to say anything.

"I had supposed at first that this woman was his mother-in-law. I couldn't help laughing aloud at Mother's reaction. Mahmud was embarrassed and the bride's face bristled and I reckon she hated us all from that instant."

"Is that how people greet their newly wed daughters-in-law?" commented Adil. "By Allah, you've made me sympathize with the bride. This concerns nobody else but Mahmud. What have his concerns to do with you? He has perhaps found happiness with this woman, more than he would with any other woman, however beautiful and perfect she might be. When will we realize that marriage is something personal and doesn't concern anyone else?"

"Mother will never be able to understand that, Adil. She had dreamt of a young girl of fifteen who had attached herself to Mahmud. A girl, fresh and virginal, blonde, with green eyes. A girl who would be content to live with her and respect what Mother told her and would present us with sons and daughters."

"And supposing Mahmud did not care for green eyes?"

"Mahmud's views are unimportant. Mother wanted them to be green and that was that. And so Mother felt cheated when she saw that the bride was the exact opposite of what she had dreamt of. She nursed the idea that the bride's mother had bewitched her son and had abducted him from us and had married him off to her old maid of a daughter. If only he had left Homs and come back to us. And so Mother fell ill just a few days after Mahmud left."

"Look after her as much as you can. You are the only one who can persuade her to accept what has happened."

"I'll do what I can. But time has flown and we've been talking about personal matters. Tell me, what's been happening?"

"There's good news this time. After the demonstrations and disturbances, the French have found that there is no alternative but to go along with the will of the people. The strike did not stop and the demonstrations did not quieten down until the French agreed to hold elections to the Constituent Assembly in a few days' time. We are now busy getting the names of the candidates ready. What makes us younger folk anxious is that some of those who have fought the good fight for the sake of the nation and have made enormous sacrifices want to have themselves placed on the list."

"That would be all right only if they had the right qualifications."

"You're absolutely right, Sabriya. We've got to put on the list people who are competent as well-educated nationalists who know about legal and constitutional matters, so they can draw up a constitution for the country. What we, the younger generation, are afraid of is that this jockeying for position will lead to divisions in the ranks."

I looked at my watch. It was getting late. I said goodbye to Adil and hurried home, worrying about these splits in the nationalist ranks.

The following week I went to the garden more anxious about the news Adil would bring than at any other time.

He was waiting for me under the old willow tree, grinning broadly. At once he said, "The good news is that this time you are going to join a big demonstration in which we will be depending on the women."

"Why do we need a demonstration now?" I asked.

"It's become clear that French intentions are not at all straightforward. We hear that they are preparing a list of candidates who are loyal to them. They will be called the government list. They are sure to be successful, thanks to corruption and manipulating the election papers. It means that all our efforts and sacrifices have come to naught. What is the point of a Constitutional Assembly that is a willing tool in the hands of the French, who give them their orders? They will devise laws that the imperialists wish us to have."

"What then is to be done?"

"We have no alternative but to refuse to accept this list. The French will not be persuaded unless the country goes on strike, and there are massive demonstrations everywhere protesting against the official list. We discussed the matter with the merchants, but they have not responded this time. They've become bored with demonstrations and strikes that interfere with their business. Some members proposed we involve the women this time. They will arouse pride and enthusiasm. The merchants are bound to answer their call. They will close the stores and the strike, which we regard as very important, will take place. Everybody agreed to the proposal."

"I'm absolutely delighted with this news. I used to envy men for what they are doing for the sake of the nation. How I have longed to serve my country with deeds and not just with words. I've never had the chance of real service. Tell me, when is the demonstration going to take place? I'm going to start exercising my throat from now on, shouting slogans."

Adil laughed and the dimple on his right cheek deepened. I wanted him to snatch a kiss, but he did not. He was preoccupied.

"Don't rush ahead," he said. "Are you sure your family will let you take part in a march?"

"Who said I have to ask permission? I'm going to join in the march and let them afterwards do whatever they like."

"Yes, indeed," he laughed. "Independence has to be taken, not given. Take care not to give too much importance to taking part. I'm afraid you may let yourself get involved in a way that will have unhappy consequences. I know your family. They are fiercely reactionary. I'm afraid we may deeply regret what we do."

"Leave it to me. Nobody will dissuade me from taking part, regardless of the consequences. Now tell me, how do I get involved?"

"I think all the demonstrators will be from the teachers' training college, the sisters and relatives of comrades in the National Bloc. I'll pass your name to the committee and the person in charge of the women's march will contact you. She'll tell you the time and the place the march will set off from."

The march was fixed for a Thursday. We met up after we left college at the house of a fellow student in the Muhajirin quarter. There were twenty of us, all students. We were provided with open cars, which we stood up in, wearing modest black headscarves and thick veils lowered over our faces to avoid giving the men of religion any pretext to attack us. Each car was surrounded by a large number of young men, who linked arms and provided a cordon round the car so that the police could not get at us. I spotted Adil among the young men, smiling at me. He waved to me in encouragement.

The cars set off from Muhajirin, proceeding slowly. There was just a short space between each car. The cavalcade was more like a procession than a demonstration. As soon as we reached Salihiya, we started to shout slogans.

"People of Damascus . . . People of honor and people of spirit . . .

131

The French want you to elect traitors. Down with So-and-So and Such-and-Such —" and we went through the names of the government candidates — "Long live So-and-So —" and we read out the names of those on the nationalists' list.

"Close up your stores. We call on you to boycott the elections until the government's list is dropped. We ask you to do that for the sake of the blood of the martyrs."

The young men who were marching with us repeated our slogans. Then the storekeepers responded to our calls and closed their stores and joined in behind us.

When the march reached Martyrs' Square, our cars had great difficulty forging a way through the huge crowds. A tussle broke out between the police and some of the young men who were preventing the police from approaching us. No policeman was able to reach any of the cars.

As I stood up in the car, I felt I had sprouted wings that enabled me to fly high, in spite of the black headdress that hung from my head to my feet and the thick veil that covered my face. I felt that I was a defiant wave in this sea surging in front of me. I was overwhelmed by a strange sensation. For the first time I felt I was a human being with an identity and an objective, in defense of which I was ready to die. I had absolutely no sense of fear. Indeed I felt capable of facing anyone and defying the world. I felt able to confront Father, Mother, and Raghib and to tell them, "I have been on a demonstration with the young men, in defense of my country. There is no power in the world that can get in the way of what I want."

One of the girls gave an impassioned speech. There was total silence. She held the text of her speech in one hand and threw back her veil a little with the other so she could read.

After every sentence we interrupted with applause and slogans.

The march then resumed its unhurried pace to Suq al-Hamidiya, where another girl gave another speech. We then went into Midhat Pasha Suq and Suq al-Buzuriya. As soon as our cars went into these streets, all the stores closed at once. Merchants stood before their stores, applauding and shouting slogans with us. Some joined in the march.

These were the principal Damascus suqs. When they closed down, the rest of the country would follow suit. The objective of the march was thus achieved and the close-down was total, thanks to the participation of the women.

The French had called up some officers and soldiers to assist the police in putting down the march and in arresting some of the enthusiastic young men, taking them off to the police station for interrogation. Some would face trials and be given long terms of imprisonment. But our men thought they should protect the women before they were arrested by the police or by the French soldiers.

The cars would stop at a corner so one of the girls could get down, disappear into the crowds and then slip off into an alleyway. Some men would escort her until she reached her home.

I got down from my car at the corner of Suq al-Buzuriya. Adil was waiting for me.

"Follow me," he said.

We went from Suq al-Buzuriya to the silk suq. That suq seemed to be quite eerie. The stores were all closed and dark and there was nobody about. Adil took my hand, pressed it and said, "You really were splendid. Your voice could be heard above everybody else's. I'm so proud of you."

"That's because I was speaking from the heart."

"We must move as quickly as we can. I didn't expect the march to take so long. The sunset call to prayer has begun. Your family is sure to have missed you by now. It may not have occurred to them that you were taking part in the march."

"My main worry is Mother's health." I then added, "If only the march had passed by Khan al-Jumruk, in front of Father's store. Maybe he would have noticed that I was in the march. He might have been pleased with our courage. He would have been staunchly with us, like the other merchants."

As soon as we reached Suq al-Hamidiya, skirting the Umayyad Mosque, we saw some police assisted by French soldiers picking up stragglers from the march.

Adil was afraid that we would get arrested and we went into the Umayyad Mosque with those who were going in for the sunset prayers. The mosque was a sanctuary: nobody could be arrested there.

133

We took off our shoes and carried them in our hands and went into the courtyard. I was a few paces behind Adil. We left by the gate leading to the Amara quarter and went on as quickly as we could.

From Amara to the Uqaiba quarter, and then to our quarter in Suq Saruja. This route was longer than the route by Suq al-Hamidiya and Martyrs' Square.

I knew what woe would be waiting for me at home. Nonetheless, I walked at Adil's side, feeling so happy, with a joyfulness and a love of life in my heart.

As we entered our quarter I saw at a distance Raghib standing in the middle of the road looking in all directions. I knew he was looking for me. I then realized that he had spotted Adil before he went into his house. I was behind him. Raghib gave the impression of not bothering and sauntered towards our house. He stood at the door waiting for me. When I reached him he opened the door for me and followed me in. He then punched me hard in the face.

"Bitch. Where've you been?" he said.

I made no reply. I hurried in along the corridor to the courtyard. My parents were standing there in the middle, looking towards me.

"Where have you been, damn you?" Mother said. "The evening prayer has been called and you have been out of the house."

Father then shouted at me.

"Where have you been?"

"I was in the demonstration with the other girls," I said with great pride.

"You were in a demonstration without my knowledge?" said Father. "I do not have daughters who go on demonstrations with young men."

He then struck me a blow in the face that made me stagger. Then he hit me again and I caught my balance. The blows came one after the other on my face as I stood stolidly before him, challenging him to strike further. With each blow he shouted, "From now on there's to be no more college. no more demonstrations. You will not go out of the house. No college, no demonstrations."

Finally Mother tried to intervene, but she got hit too.

"Enough! Enough, Abu Raghib!" she said, out of breath. "Have you gone crazy?"

She pulled me away by the hand and pushed me into my bedroom, closing the door behind me.

Then I heard Raghib shouting, "She's lying. In the name of Allah, she's lying. Do you believe what she said, Father? Are there demonstrations after the call to evening prayer? She has been with Adil, the baker's son. I saw them coming into the quarter together. When will we be free of this bastard? What's he got to do with us? It's he who urged Sami to join the revolt, and here's this son of a dog dishonoring us. I know how to deal with him. We've always been able to hold our heads high. Now this baker's son has come and shamed us in front of others."

I feared for Adil. I left my room. I don't know how I managed to lie and to deny that I had been with Adil. But I said in beseeching tones, "Believe me, Father, I don't know Adil. I swear to you that I've not seen him, but after the march some policemen arrested us and took us to the police station for questioning. I was late because I had to wait my turn. When I left I found him in front of the police station. He walked and I walked behind him until we arrived . . ."

I was unable to finish my sentence, for Raghib burst out melodramatically, "Allah, Allah, in the name of Allah the Great! This mishap is even more damnable than I had thought. I know what the French and the police do with young girls whom they take to the police station. No one leaves them unsullied. This is fundamental . . ."

I felt confused and no longer knew what to say. I did not know where my lie would lead me.

Father struck his forehead.

"That's something I hadn't thought of," he said.

He was too weak to remain standing and sat down at the edge of the *liwan*.

Mother came back and pushed me into the room and closed the door. I looked through the window and saw the three of them whispering to each other.

Mother raised her voice.

"No, no, that's not possible," she cried. "I know my daughter. Let me find out from her first."

"Do you imagine she's going to confess to you?" asked Raghib. "She'll deny everything. That's what girls do."

"I will not be able to sleep tonight until my mind is satisfied," said Father. "Raghib, may Allah be satisfied with you, go and fetch her immediately."

Raghib went out.

Who, I wondered, is Raghib going to fetch this evening? Can it be my aunt, Umm Rashid, to whom we usually turn in difficulties? Doesn't she have enough to worry about?

Shortly after that Mother came into the room. Her breathing was irregular. There was a reddish ring around her dull eyes. I realized that she was going to have a bronchial attack.

"Take it easy, Mother," I pleaded. "In Allah's name, don't let my concerns trouble you. Your health is the most important thing in the world."

"Confound my health," she said. "I wish I could die so as to be free of you."

She then came up close up to me and whispered, "I'm your mother, my dear. Speak openly to me. Has anyone misbehaved with you? Have no fear. I can fix everything with Umm Fawzi, who'll be here shortly. Everything can be kept from your father and your brother."

I leapt up as if I had been scalded and stared hard at Mother.

"That old hag, Umm Fawzi?" I exploded. "Has Raghib gone to fetch her? Have you all gone mad? What's the point of it all? Who would put themselves at the mercy of Umm Fawzi's tongue? This is a scandal she would spread through the whole quarter. Tomorrow she would go from door to door and tell everyone the tale, making an enormous drama out of it all. Oh, the indignity of it! I wish the earth would open and swallow me up. You can be quite sure that I won't let Umm Fawzi touch me, even if I were dead. I'd rather die than let her."

Mother looked at me with sad, imploring eyes. Her breathing was even more irregular.

"Have pity on me, my child," she begged. "I feel that my hour has come. So long as you have confidence in yourself, why not just let her have a look at you and we can then avert the Evil Eye? We can make her swear a solemn oath on the Holy Book to conceal this whole business and talk to nobody about it."

I looked anxiously at her as she struggled to speak through her uneven breathing. I felt obliged to give in to what she said, not out of conviction but out of fear that she might have a fatal seizure. "I'll let her examine me but only for your sake, Mother. But I'd rather die than suffer such an outrage. Who says that Umm Fawzi is capable of concealing things even after she has sworn on the Qur'an?"

I then hurried into the kitchen and brought out a glass of water. I poured into it twenty drops of the medicine prescribed by the doctors for whenever Mother had an attack. She sipped it slowly. I then fetched a pillow, put it behind her back, and asked her to put her feet up and rest as much as possible, again as the doctors had ordered. After a little while, she seemed to be more at ease and her breathing became more regular. I then heard footsteps in the court-yard and realized that the old woman had arrived. I shuddered all over and was filled with feelings of utter repugnance and humiliation. The door was pushed open and the old hag called Umm Fawzi the midwife came in. I had always loathed this fat little woman with her evil glance and her poisonous tongue. She used to come and see us every now and then and bring Mother the neighborhood gossip and tell her of any scandals that had occurred. I used to escape when-ever she called, in spite of her cloying words reminding me always that she had been the first person to welcome me into the world.

"Umm Fawzi," Mother said, greeting her, "we want to be quite sure about Sabriya. She fell over today in the *hammam* on some-thing that was very hard and I am afraid that something awful may have happened."

Such a crafty old crone as Umm Fawzi was not in the least de-ceived. She nodded and clucked meaningfully.

"Come here, you little devil," she said to me. "I won't do you any harm."

I let her do whatever she wanted to do and then kicked her with-out looking at her or saying anything. She smiled.

"I can take anything from you," she said. "You are intact, praise be to Allah."

Mother sighed with relief.

"Up you get, Umm Fawzi," she said, "and go and tell Abu Raghib that."

Umm Fawzi left the room. I heard her say to Father in her harsh voice, "Allah above, offer prayers to the Prophet. My girl, Sabriya, praise be to Allah, is as sound as a golden pound coin."

By which she meant she wanted a golden pound coin as her fee.

Father of course paid that willingly, having been reassured of the fine honor of the family that lay concealed between my thighs — my thighs, me, alone of all the family.

When Umm Fawzi left, I came out of the room and went towards the stairs. I did not turn towards the *liwan*, where Father and Raghib were, but stamped past them to let them know of my anger. I hurried upstairs to my room and threw myself on to my bed, feeling as if I had been torn to pieces by wild dogs. Degradation and misery oozed out of every pore of my skin.

They want to take me out of college just one year before I get my certificate.

They want to incarcerate me in the house.

An insensate scream rose up from deep inside me and was stifled in my throat, like the death rattle of a wild animal that is wounded in the jungle.

Ohhh! Even screaming is beyond me. My nerves twitched and with my teeth and fingers I set about ripping the sheets into tiny shreds.

Where are you, Sami? . . . If you were still here, they would not humiliate your sister in this way.

Where are you, Adil? . . . You won't be seeing me next Thursday. They have slain the joy in our hearts. They have killed our aspirations. I feel that you are as far from me as heaven is from earth . . . But no, no. They won't be able to keep us apart forever. I will run away to you, even if you are at the end of the world.

I felt as if a fever was coursing through my veins, like the intense heat of the sun. I felt pain in my cheeks. I did not have the power to stand up and walk even the two paces to the wardrobe mirror to examine my face. I felt it with my hands. It was swollen. There was no doubt that Father's hand had left its mark in red or blue. The hand that had exuded compassion when he used to caress my shoulder. How could those fingers go wild in an instant? How could that hand lose its tenderness and humanity? What a destructive power these acts have! We have been conditioned since we first become aware of things. Time reinforces these ineradicable qualities which over the years become stronger than love, stronger than compassion. Then a quiet human being can be transformed into a violent criminal. I have no doubt that if Umm Fawzi had been unable to convince Father about that honor that is concealed between my legs, he would have killed me and carried on living, mourning me. I imagined that he was suffering now, and was wanting to take me to his bosom and to wipe away the pain which he had caused. I was totally aware of how much he loved me and how precious I was to him. But he could not acknowledge this because he would see in it a frailty that challenged his manhood. Nothing could be as bad as to question this holy of holies. What a flawed concept is this manhood!

Is not the man with perfect manhood the one who stands in the face of the current or who disregards it? He acts as his conscience dictates and take no heed of others. He speaks the truth and is unconcerned with appeasing or angering others. In spite of what he has done to me, I do not hate Father, because I know how much he is a prisoner to these beliefs that have embedded themselves in his innermost being, the work of generation after generation, for hundreds of years.

But I do hate Raghib. It was he who egged Father on, spurred him on. But for Raghib, I would have been able to persuade Father of my own point of view. Why was I compelled to tell him a lie, a clumsy lie that brought upon me this degradation that I will never forget for as long as I live. I wonder whether, if I refuse to eat or to talk, I could arouse his sympathy so he would send me back to college? I will stay here in my room. I shall not leave it until I get what I want.

Two days passed and I kept to my room. I didn't leave it and all I tasted was water. Father and Raghib made no attempt to see me or to talk to me. Ill as she was, Mother was the only person who came upstairs to bring me some food. She tried to tempt me with tasty morsels, to draw me out and get me to talk and to awaken my sympathy for her state, but she failed utterly.

On the third day I lost my strength and could stand only with

139

the greatest difficulty. Mother did not come up. She sent me some food with Umm Abdu, who had been coming to the house for a few hours every day since Mother fell ill. She would clean the house, prepare some food and then leave. What I liked about this woman was that she knew what she could do and what she could not do. And she showed no curiosity. When she brought me food, she would look at me with sympathy and sigh and ask no questions. I don't think she knew anything about what had been going on in the house or made any effort to find out.

Shortly after Umm Abdu left, I heard a row coming from the ground floor. It seemed as if Raghib was shouting and quarreling with someone. Why wasn't he at his work, I wondered. Had he taken leave so as to keep an eye on the house? Who was he arguing with? I pulled myself together and went and stood at the window, but I couldn't understand anything he was saying and I couldn't see anybody. You can't see the whole of the courtyard from my window.

What are his concerns to do with me, I said to myself. He can have a row with whomever he likes.

I felt a bit giddy and staggered back to my bed. I looked at the tray of food on the bedside cabinet. A tasty smell came from it and my resolution almost crumbled. I turned my back to it and stretched out on the bed. I would stay firm, however much pain and torment I suffered, even though it were to end in my dying.

Next morning the door of my room was pushed open. I was terribly feeble. In came Umm Fawzi the midwife. I felt a sudden strength come back to my limbs and I sat up.

"What on earth has brought you here?" I said. "What do you want from me now? Get out of this room."

She placed a finger on her lips.

"Hush," she whispered. "I've brought you a letter from Adil. He wants you to reply immediately."

Her evil eyes sparkled as she took a letter from her bosom and handed it to me. In confusion I opened it, glanced at it, recognizing Adil's handwriting. I started to read it.

"Dearest," I read. "I have heard of the difficulties and humiliations you are having to put up with ..."

I paused in my reading and gave Umm Fawzi a look of contempt. What I had anticipated had happened. How could Adil know anything about me except from Umm Fawzi, who would be spreading the news all round the quarter?

I carried on reading.

"I sent Mother to your family today to ask for your hand in marriage, and to rescue you from what you are going through. Your brother Raghib chased her away. He treated her very badly and told her, 'We don't marry the sons of bakers.'

"She left your house in a state of distress, brokenhearted . . ."

As I read I recalled what had occurred yesterday. This is what had obviously happened when I heard the row coming up from the ground floor, and the voice of Raghib echoing around the place. I didn't then understand what it was about.

What a mean, wretched man! Why should he stand in the way of my marrying Adil? What on earth does it matter so long as I love Adil? I carried on reading.

"I have given it a lot of thought and have come to the conclusion that the only way of rescuing you is for me to give up my studies now, and to work as a teacher in a village far from Damascus to which you and I can escape. There we can get married properly and can live the life of our dreams. We can present your family with a *fait accompli*. I will instruct you so you can enter for your exams with your fellow students and you will have lost nothing.

"After the march, some of our comrades were arrested and thrown into prison. I feel I am currently under surveillance by the authorities and so flight away from Damascus would be in my interests as well. I have already been to the Education Department and they gave me a warm welcome. They are in acute need of teachers and I was at once appointed to a village school in the far north. I leave it to you to choose a suitable time to join me. We must move as quickly as we can. I prefer to get away today. If you consent, do write to me. Fix a time and I'll arrange for a car to be waiting for you some time after midnight at the first alleyway outside the quarter. Be of good cheer and have no fear, so long as I'm at your side."

I took a pen from the desk drawer and wrote at the end of his letter, "My love, Mother is very ill. I have no doubt that if I ran away it would be the death of her. I would be miserable and have a guilty conscience for the rest of my life. You must go first to the north and I'll write to you. When Mother's condition has stabilized, you will find me ready for a sign from you and ready to flee with you to the end of the world. Nobody will be able to keep us apart until death. I am dismayed to hear what happened to your mother in our house. Give her my apologies, and look after her as much as you can."

I folded up the letter and gave it to Umm Fawzi, without looking at her vile face.

"This is my answer." I told her. "Hand it over to Adil in person."

"At your command, my dear."

She hid the letter in her bosom and added, "Why are you sitting here alone by yourself? I asked your mother about you. She told me you were sulking in your room, that you aren't leaving it at all and that you aren't eating or drinking anything. Your mother is very worried about you. She's ill, alas. Last night she could not sleep at all, with one attack after another until morning.

"I told her, 'I'll have a word with my little girl, Sabriya.' I saw you into the world and am like your own mother. Get up now, may Allah be pleased with you. Come down with me to your mother — my Allah bless all parents."

"This is none of your business," I said firmly. "I'll go down when I want to."

She gave me a mean look and got up sullenly.

"It's for the best, if it is the will of Allah," she said. "You know your own interests better than I do."

Adil's letter gave me a great boost. Hope was revived. What was the point of continuing to go without food if my poor Mother was the only person who bothered about me, even though I might be at death's door. And Allah knows how much she has suffered for me. She is sure to have been doing what she could to persuade Father to send me back to college. But that no longer matters, for Adil will be able to instruct me and I can take the exam at the same time as him. Tomorrow morning, when I know that Father and Raghib will have gone out, I'll go down and see Mother, get into her bed and bury my head on her tender breast. I'll make up for the anguish I've caused her.

I looked at the desk by the bed. There was a tray of food on it which Umm Abdu had brought up. I had eaten nothing from it even though I was in an agony of hunger and was tormented with feebleness. I took the cup of buttermilk and sipped half of it, and then I slowly chewed a piece of fried meat, swallowing it with difficulty, for my throat was very dry. It was as if my throat was lined with thorns. I took a second piece of meat and tried to swallow it with the help of a mouthful of the buttermilk. Then I ate a third with some salad and enjoyed it. The pains inside me abated and I lay out on the bed. It was beginning to get dark. I pulled the blanket up, closed my eyes and dreamt of flight with Adil, imagining what it would be like.

That night, after midnight, a car would stop at the entrance of our quarter. I would go out under cover of darkness. I would go on tiptoe to avoid making any noise. I would have with me a small bag with a few essentials — just as in the storybooks. Adil would greet me anxiously, restlessly. I would be perfectly calm, full of self-possession. We would get into the car and it would set off. I would put my head on Adil's shoulders and cast off the agonies of so many years. The car would take us a long way away and I would remain silent. If Adil said anything, I would make a sign to him to be quiet. I do not want to sully the delight of this magical silence. When my family wake up and find me missing, Raghib will search the house from top to bottom, but we may already have reached our village far away. I will insist that Adil and I go first to the *mukhtar* of the village to get him to marry us. This can be done with the utmost ease.

There are not the complications in the villages that exist in the cities. We will then go into our house, which will be at the top of a little hill, concealed among vines and fig trees. There will be only a small courtyard and one room with a smell of the whitewash which peasant women use to paint house walls. I love this refreshing smell, a smell of newly dug earth. In the middle of the room there will be bedding, and near the stove a carpet and a few cushions. A village teacher's room. We will embark on this simple life and learn all about magic and beauty and love and affection, about triumph and joy. We will stay up late under the stars and will wake to the colors of the dawn and to the chirping of the birds.

I dozed off amid this fabulous dream and to these sweet yearnings. I was as hungry for sleep as I had been for food. I plunged into the deepest of sleeps.

I woke up late the next morning to the sound of Umm Abdu talking loudly to Mother downstairs. I could not make out what they were talking about. I called out to Umm Abdu, who came upstairs, weeping and beating her breast.

"There's been the most awful tragedy in the neighborhood," she said. "The whole place is upside-down. At the hour of the morning prayer the French assassinated Adil, the son of Sa'id the baker."

The noise of her sobbing was like the sound of cold water thrown on hot metal. My gaping wound felt no further pain at first. I repeated what had been said in a hushed and dazed voice, adding, "Adil is dead. Then everything is finished."

I did not shout. I did not burst into tears. Stupefied, I looked at Umm Abdu, who was talking and crying, describing how handsome Adil was, how he was in the prime of life. "They say Adil had no enemies but the French. Who but they would have killed him, my lady? May Allah avenge his death."

Like a flash of lightning it occurred to me — Raghib. But no, that was impossible. Was he so consumed with hatred and ill-will that he would actually commit such a crime? And besides, he knew nothing of my relationship with Adil except that he saw us on the day of the march walking together. Would he commit a crime on mere supposition? No, no, impossible.

In Adil the French had found a doughty opponent. It may be that they had found out that it was Adil who had brought down an airplane during the revolt and wished to get even with him. Or they liquidated him in order to make an example of him to other enthusiastic young men. Had he not written only yesterday to me to say that he felt he was under surveillance? If I had agreed to elope with him last night and go away to the village far away, could I have saved him from being killed?

144

I am the criminal . . .

I felt a chill go through me. Red-hot skewers stuck into my eyes and the tears gushed out. A hive of bees buzzed in my head. I closed my eyes. Life was a game, a foolish game of mockery, not worth bothering about.

I opened my eyes. I did not see Umm Abdu in front of me. I don't know when she went away. I looked hard at the window. With one leap I could throw myself to the courtyard, end it all, and enjoy eternal peace.

Then I visualized my ailing mother running out and throwing herself on to my broken body. She would flap around like a chicken with its head cut off. When the news reached Father, he would shed copious tears like a miserable old man. He would forget those manly traditions to which he had committed himself.

No. No. I cannot cause such distress to my aged parents. I am not that self-centered. Has not the tragedy of Sami been enough for them? I will carry on harboring my grief in silence. I will conceal it in the depths of my soul and disclose it to nobody. I will hoard it as a miser hoards his money. I will cope with it in solitude. I will stay up all night with it and, when morning comes, my wits will be dulled and I will live like a corpse untroubled by any worldly concerns. I will toil away like an automaton, without reflection, without sensation. And when the old folk move on from this world, I will know how to put an end to this life of mine.

Another page is pinned to this page of memories. This is what was written:

About ten years after these events a young woman whom I did not know came to the door.

"Are you the lady Sabriya?" she asked.

"Yes, I am. What do you want?"

"My grandmother, Umm Fawzi the midwife, is on her deathbed. She wants to see you."

My immediate instinct was to say no. What did I have to do with Umm Fawzi? But curiosity got the better of me. What could this woman at death's door want from me? I left my paralyzed father alone in the house and went off with the young woman. Umm Fawzi's house was not very far away. I was led to a room in the middle of which an emaciated body was stretched out on some filthy bedding. There was the sound of gasping and a foul smell. I could hardly believe that this bundle of bones was that stout woman, Umm Fawzi the midwife.

The bundle of bones made a sign to the girl to leave the room. She then whispered to me, moaning and talking in snatches, "Pardon me, my girl. I am to confront the face of the Lord. I have wronged you. Do you remember the letter I brought you from Adil, the baker's son?"

"I do."

"When I left your house with your answer, I saw your brother outside. He played the devil with my mind and beguiled me with money. I traded the letter with him and pocketed the money he gave me. He read the letter and gave it back to me. Adil was killed the same night. I really don't know whether it was the French who killed him, as everybody imagined, or your brother who was the murderer. I have lived a life of torment since I committed this grievous error. I have enjoyed no peace of mind. Forgive me, dear girl, before I die."

I looked at her with disgust. I spat on the floor and walked out without saying a word. This evil hag wants me to forgive her for having been the cause of Adil's murder and the destruction of my own life!

So it was Raghib who committed the deed. It is now clear. What had been just a suspicion in my mind is now a certainty. Black hatred.

Raghib then killed Adil after reading the letter. Didn't he say on the day of the march, "I know how to deal with him?" Perhaps he got someone to do the killing. That kind of thing was not difficult in those days. There were plenty of people to hire and lots of weapons around. For just a little cash, people carried out what was requested of them without delay or fear. Who did they have to be afraid of? The French would have supported them and may even have rewarded them for getting rid of the likes of Adil.

That venal evil old woman has lived on after committing her

heinous deed, her conscience in torment. But Raghib does not seem to have suffered any torment or remorse. He is living with an easy conscience, full of self-satisfaction. Was it not sufficient that he had redeemed the honor of the family and had prevented his sister from marrying a baker's son?

What has impelled this woman in the throes of death to poke around in the ashes of my heart, breathe on a live ember buried inside and inflame it anew?

I have not erupted like a volcano on becoming aware of the awful truth. I feel rather that my heart is smoldering away like a ball of wool on fire. The fire consumes it slowly and it does not flare up or burst into flames. Oppressive smoke settles deep in my throat. I am suffocating but I am not dying.

A strange lethargy falls on these memoirs. There are blank pages followed by other pages on which nothing is written except the date at the top of the page. This suggests that Auntie was enduring in reality a living death. She was not moved to record any of the events of the day in her memoirs.

Sometimes she has written a line or two without comment. It is as if she is writing down an item of news that is of no importance. For example:

I did not get any sleep at all last night. Mother had an attack that went on until the morning.

Or there is this remark written in some confusion:

When will her agony end?

It was as if she was wanting her mother to die.

After a lot of uneventful jottings like these, Auntie then recorded the following:

I am the subject of a conspiracy that is being hatched. My parents want to send me back to college. It seems that Father is suffering from remorse. My dignified, wounded silence in all its dimensions is giving him pain. Mother believes that my wretched depression is because I have been removed from college. I have refused their request to make them feel bad. They still do not realize that I am a living corpse only because of them.

I find it painful to burden them with the death of another of their children. Why should I go back to college when I have nothing to strive for afterwards?

Adil, you who are in the very depths of my heart and have left this world but will never leave me. My going back to college would be a betrayal of you and of our shared dreams and hopes, which have shattered like a piece of translucent crystal on some massive rock.

I have cut off all connection with the college. I have burnt my textbooks and my notebooks. I shun my former fellow students and have asked Umm Abdu to say I am not at home if they come to see me. They have now given up calling.

The only human being I want to see is Nirmin. I don't know why she has stopped coming to see me. I have sent her a letter via Umm Abdu.

A few days later. Nirmin has come to see me. I hardly recognized her. She was as pale as I was. We went up to my room.

"How are things with you?" I asked. "In the name of Allah, I hardly recognized you. Why haven't you come to see me?"

She gave me a look that was a mixture of pain and scorn. Her upper lip quivered and she was chewing on the lower. She closed her eyes, held back her tears and said in a shaky voice. "I've got married."

"You've got married!" I cried out in amazement.

She nodded.

"Yes, I've . . . got . . . m-married," she repeated.

She then opened her eyes, laughed and said derisively, "What's the matter with you? Aren't you going to congratulate me? Aren't you going to congratulate the bride?"

"Your attitude doesn't encourage me to congratulate you."

"Offer condolences then. At least say something."

"I don't know what to say. I know nothing of the background."

"Do you want to know the story then?" she asked. "Rest assured, it's not a strange story. It's like thousands of stories that have happened in this country from the earliest time . . . My dear, I've married a rich old man who used to be a friend of my father's. His wife died a long time ago and when he married off his three daughters — and the youngest of them is my age — he found himself all alone. He started to call on us from time to time, to find something to cheer him up. He already knew how things had gone with us since the revolt and made some generous offers of assistance, insisting that we consider him as Father's brother, for indeed there had been a brotherly affection between the two.

"At first I thought he was interested in Mother. I wondered whether he was going to ask her to marry him and whether she would accept. She was, after all, in her fifties. Whenever I saw them together in the evenings I would have my suspicions. Perhaps they had been in love when they were young and, out of loyalty to their partners, had had to conceal and suppress that love. Perhaps, with more and more encounters, they were affected by their memories of the past. I often tried to talk to Mother about my feelings and to reassure her that her marriage to Uncle Shukri would not upset me in the least. But I never had the courage actually to bring the subject up. I was in great awe of her.

"But that awe crumbled when she married me off to this old man. We found ourselves quarreling every day. Whatever I did to hurt her did not make me feel any better. I don't know how but she had an almost magical power over me. I did not wake up from it until after the marriage. I felt soiled by this old man every day. I now know the meaning of desecrated territory, and what humiliation, what shame and defeat. Mother took advantage of my desperation, of my inability to love any other human being but Sami. She was able to do just what she wanted."

I listened to her in silent amazement. When she finished her story. I said, "I can hardly believe my ears, Nirmin. What led your mother to sacrifice you? She is, as far as I know, a woman of education, with experience of the world, a person of understanding and intelligence."

"Why can you not believe it? It's as if you are not living in this country. Don't you realize that we have to sacrifice ourselves. That is woman's thankless duty."

And she's saying this to me of all people, I smiled grimly to myself.

Nirmin went on, "Mother sacrificed me for the sake of my brother. Is he not the male and I the female? My husband sent money to my brother until he passed his exams. He bought medicine for a clinic, tickets for his travels and also for his French wife. As soon as my brother arrived in Damascus, he rented a clinic for him and a house for both of them. It's all paid for by my husband, who crushed the life out of me. My brother is totally unaware of what I'm going through for his sake. He's never asked me if I am happy with my old man. Or why I married him. He's completely wrapped up with his French wife. I fear what he fears and that is, she won't fit in with our conservative traditions. It doesn't occur to him for a moment that he could make my life sweeter by inviting me to join them on one of their outings. What makes me even angrier is that Mother is completely satisfied with him. All she's bothered about is his success and happiness. I'll never forgive her for the way she's treated me. A great gulf has opened up between us. Harmony and affection have turned into aversion and loathing.

"And the worst of it is that the old man is jealous. He won't let me go out of the house unless Mother is with me. I've stopped going out because I can't bear my mother's company. Today I seized the chance of him being out of the house. I got dressed quickly and left the house without Mother seeing me go. I have to return now before he gets back. It's not for me to quarrel with him or to be blamed by him. Getting into trouble from Mother utterly crushes the spirit."

Nirmin rose. We hugged and kissed each other affectionately. She then left before I could tell her anything of my own woes. If I had thought I was the most unfortunate individual on the face of the earth, then here was Nirmin, even worse off than myself. Indeed, there is much in common with our two lives. I am cut off from my studies. She lives with her family in a more hateful atmosphere than I do. Isn't it enough for her to sleep and to be involved every day with somebody she hates from the depths of her being?

Allah, how awful it is. This gentle, sensitive girl lives in a state of humiliation. I, on the other hand, do not hate my parents. Indeed, I do whatever I can for them and find a certain amount of comfort in what I do for them. I do hate Raghib, but I am not forced to spend time in his company. I can get away from him whenever I want. There is some consolation in this.

My aunt no longer dated her entries by days. Instead the month was recorded. This means that one day must have seemed very much like another, one day being dragged out after another like so many corpses. She occasionally recorded events she saw as significant.

Father can no longer put up with it. He is always impatient, his face full of gloom. He's short-tempered and never stops complaining and mumbling about things folding up and himself going bankrupt. He complains incessantly to poor Mother and that makes her ill and depressed.

Hasn't the old man had enough of this world? Enough of profit and loss, and of unremitting toil? Even if his business fails, he knows that we won't die of starvation.

Raghib comes back late every night. I avoid seeing him or talking to him if possible. We talk to each other only when we have to, and when that happens we do not look at each other.

I live without sensations like a tortoise in its shell. I am unconcerned with what is happening in the country. In the past I used to follow events avidly. I do not appear before guests except to offer them tea or coffee. I then go and hide myself in my room. I leave the house only to fetch the doctor whenever Mother has an attack and when I am the only one at home. Or to buy some medicine from the nearest pharmacy.

Mother is trying to persuade me to go to the dressmaker's to have a dress made from some cloth from Father's shop. Poor Mother! She thinks I am like other girls, happiest when I have new clothes or new shoes.

I have said no. It's absurd. Why does a girl like me need new clothes? I've got enough to last me for the rest of my life.

My happiest times are when I retreat to my bed. In the middle of the night I summon up the image of my precious lover. Rays of light appear before me, in the middle of which is the face I love. In my ears I can hear his merry laughter, which is like the melody played by a young lover in the light of a new moon. His pearly teeth glint amidst his swarthy face. The dimple deepens. I talk to him and he talks to me just as we used to do, exchanging news and never tiring of repeating ourselves. I make no complaint to him of my misfortunes or of the emptiness of my days. Yesterday morning at dawn I woke up from a very clear dream — it was as clear as if I had been awake. I was hugging the pillow to my breast and panting with desire. It was as if I was clinging to Adil. We were talking to each other, saying things that lovers had never uttered before. I pushed the pillow away and got up. "Allah," I said to myself, and wondered if I was going mad.

I laugh at myself. Is somebody who is mad aware of the fact that they are going mad?

But then, has not all my behavior since I started to fantasize about my lover every night, has not all this been a madness within a madness? What have I got to be afraid of? Isn't madness gentler and pleasanter to me than this loathsome sanity from which I get nothing but weariness and travail?

I went back to bed. I hugged the pillow with even greater passion and said, "Come, waves of madness. Let me drown myself in you and forget my past, my present and my future."

An interesting event took place yesterday.

Raghib came into Mother's room before he went to work.

"I'm going to bring you, Mother," I heard him say, "a nice intelligent girl who can help Sabriya with the housework and look after you. Then Sabriya can enjoy this girl's company."

Mother was surprised.

"Where did you find this girl? Who is she?"

Raghib replied carelessly, speaking quietly and quickly, "She's a Christian girl. I've got to know her through my job. She came in search of some government assistance. She's a foreigner and an orphan. She came to Syria with her parents but they were killed in a road accident. The poor girl escaped and has been by herself, a foreigner without any means of support."

"Heavens above," said Mother. "Allah preserve me from such misfortunes . . . But not so fast, Raghib," she added. "We must get your father's permission before you bring her here. Are you sure she's telling the truth? We don't know anything about this girl who's coming into the house, do we?"

"You can rest assured, Mother. I'm not as foolish as all that, am I? I've got to know everything about her. She's a poor, innocent orphan. I'll go straightaway and see Father at the shop and talk to him about her. If he agrees, I'll bring her to you at lunchtime. I want her to have the cubbyhole to sleep in. She can live with us as if she is one of the family. Our reward will be in Heaven."

He then went off hastily, as if he did not want the conversation to go on or to hear what else we might have to say on the matter.

"I've never complained to Raghib," I said to Mother, "about being fed up helping you or about being alone in the house. Why should he bring in this girl?"

"Allah in heaven. He is your elder brother, girl. Why do you always think ill of him? He's concerned about you and has been thinking of your interests. Let us wait and find out about her. If we don't like her, it will be quite easy to get rid of her. Perhaps you are apprehensive of something that may actually be to your benefit."

"I don't like our arguing about Raghib. We've been doing that for a long time. You always give in to him. You should have said no to this girl as soon as he raised the subject. But once she is in the house it's going to be hard for her to leave quietly, so long as Raghib is behind her. I know your son better than you do. He is only bringing this girl into the house for some purpose of his own. Just you wait and see how right I am."

I left the room feeling furious. When the time came for Raghib's return, I stayed in the courtyard and busied myself with pruning the rose bushes. I waited, full of curiosity about the girl.

Exactly at the usual time the door opened and Raghib came in, followed by a blonde girl carrying a small suitcase. She had a pretty face, but also a pert expression. She was wearing cheap clothes and makeup. She walked behind him, swinging her hips in a vulgar way.

I could tell at a glance why she was being brought into the house. I looked at her in amazement without moving a step towards her. Raghib said to her as they came up to me, "This is my sister, Sabriya."

She put out her hand. I put out mine and we shook hands.

"Welcome," I said quietly and languidly.

"This is Sophie," said Raghib. "We call her Safiya, as that will be easier for Mother and Father."

The woman raised her penciled eyebrows and said with a slight foreign accent, "Perhaps I won't reply when I am called Safiya, because I'm used to hearing my name as So . . . ph . . . ie." She spoke, drawing out the name with a coquettish pursing of the lips. Raghib turned towards her and with a gesture of his hand and head seemed to say, "That's agreed then, isn't it?" She did not seem to be at all disconcerted by the coldness of my greeting. Raghib left and she followed, swinging her bottom from side to side as she went towards Mother's room.

I looked at her from a distance. They stayed with Mother only a little while and then Raghib took her up to the cubbyhole and left her there to unpack her case. He came down whistling cheerfully and asked Umm Abdu to prepare lunch.

The woman came out of her room and joined us all at the table. The meal consisted of burghul and lentils with pickled turnip, fried eggplant with chopped parsley and crushed garlic.

"Is this all we're having, just burghul and eggplant?" Raghib said. "Although I'm very fond of them both, we've never had a meal like this before. Mother usually gives us lots of different kinds of delicious things."

He looked at me as if to say, "This is your doing." But as Allah is my witness, I can say that it had nothing to do with me. Mother had arranged it.

"In Allah's name, my son," Mother said, "this is the kind of food I wanted to have today."

"But it doesn't suit you at all," Raghib said peevishly.

"I'm tired of broiled things, so I asked Umm Abdu to prepare this meal. She's better at it than I am."

As we were talking, the woman filled her plate with burghul and lentils and ate them, along with the pickled turnip, licking her lips with great relish.

"Very nice," she said. "This food, it's really nice."

She then took the eggplant and crushed it with her fingers with the parsley and garlic in our Damascus fashion. It was as if she had lived among us and eaten with us many, many times.

After lunch Raghib showed her round the house. They went into every room and then up to the Eyrie and on to the roof. They stayed there until just before sunset. Father came home from his work after sunset prayers. He had only just sat down at his usual seat in the *liwan* when Raghib came and introduced the woman to him. She leant over to kiss his hand, but he withdrew it without a word. He remained silent, looking at the floor. He was obviously very angry. Silence hung over all. Raghib was embarrassed, while the blonde woman fiddled around with her hair. She looked at our faces searchingly, but without being aware of all that was going on around her.

Father turned to me.

"I don't want any dinner," he said drily. "Bring me a cup of tea and a piece of cake."

He then got up and went up to his room.

Then Mother said, "After all that heavy burghul and lentils we had for lunch I can't face eating any dinner either. I'll just have a cup of tea."

I got some tea ready for them and took it to their rooms. Raghib and the woman went to the kitchen and had dinner there. I could smell the aroma of fried eggs. I avoided going into the kitchen and went to Mother's room.

"What's your impression, Mother, of this strange woman your son has brought in?" I asked.

"May Allah forgive us. Don't let us use obscene words. She's a girl of easy virtue, I shouldn't wonder, my girl. May Allah put you on the right path, Raghib. How did you allow yourself to be persuaded to bring this woman into our house? Allah! My girl, when he told me about her I supposed her to be a poor young orphan, a sprig severed from a tree. And so your father thought, from how Raghib described her. I said to myself, we'll bring her up ourselves, and she can help you in the future, because Umm Abdu will leave us one day soon. Her sons are starting work, and she is getting old and tired. It's time for her to take things easier. It never occurred to me that Raghib would bring a brazen tart of no background like her. I don't think your father will allow her in the house. I can tell that from the expression on his face. If I were able to get upstairs, I'd go to him now and find out what he plans to do tomorrow."

"The main thing is that Raghib shouldn't come to you to manipulate you as he usually does, getting you to persuade Father to let this plague stay in the house."

"May Allah help you to watch your language. Am I a child to be manipulated by Raghib?"

I laughed.

"You know it's happened before," I said.

I then got up to fetch her medicine. She took it and retired to bed.

I went up to my room and closed the door. I wanted to cut myself off from this world with all its complications. I wanted to relax with the image of my lover for a few hours. I would then be able to laugh to myself at the world and escape from the bitter and banal reality of my circumstances.

But it seems that Fate wished to give me vengeful gratification even after the passage of time. At dawn the following day when Father rose to say his prayers I heard his voice booming around the house. It reminded me of the day I had heard Raghib's voice reverberating round the courtyard, when he chased Umm Adil from the house shouting, "We don't marry the sons of bakers." I got out of bed and opened the door slightly, concealing myself behind it. Father was at the top of the stairs, speaking to Raghib, who seemed to be halfway up the stairs by the door of the cubbyhole.

"Get out of my house this instant, you dog," he shouted. "You and this foul woman you have brought here. Are you out of your mind? . . . Have you forgotten that you live in the house of a respectable family? Or do you imagine that this a whorehouse? I'm not dead yet to leave you to treat this house as you would wish, you wretch!"

Raghib went up a few steps until he was level with Father.

"I love this woman," he said defiantly. "What's that got to do with you? I will get married to her in accordance with the procedures laid down by Allah and his Messenger. I brought her here so you can get to know her before we marry."

"You're going to marry a harlot?" Father said in amazement. "A son of mine is going to marry a harlot?"

"In the name of Allah, she's an honorable woman, the daughter of a respectable family."

"Silence! This, a woman of good family? We don't know the standing of her father or where she is from. If she was honorable, she would not have permitted you to slink to her room at midnight before you were married. I've been watching you. I saw when you went into the cubbyhole and when you came out."

"She's my wife in the presence of Allah," Raghib said in a shaking voice. "All that remains is for the shaykh to sign the marriage document."

"But he has not signed it yet. You are not married yet. I will not give my consent to you marrying a whore. Do you understand? If you insist on marrying her, take her and get out of the house at once."

"Leave now?" said Raghib in a tone of defeat. "Where do you want me to go before it is daylight?"

Father placed one hand on his hip and pointed angrily with the other.

"To hell . . ." he said. "To the brothel you took her from. Do you think I cannot tell a brothel woman? I can tell one from among a hundred women. I can tell them from their wanton behavior and their impudent looks."

Raghib then said in a poisonous and threatening tone, "Very well then, I'll take her now. And I'll never show my face to you again for as long as I live."

"Good riddance. Who says we want to see your face of ill omen? Sami died and we survived that. Can we not live after you, you who've been the despair of us all?"

He then turned back to his room, muttering to himself, and slammed the door behind him. It could be heard all over the house.

Raghib went back to the cubbyhole and closed the door. I tiptoed out of my room and went downstairs to the sitting room, where Mother slept whenever she was unwell and could not get upstairs, I saw her leaning on the doorway, gasping.

"Allah," I said. "I guessed I'd find you out of bed."

She shook.

"We've become the subject of scandal," she said. "We've become the subject of scandal in front of the neighbors. I feel so ashamed, I cannot face them. Ever since we came to live here they've seen no reason to think any the less of us. Has your father gone out of his mind? Can't he just be patient until the sun is up? He can talk calmly to Raghib. He may then have been able to persuade Raghib to get rid of this woman."

"Huh, as if your son could change his mind! Father wanted to catch Raghib red-handed so he couldn't lie about it afterwards or be up to his usual tricks and escape the consequence of his outrageous behavior. I think Father stayed up all night watching the stairs from the window of his room until he caught Raghib leaving the cubbyhole. By Allah, Father's got it right. He saw the wickedness of his son, his shamefulness, his disdain for the rest of us. Father could contain himself no longer and exploded as you saw, without giving a thought to anyone else."

Mother made her bed and then sat on it. She sobbed and bemoaned her fate: "One splendid son meets his death in battle in the prime of life. Our second satisfactory son, poor fellow, is spirited away from us by some old woman who marries him off to an old maid of a daughter. Our eldest son gets rid of us for the sake of a woman."

She said an obscene word — quite contrary to her normal custom. It made me laugh and I had to stifle my laughter. I was filled with a sense of happiness. How sweet was this feeling of satisfaction. Has he forgotten, I wondered, how he turned the house upside-down to prevent me from marrying Adil, a man of worth? Now he wants to marry this tart, a woman of no importance whatsoever, because he is a man, and men are permitted to get away with anything.

When will this male myth be expunged from our society? Or will we carry on passing it down from generation to generation to the end of time?

I stayed with Mother, talking to her and soothing her as far as possible and hoping she would not have another seizure.

When the sun was up, I saw Raghib and the woman coming downstairs. Raghib was carrying two large suitcases into which he had packed all his things. The woman was carrying her suitcase and they were heading for the corridor. Raghib put his cases down and came into Mother's room. He looked a bit surprised when he saw me at her side. I was smiling grimly with apparent satisfaction in spite of myself. He stood at the doorway, ignoring my smiling self.

"Don't be cross with me, Mother," he said. "I can't help it. This is our fate. Don't blame me for having upset you."

He then left with the utmost casualness and nonchalance.

As soon as he had gone, Father came down from his room fully dressed. He looked at Mother, who was holding back her tears.

"Why are you weeping, you crazy woman?" he said passionately. "Your well-being is worth a hundred Raghibs, a name I don't want to repeat. From this day on I do not wish to hear any mention of Raghib in this house for good or for ill. Be reasonable, woman, what have we gained from Raghib ever since he was born? Nothing but problems and headaches. He has finally tried to sell us a harlot. He's now fully grown and has a job in the government. Don't worry on his behalf. So long as he doesn't ask about us, why should we ask after him? Let him live his life as he wishes."

He turned to me.

"May Allah be content with you, Sabriya. Look after your mother. These scenes don't do her any good."

He then turned to leave.

"Wait a little," I said, "and I'll make you some coffee."

"No, I'll drink some at the shop."

After he left, Mother asked me to write a note to Mahmud and to send it off at once. I described the situation and how Raghib had been turned out of the house. I told him about Mother's illness

160

and how she was getting worse day by day because her children were far away.

"I hope when he receives this," Mother said, "he will take pity on us and bring his wife to Damascus. Since her mother died there's no longer anyone to keep them at Homs."

A few days later we had a reply. Mahmud seemed to be in some difficulty. He wrote, "Whenever the question of my being transferred to Damascus arises I request a postponement. My wife refused absolutely to come and live with you. I have insisted and she now proposes that we sell this house and also the shop she owns in Homs and with the money buy a house in Damascus. This is embarrassing. How can I live a long way away from Mother and Father for so long in my wife's house and then refuse to live in our spacious family house? Can you prepare the way, Sabriya, and explain the matter to them? I will come to Damascus as soon as I can to have the pleasure of seeing them."

I did not think I would succeed as quickly as I did. Mother and Father were, however, happy that Mahmud was returning to Damascus, even if he and his wife would be living away from us.

I hadn't seen Mother so happy for a long time as she was during the week when Mahmud and his wife came to see us. Father found a house for them and Mahmud's wife bought it.

We started to feel some sympathy for her. She did what she could to lower the barriers that had grown up between us, trying to make us feel that she was one of us, helping us in the housework, getting close to her mother-in-law and showing concern for her health. Mother grew to like her, especially after the experience of Raghib's woman — "the slut," as she called her.

"Mahmud's wife is a sensible woman," she would tell me. "She knows how to run a house and keep it of good repute, although upon my word, I do wish she were younger and prettier. And I wish she would have some children. She would then have no rival."

Once Mahmud and his wife were living in Damascus, they would come to visit us twice a week. This did Mother a lot of good. But she began to complain to them that I was always in low spirits, that my thoughts were all over the place and that I preferred to be alone in my room. I showed no interest in my clothes or having my hair combed in the way she liked. I would not appear before guests and would not go out visiting. As a result people were cut off from us and we lived in semi-isolation.

Time passed rapidly, with the days much like each other. A year has gone by since Raghib was thrown out of the house. I have heard that he has married the blonde woman and has rented a house far away and is living with her in a state of agreeable bliss.

On Friday Mahmud called with Aunt Umm Rashid, whom we had not see for many months. Father greeted her warmly and affectionately. Mother chided her for not coming to see us, especially as she had been unwell and unable to leave the house to see her.

"In Allah's name," said Aunt, "I've longed to see each one of you, but I'm sorry to say I've only occasionally managed to get out of the house myself. It's not easy to leave Rashid by himself. After his injury he likes to be alone but has become addicted to strong drink. This upsets me more than anything else. He often has rows with his brother over matters of no importance. He wants Salim to give up his studies and work all the time with us as he used to do, but Salim is not really capable of doing that kind of work. And I'm old and can no longer do the work of my young days."

"This cannot be," said Father. "Rashid is a man of reason. He must overcome his handicap. Is he the first person to have his leg amputated? We must encourage him to get back to a normal life."

"We've got nobody but you, brother-in-law. Rashid is very fond of you and will listen to you."

"If Allah wills, I'll have a word with him from time to time. I'll try to persuade him."

I prepared a couple of *nargilas*, one for Father and one for Aunt Umm Rashid, who used to smoke the hubble-bubble like a man. Aunt drew a long breath from the mouthpiece and the *nargila* bubbled steadily. She turned to Father and, looking very serious, said, "Is it true, brother-in-law, that woman was created from the rib of the man that married her?"

"Do you have the slightest doubt on the point, Umm Rashid?" said Father, with some surprise.

"I wanted to be quite sure about that because it is the will of Allah that you are learned about these matters."

"May Allah strengthen our faith and keep us from doubt."

"Tell me then, what is the offense of your son Raghib, when Allah has created from his rib this woman and made her his destined partner?"

"I need help in dealing with you. Nobody is smarter. I understand now what you are getting at. I do beg you not to try and reconcile me to Raghib. I have not stood in the way of him marrying whomever he wished, but I will not allow that shameful woman to live with my daughter and my wife."

"I'm not asking to let them live with you. I am only asking you to allow him and his wife to visit you just as Mahmud and his wife do. In this world, brother-in-law, there is death and there is life. It is not right that you are deprived of your son while he is still alive. A few days ago Raghib and his wife came to see me. The woman has become a Muslim and was wearing a veil and a headdress just as we do. If Allah can accept repentance, how can we fail to do likewise?"

Mother than said, her voice quaking, "Abu Raghib, I am sick and am at the edge of the grave. I want to be able to see all I can of my children before I die."

Father sighed.

"There is no power or strength save in Allah. I resign myself to the will of Allah and trust in his mercy. Do whatever seems right."

"Raghib and his wife are at my house," said Mahmud. "I'll go and fetch them now."

All this was Mahmud's work. He was working as a peacemaker among members of the family. I felt hatred inside me, depression in my heart, and resentment towards my aunt. Only she was able to persuade Father to allow Raghib and his wife to enter our house. I greatly feared lest they come back to live with us permanently. That would bring back to our gloomy house all the old problems and rows which in my state I could no longer abide.

I did not think our complex affairs would be resolved so rapidly. The reunion took place. Raghib and his wife, together with Mahmud and his wife, all came back to the house. Cups of coffee circulated along with little courtesies. The name of the martyr Sami was not uttered by anybody. He had sunk into oblivion. Each member of the family had got what they wanted except myself.

Nobody is aware of my tragedy, least of all Mother and Father. They are all used to my silences, my depression, and my low spirits.

There is no doubt that the two daughters-in-law, the two new members of the family, suppose that this is my nature, that I am a simple girl, shy and introverted, a person of no great consequence among members of the household, my only function being to serve my parents in a kindly manner and to look after the house.

But they do not know Sabriya, the girl of ambition, the educated girl. They do not know the days when she had been fired with enthusiasm and passion, when she radiated joy in the house with her talk and her sound comments, the days when each of her brothers took careful account of her acute and critical observations. No. They know me only as a person dead in feeling and sentiment. I sit among them as if I am not there.

The day I hate most is Friday, when the whole house gathers together after midday prayers. We have lunch together. Sometimes the meal comes from Raghib's house, sometimes from Mahmud's. I am unable to manage all the cooking as well as clean the house and nurse Mother in her illness, especially now that Umm Abdu has left us.

I feel forlorn and lonely among them. Raghib's wife in particular infuriates me. That unspeakable woman knows exactly how to win over Mother and Father. Whenever she comes to call she is wearing a modest dress and there is not a trace of makeup. She weighs her words when she speaks. She gets close to Father to show her concern for him and her solicitude for his peace of mind. I hate it when he is pleased with her. I was so worried Father would agree to Raghib living with us if he chose.

Self-centeredness seems to be an inescapable characteristic of humankind. Nobody — not even mothers — are immune.

Frequently Mother used to offer this prayer to me: "May Allah

send you, my daughter, a handsome young man who will delight
your heart and mind."

She would then turn to those around her and say, "I make this
vow that when Sabriya gets married, I'll present her with this magnificent carpet. My father gave it to me on the day I got married."

She used to point to the huge carpet that covered the whole of
the reception room. But now she is ill, her tongue no longer utters
this prayer and this vow. She seems to have forgotten about the
matter of my marriage. Who is going to tend to her and to care for
her in her loneliness if I wed?

What preoccupies Mother's mind at present is that her two daughters-in-law have not produced children.

"How unfortunate I am!" she tells me. "The name of our family
will disappear. Mahmud has married an old maid and Raghib has
married a woman of dubious reputation. Such women rarely have
children."

Mahmud brought Mother news today that has made her weep with
joy. After a period of five years his wife is pregnant. She's now in
her fifth month. She concealed the news until she was completely
sure. The fetus has moved. How cunning she is. She was afraid
unkind people would gloat if the pregnancy was imaginary, especially Raghib's wife.

When Father returned from his work Mother trumpeted the glorious news to him in a voice full of delight.

"Great news, Abu Raghib, great news. In four months' time you
and I are going to become grandparents. Mahmud's wife is pregnant. She's in her fifth month. I beg of you, Allah, to make me live
long enough to enjoy the sight of my grandchild. I don't care when
it will be Your wish to call me to You after that."

Father was delighted with the news.

"Why has she kept the news from us till now?" he asked me.

The four months went by without my being aware of them. This,
however, was not unusual for me. But Mother found them dragging much too slowly.

Early one morning Mahmud called to announce that his wife

had given birth to a girl. I had never seen Mahmud so overjoyed. He hardly seemed to be aware of anything else.

Mother was a little cross. She had been dreaming of a boy who would bear the family name. But she soon brightened up.

"Whoever brings first a girl will follow with the gift of a boy. A boy will follow, my son. I'll give your daughter my name. You must call her Salma."

"Yes, by Allah," said Mahmud. "It's a lovely name. It's enough that it is the name of our dear mother."

"Then the name will not disappear from the family. For I am near to death, my son."

"May Allah forbid. After all this, Mother, with the will of Allah, you'll be restored to full health."

"By Allah, if I weren't ill, I'd ululate for joy. I'd boil some caraway seeds and invite the family and neighbors to give us their blessing for this precious delivery. It is as Allah willed."

Mother then untied a golden necklace from her neck. She had never removed it before. A triangular carnelian stone hung from the chain. On one side was carved the Throne Verse from the Qur'an. On the other was the name "Salma."

"Take this, Mahmud," she said, "as a present for the occasion from me to young Salma. It will ward off the evil eye."

After Mahmud left, Mother remained deep in thought. She then said to me apprehensively, "I fear, my girl, that this newborn girl is the fruit of barrenness, as they say. She is female and has turned up after a long period of childlessness."

"In the name of Allah," I said sarcastically, "save us from such a misfortune that could afflict us, that the name of this noble family be effaced from existence."

Mother's health steadily got worse and she became bedridden. When Mahmud brought in the precious newborn babe, we got Mother with some difficulty to sit up in bed. We placed the little one in her lap. Mother hugged the baby and wept. She then said, "Take her from me, I'm no longer fit for anything."

Mother's only concern has become the visits of the doctors, who relieve her of some of her discomfort. She has given Mahmud her jewelry without telling Father, who has now fallen deep in dept. Mahmud has sold the jewelry and with the money has paid for the doctors and for the medicines, which have had no effect whatsoever.

The doctors says that she is in a serious condition. The arteries of her heart are almost blocked up.

For three nights I have had no sleep at all. I have sat up with Mother, who has been suffering torment beyond description. She has died and revived before me several times in one night. I complain to nobody about my exhaustion and seek no assistance from any other member of the family. I hide what I am going through. I also hide what Mother has been going through — even from Father.

Mother has died.

The light that has illuminated our house has finally gone out. She has swamped it with her great love and tenderness. On the day the mourners called I felt very awkward in the presence of other people. Aunt Umm Rashid wailed and wept and lamented her sister. But I shed not a single tear. I did not know how to mourn Mother with words. It was as if I was a speechless rock that nothing could disturb.

I suffered a lot on the three afternoons and the following Thursday, when people called to offer condolences. I sat to the right of Aunt Umm Rashid. To the left were my two sisters-in-law and then the rest of the family. We wore heavy dark clothes and put white coverings on our heads. We sat in silence, listening to the Qur'an being recited by a blind shaykh sitting in the next room. People came, usually in threes, to offer condolences. They stayed a while and then left without saying anything at all. We would get up and then sit down as they come in or left, acting like puppets responding rhythmically.

One day, after the period of mourning was over, Father said to me, "It's hard for me to know that you are all alone in the house after I go to work. What do you think of the idea of our asking one of your sisters to come and live in the house to keep you company?"

"If you love me, Father," I replied, "and want me to enjoy peace of mind, let me live with you alone. I do not want even a young servant girl. It does not bother me at all to be alone. Indeed, it is other people who bother me. While you are away, I amuse myself with reading and housework."

"As you like."

Father is awkward in things that concern me. He wants to make things easy for me but does not know how to. The other day he brought me a pair of canaries in a beautiful cage. I showed my appreciation out of respect for him. That pleased him a lot.

Mahmud's wife comes to see us from time to time. She is a good soul, but even so I feel ill at ease during her visits. When will people near me realize that I do not need them, that I feel isolated when I am with them and that I am perfectly happy to be alone with my own fancies and dreams?

Yesterday Mahmud's wife came for a short while in the early afternoon. We sat on the *liwan*. She saw that I was gloomy and depressed as usual and tried to amuse me.

"For those who look at the misfortunes of others," she said, "their own troubles become easier to bear. I'm going to tell you a tale that happened in Homs a long time ago. You've heard the song that begins, 'Tears have been shed, have been shed, and for our beloved ones our clothes have been rent.' There is a distressing story attached to this tale that the people of Homs used to tell each other. My mother, who was around when the events took place, used to tell the story to people who came to see us.

"There was once a very rich man in Homs. He had servants, attendants, orchards, villages, and a coach that was drawn by the most beautiful horses. He lived with his sons and daughters and grandchildren in a house that was really like a palace. It was surrounded by a big garden through which flowed the Orontes River. His youngest daughter was a very beautiful teenager. She liked going every day to the orchard to play with the handsome young son of the coachman, who was just a few years older. Sometimes the girl liked to ride a horse without her family knowing about it. The young man was not slow in providing her with a docile horse from the stables and in helping her get on. He would then lead the horse through the luxuriant trees by the banks of the Orontes. He would sing tuneful, happy songs. The two young people took great pleasure in these outings. It was not long before they fell madly in love. But in the course of time the girl was affianced to a cousin. There was a problem. She talked it over with the young man and they agreed to elope to a distant village where the young man had an old aunt, widowed and alone. There would be no difficulty so long as they took some money for her. They could then live together as man and wife.

"But it was not difficult for her father and her brothers to find their way to the young lovers. They killed the young man instantly and threw his corpse into the Orontes River. They then brought the girl back home. They feared that if they killed her the story would get around and that would not be good for the family's reputation. Instead they tied the girl up and fetched her youngest brother, who was only twelve years old. They handed him a gun and told him to shoot her, so they would afterwards be able to say in the presence of the servants that it had been an accident and the will of Allah. The boy opened fire on his sister. She collapsed in a pool of blood before his very eyes and when he saw her in the agonies of death he went completely and utterly out of his mind. The unfortunate mother of the murdered girl and the demented son was no longer able to remain at the palace. She would leave in the morning and wander along the banks of the Ornotes, crazily weeping and singing in great distress, 'Tears have been shed, have been shed, and for our beloved ones our clothes have been rent.'

"One day she went out as usual and never came back. The story spread throughout the area. And so did the song. In the course of time people forgot the story but not the song. That was the product of a broken heart. People added verses to the song that had no connection with the original story."

As she was telling me the story, I wondered what it had to do with me. What made her tell me this story? Was it told spontaneously or deliberately? Did she know something about my tragedy with Adil? It was similar to her story. Did she want to comfort me by telling me a tale that was more harrowing than my own?

But no . . . no . . . How could she know? Living in Homs, she had been isolated from us. Even Mahmud knows nothing of my misfortunes, unless Raghib has spoken to him about what happened and my distress when the French killed him. Perhaps Mahmud then repeated the story to his wife.

The story upset me but I did not let her see. I made her feel that however much she might try to get me to open my heart to her, I would not respond.

Mahmud's wife no longer calls to see me. I see her now only on Fridays, when the whole family gathers.

Since Mother's death the house seems to be abandoned. Silence and gloom prevail. When I have finished the cleaning, I wander around the rooms like a lost spirit. Every day I make three cups of coffee and take them up to the Eyrie and pass through my mind that brilliant episode of my life. I sit where I used to sit with Adil and Sami. I picture them sipping coffee in front of me. We talk about the revolt and books and our hopes for the future. Since Adil's death my feelings have become so numb that I find no pleasure in reading books or in any novelty. I used to read the classics and recall comments Sami and Adil had made on them. I used never to get bored ...

When the whole family gets together and Father and my brothers talk about the political situation, or about the merchants' strike and the detention of the nationalists, or about the marches organized by the students, or about the nationalist delegations sent to Paris to demand the ratification of the treaty between Syria and France, or about the stubbornness and delaying tactics of the French, I hear it all but with detachment and diffidence. What is the point of being moved if I cannot participate effectively in these events so important to our country? If I had been given the opportunity, I would have carried on after the deaths of Sami and Adil. I would have become more passionate and more involved than I had been before. When I was at college I proposed to my fellow students that we set up a women's society that would struggle alongside men with national problems. Most of them were ready to agree.

But after what happened at the march I have been sentenced to live away from all these questions, to live as one outside the system, as a spectator from afar. I have been too weak to resist this current that has swept me along. I have made up my mind to live as one who is dead. This is the only way to cope.

Today Father went to work. He came home, one hour later, looking very anxious.

"The whole country is on strike for the sake of the treaty," he told me. "I don't know when there'll be an end to the strike. We've gained nothing from it so far. Conditions are becoming intolerable. I'm being dogged by bad luck. The strike was announced the very day some goods arrived for me at the customs. I've borrowed money and, in the name of Allah, the interest payments are crippling. I have been hoping to sell these goods at a profit and so pay off my debts and escape from the stranglehold I've been in for years. And now there's this strike. If it goes on for long, the season will be over and the goods will be useless and your poor father will be bankrupt for the rest of his life."

"Allah forbid that that should happen, Father. The season has only just started and the strike can go on for only a few days."

"A few days! . . . They say it can go on for a month or more, or until the treaty is ratified, and when will that be?"

When we were all together on Friday, Raghib said to Father, "There's never been a total strike like this in Syria before. People are solid and keen in spite of the economic hardships everyone is complaining about."

Father refrained from saying anything about his own circumstances. He didn't want his daughters-in-law to know anything about them.

"How do you think people will manage their affairs when the strike goes on and on?" he asked Raghib.

"Committees of nationalists have been set up in each quarter to collect money and distribute it to the workers and those in need, so they can manage till the strike is over."

"The bakers and the butchers," said Mahmud, "have been allowed to keep their stores open for two hours every morning only, so people can buy whatever they need. I'll drop by to buy what you need before I go to work."

171

Father was being optimistic when he suggested the strike might go on for a whole month. It has now gone on for almost two months and there is no sign of an end yet.

I have had a tough job all the time keeping Father happy. He doesn't go out of the house nowadays. He can't talk about anything except his merchandise that is becoming worthless and the bankruptcy that is impending. I listen to him with enormous forbearance until I am bored to tears. There's just nobody else in the house to listen to his endless complaining.

Mother, may Allah have mercy on her soul, must have had to put up with a lot. I have sometimes imagined he was on the verge of collapse or suicide. I have done everything I can to ease his burden without entering into any arguments. I realize that arguments would be no use at all. How I wanted to tell him, "If the country benefits from this strike in any way, what does it matter if people like us go bankrupt? You lost your son for the sake of the country. Is it so hard to lose your money when you are perhaps towards the end of your life?"

But I do not believe that money alone is the cause of his distress. He is jealous of his reputation as a respected merchant. The store in which he has spent sixty years of his life is very dear to him. He was ten years old when he started working there with his father. From that day he was never separated from it. He went there every morning and didn't come back until after sunset prayers. He has spent more time there than at home. The store is part of him. How can the thought of being evicted from it and facing his fellow merchants be a trifling matter? I have seen him raise his hands to heaven in supplication when he prays, with the words, "Allah, I ask no more of You than that I die with an untarnished reputation."

The strike is at last over and the French have yielded to the people's will. A nationalist delegation has gone to Paris to negotiate with the French government on the ratification of the treaty between Syria and France.

Father has resumed his business. What we feared has happened. Winter is over and the goods he bought on borrowed money are all useless. He came home in the depths of despair.

"I've not sold any cloth at all," he told me. "I've not put my hands on a single piaster. People have been ruined by the strike. Who now thinks of buying clothes? They need food more than they need clothes."

The creditors called unannounced, with an official who dealt with the distraint of goods and sealed up the store with red wax. Father left it, utterly devastated.

The blow was more than an old man of Father's age could bear and he had a stroke and collapsed. His merchant neighbors sent for Raghib and Mahmud. They came and bore him away and brought him unconscious back to the house.

I felt chilled when I received the news. It was as if I had been expecting it. I reckoned that Father's end was at hand and I was sorry that it had come in this tragic manner.

I asked my brothers to bring Father's bed down from his room upstairs and to put it in the sitting room, which was not far from the toilet.

We hauled Father on to the bed and Mahmud went to fetch the doctor.

The doctor examined him carefully.

"He may recover consciousness, but I cannot say when. I am afraid to say that it is a hopeless case of paralysis. He has a sound heart and his life is in the hands of Allah."

I repeated those words to myself: "The heart is sound." Allah, Allah, how long will his life stretch out for? What further calamity has overtaken my life? How can I cope with it all by myself?

The doctor wrote out a prescription and handed it to Mahmud.

"The instructions are written on the label," he told me. "You can feed him milk or fruit juice with a spoon. Follow that with the medicine. One teaspoonful every six hours. If things become serious, get in touch with me whenever you wish."

The doctor left. There was silence for a few minutes. It was as if we had not absorbed the full impact of what had happened. It was clear that my brothers were thinking that they could leave me alone with my paralyzed father. But each of them appeared to be too awkward to be the first to leave. I wanted to relieve them of their embarrassment.

"There's no need for you to stay here with me," I told them. "Why don't you both go home? It's almost time for the sunset prayer."

"How can we leave you all alone?" said Mahmud. "I'll go and fetch my wife and Salma. They can sleep here and help you nurse him."

"It'll be enough," said Raghib, "for you and me to take turns in calling here."

He obviously didn't want to upset his precious life.

"Let me try and nurse him by myself," I said. "If things are all right, there's no need to trouble you. The problem is going to be with us for a long time. We don't know how it started or when it will end."

It was as if I had provided them with a way out. They did not insist on staying behind and wasted no words in courtesies.

Raghib got up to go first and glanced at his father. He sighed and assumed an attitude of grief. Father seemed to be in a deep, deep sleep.

"I'll go and get the medicine," said Mahmud.

It was a heavy, oppressive night. I fed Father with a spoonful of milk and then a spoonful of medicine. His lips would open as soon as the spoon touched them. His eyes remained closed and he received the milk with no difficulty, instinctively, like a child at its mother's breast who, at the touch of the nipple, responds with open mouth and unopened eyes.

I myself ate a few pieces of cheese and some olives, and then brought my blanket and pillow and stretched out on the sofa opposite Father's bed. I crawled inside the blanket and wondered, "Have I been created a unique individual? I have been so buffeted by misfortune that my feelings are dulled. I no longer care about anything. I do not like to complain or to grumble. That's a humiliating sign of weakness. I accept the situation whatever it is. What upsets me most today is that I have left my own room and have to sleep here to keep an eye on this helpless invalid who is my father."

174

The fantasies that I used to enjoy each evening have left me. The atmosphere did not encourage such fancies.

When I turned the lights out I felt desolate. The light of the moon shone through the window into the room and glimmered on the wall opposite, producing the faint shadow of the branches of the citron tree in the courtyard outside. The shadow flickered rhythmically whenever there was a slight breeze. I stared at it without thinking. The absolute silence in the huge house frightened me. Specters changed into ghosts. I felt extremely alert. My ears picked up every movement, every sound. I heard a scratching at the foot of the door. I could see in the light that it was the cat, Zarif, trying to get out. I let it out, closed the door, and went back to my makeshift bed without bothering about the light. I was unable to sleep and, in spite of a sense of oppression, kept tossing and turning on the sofa until I heard the dawn call to prayer. My poor Father! Every morning at this time I would have heard the tread of your footsteps as you came downstairs to perform your ritual ablutions. I would hear your gentle voice as you repeated your prayers in praise of Allah and performed your devotions. You would pray and then recite from the Qur'an. I would feel that life was still continuing in our house. Most of the family have now left, but you, Father, are the head of the family and our house is an open house so long as you are alive, even though paralyzed.

I got up and stood by Father's bed. His eyes were still closed, his chest rising and falling regularly. I gave him some milk and some medicine. It was now my job to care for him and to clean him up.

I was in a quandary. How, dear Allah, was I to begin? I summoned up courage and lifted up the blanket and removed his trousers. I shook with a feeling of nausea. But I did not give up. I raised his cold flabby legs and withdraw the wet soiled pieces of cloth that I had placed beneath him and on top of the plastic, waterproof sheet. I then wiped his legs with a damp cloth and covered him up with the blanket. The whole task was easier than I had expected. I felt like a mother cleaning a small baby and I was filled the passionate tenderness.

The next afternoon Mahmud and Raghib called and stayed for a little while. They asked me before they left if I needed anything from them. Nothing at all, I assured them.

What I wanted most was for them to go away and leave me in peace.

Two days later. Father has slowly started to regain consciousness. He opens his eyes when I call his name, but looks at me vacantly. He then mumbles some words which I cannot make out.

A few days later. He has recovered total consciousness. He wept bitterly when he realized he was paralyzed and started to blame his Lord.

"What, O Allah, is the reason for this torment? Why didn't You take me to You all at one go?"

He then begged forgiveness and asked Allah to pardon what appeared to be insolence and impatience.

News spread throughout the quarter of his illness. I felt overwhelmed by the visits of family, friends, and neighbors. Not for a moment was I able to rest from running around. I would be up at sunrise, clean Father up, change his clothes and his bedding, feed him and give him his medicine, rinse down the floor of the courtyard, tidy up the house, wash, cook, prepare coffee for guests, and go to open the front door whenever there was a knock. When evening came I felt shattered.

The flow of visitors has started to trickle away. Even Raghib and Mahmud drop in only once or twice a week. Father has become aware of the state he is in and has started refusing to take his medicine.

"He who has thus humbled me can cure me as He chooses," he says.

I never saw Father after the collapse of his health so pleased or so grateful as he was after the call of one of his merchant friends. This friend brought him the news that his creditors have released him from his financial obligations. He now no longer owes a piaster to anyone. This is thanks to his merchant friends, who thought highly of him. When his goods were put on the market, they all bought them up, paying well for them. This paid off his debts and one merchant has rented the store for a good price.

"I can die now happy and blameless and with an easy conscience,"

I heard him say. "I am neither a creditor nor a debtor. The rent from the store is enough to keep Sabriya and myself for the rest of our lives."

Nirmin was my window on to the outside world. I looked forward to her visits every Tuesday morning. When she left the hairdresser she would pass by and we would be together for an hour or so. We would share our concerns and this would make us both feel much better. As soon as I heard her knock at the door, my heart would beat a little faster. I would rush to the door and we would hug and kiss each other. I would feel as if I was alive again and my blood would course warmly again through my veins. But for Nirmin I would be insensible to the passage of time. I might have been unaware of the day of the week, so monotonously did the days pass, with one so much like another.

Last Tuesday she did not turn up. I was most upset. I had been irritated by Father's demands and my nerves were on edge. I did not know what to do. When I gave up hope that she would call, I poured away the citron drink I had prepared, untasted, into the fountain. I wondered whether she was ill. Or had she grown bored with my company, preferring to call on another friend, more amusing and more spiritually comforting? The only time she left the house was to go to the hairdresser. I thought of slipping out and looking for her at her house. Then I thought that this might annoy her. I had to be patient until the next Tuesday. I thought that if she did not come, then I'd go and see her.

The week dragged by. This Tuesday I tidied up the house, squeezed some citron juice and put it in a crystal jug on the ledge round the fountain.

She came at the usual time. I took her in my arms and kissed her warmly.

"I've been on the rack all week," I told her. "I've been so worried about you."

She looked very pale.

"Do you know what I did last Tuesday?" she asked me. "Instead of coming here I went to see one of the old midwives. I was afraid two weeks ago that I might be pregnant. The midwife gave me a drug that brought on a miscarriage. My husband and my mother were in mourning and in tears, but I was laughing triumphantly inside. They don't know that I brought it on."

"But, Nirmin, are you crazy? You took some drug from some ignorant old midwife? You could have done yourself enormous harm."

"As far as I'm concerned, life isn't worth an onion skin. Death means less to me than to bear the child of a man I don't love."

She then added, angrily, "Isn't it enough that I hate my mother, my husband, and my brother? Do you want me to hate my child as well? This is the most awful kind of hatred."

"But what harm has this innocent little mite done? He may have become a delight to you."

She turned away.

"In my opinion a child should be the fruit of love and harmony, not of hatred and aversion. Do you want me to bring up a child in such a poisonous atmosphere to be mixed up and miserable? Do you think I can spend my life with this disgusting old man? Am I to do nothing but feel sorry for myself and bear children?"

I looked at her in confusion. This was not the Nirmin I used to know.

"I'm beginning to wake up, Sabriya," she went on. "Or rather, to recover from my illness. You and I have seen our youth end up in dust."

"It is circumstances that have decreed our fate."

"No! No. A thousand times no. We've got to fight back. We've given in and surrendered like stupid goats."

"What then do you think we could have done?"

She spoke quietly, choosing her words with care.

"Run away. We could have run away from this useless country and its stupid people."

"Run away? . . . But where to?"

"The world of Allah is wide. Palestine. Lebanon. In these places you're able to work and live in complete freedom. If every route before you is blocked, then you can work as a servant. Nobody knows you. That, in my view, is more honorable for you than to be imprisoned in this empty house with this helpless invalid, where you mull over your misfortunes night and day. Doesn't your father have other children? They too have a responsibility towards him. Here you are, working as an unpaid servant, a prisoner. But if you worked as a servant anywhere else, you'd get paid for all your efforts. You'd be able to live as freely as you like and not as other people want you to live."

"I died when Adil was killed," I said, perhaps rather pompously. "All my hopes were crushed then. I no longer have any hope in this world. I live the life of a corpse so as not to distress Father with yet another bereavement."

Nirmin smiled scornfully.

"That's a load of blah. Dead people don't feel as others do. Do you imagine if you and I had died that Adil and Sami would mourn us for more than a few days, perhaps stretching to a week? Why then should we spend the rest of our lives in mourning?"

I was astonished at her words. I swallowed hard as if I was unable to digest something.

"Adil and Sami are men. Life was opening up for them. We are women and everything in this country is blocked for us. Do you want me to marry as you have married? A successful marriage in a country like ours is rare. It is better for me to stay as I am than to marry a man I do not love. I loved Adil. I was madly in love with him. Where is the man who can replace Adil and make me forget him?"

"Are you wanting another such man to turn up in your life, knock at your door and say, 'Hey, you, here I am. Come to me, my dear.' No, get out of this prison of yours. Look for him and you're sure to find him."

"How can I when I'm forced to stay in this house? I did what I could to resist, but I failed. You're talking as if you're not a woman of this city. Are you capable of leaving as you wish and finding the man who will make you forget Sami?"

She blushed in some confusion, hesitated and said without looking at me directly, "Perhaps I have found him. Perhaps one day . . ."

It was as if she was stabbing me in the heart.

"You've actually found someone?" I said intensely. "You are concealing things from me. What have you committed yourself to, Nirmin?

What's come over you today? You are not that paragon that Sami so worshipped."

"Paragon!" she said scornfully. "Didn't I tell you that I've woken up from my slumber? I've at last been cured of my unglorious virtue."

She looked at her watch and got up.

"I should have gone by now. I really must go this instant."

I had the feeling that she wanted to get away from me and my persistent questions, to escape my disapproving look. I did not press her to stay and have some citron juice, which she used to love. Nirmin left without our exchanging our usual kisses. Just before I closed the door, as she left she said, "Do think about what I've been saying. I want the best for you. I want to take you out of this living hell you're in. Maybe some day I can do just that."

"Thank you for your kind sympathy," I said. "You look after yourself, I don't need anybody."

I went back to the courtyard shaking with anger. The first thing I saw was the jug of untasted citron juice on the edge of the pool. I picked it up and threw it to the far end of the courtyard. It shattered into tiny pieces and the golden juice poured all over the marble floor. I felt that my relationship with Nirmin was similarly shattered.

Father called out. The sudden noise of the breaking of the glass had disturbed him. I leant my head against the trunk of the lemon tree and closed my eyes. I stayed like that for a while, listening to Father's call but not doing anything until I had pulled myself together to some extent. I went to his room and found him in tears.

"What was that noise?" he asked. "Why didn't you answer? I was afraid that you had fallen over and something terrible had happened."

"There's no need to worry, Father. I'm all right. My body of clay has not been broken."

"You're made of clay? Allah forbid! You're made out of the finest porcelain."

I laughed at the thought. "Perhaps I am, but only as far as you are concerned."

I was more upset by his helplessness and by his tears on my account than I had ever been before. I stood by his bed, took his hand, and kissed it. He looked at me contentedly.

What a harsh person you are, Nirmin, I said to myself. To whose mercies do you want me to abandon this helpless old man so we can run away together? To my weird sisters-in-law, who would treat him unkindly without any respect, when he's at the end of his life?

A few days later. The last week has been agony. I am full of anxiety, wondering whether Nirmin was serious in what she was saying. Or was it just one of her outbursts that won't last very long? Will she come at her usual time next Tuesday? Or will she be going to this man who seemed to be displacing Sami in her affections?

I am strangled by the torment. Devoured by jealousy. Was our friendship destroyed forever? Or would she come and see me, full of remorse, so we would take up again our old affectionate relationship? Please, Allah, let her be within reach until the end of my days.

On Monday evening after sunset there was a persistent knocking at the front door. I went quickly to open it. I knew it was Nirmin. Since Father had become ill, nobody called at this time of night. I put a light on in the corridor and opened the door. It was as I had expected. Nirmin came in amid a cloud of expensive perfume. She was dressed elegantly, gorgeously. Her eyes were so bright they seemed to be dancing. She took me in her arms and came to kiss me passionately. I did not respond but tried to recoil from her and keep my distance. I was afraid of what she was up to. She grabbed both my hands and looked me in the eye.

"I can't leave this town without seeing you and saying goodbye," she said. "I'll give you my address and we can write to each other."

I stared at her angrily.

"You've done it then, Nirmin?" I said. "Who are you running away with? . . ."

I was unable to say more without hurting her.

"I'm running away," she said automatically, "with my hairdresser, Wanis."

She had already mentioned her hairdresser, but I had not given him any thought or any importance. Involuntarily, I removed my hands from her and slapped her on the cheek with all the force I could muster.

"You stupid girl, aren't you destroying your reputation and risking the wrath of Allah, all for the sake of an Armenian hairdresser? No. No, Nirmin, you're worth more than that."

"You're crazy," she said with feeling. "Hysterical. Don't you know that what brings on the wrath of Allah is treachery, dishonesty, and hypocrisy? And that what pleases Him is loyalty, honesty, and openness? And with Him all people are equal? I love this man. I have found in him a nobility, an honorableness and manliness. I am convinced that he is the only person who can take me away from my hell and rescue me from my unrighteous marriage, which is pleasing neither to Allah nor to anyone with a conscience."

"Enough. Enough," I said. "You've found all this only in this Armenian hairdresser?"

"You reckon all people are equal, but you know nothing about him except that he is an Armenian hairdresser. I had expected you to have a little more understanding, to be a little more discriminating and farsighted and less temperamental than I find you at present. I thought you'd be the only one who would understand me and excuse me. After all, you have been madly in love with the son of a baker."

She said this and turned to run off to the front door without giving me another look. She had forgotten about her address. I stood in my place, still as a statue. I felt bolted to the floor. I was dumbfounded by Nirmin's logic. I also realized that I had said what I had said about the Armenian hairdresser because I was jealous of him. He was depriving me of Nirmin forever.

Nirmin was the last of the trinity whom I had loved in this world.

Where in all this wide word was this Armenian taking her?

I suddenly realized that, as far as I was concerned, Nirmin was dead.

My window on the world was slammed shut.

I wish I had not behaved so impetuously. Receiving letters from Nirmin might have been some consolation. Or we might have met again one day.

I had behaved as if I was Sami, the passionate lover, surprised by a rival. I walked back from the corridor, dragging my feet, shoulders slumped, as if I was walking away from a funeral after having buried a dear friend.

I went into Father's room. He had sunk into a deep sleep. His features were relaxed and on his face was contentment, peace, and resignation. I looked at him with loathing.

"Whatever happens," I muttered, "you continue to lie there, paralyzed but breathing normally."

I threw myself on the sofa. Why was I unable to shed tears when I had more need to weep than ever before?

I felt as if I was choking, as if my throat was about to explode.

Auntie used to break off writing whenever she was buffeted by some new disaster. It was as if she could not concentrate until the wound was partly healed. Then she would have absorbed the tragedy in all its dimensions. When she resumed her record, I observed a radical change in her reflections. It was as if she was convinced of Nirmin's views without realizing it herself. But she would not admit it, even to her diary.

She no longer mentioned the three loves of her life — Adil, Sami, and Nirmin. She gave no thought to anything but herself, her misfortunes, her wasted youth, her lost years. She grumbled about servicing her father and wished he was dead. There was an intensity in her hatred for her brothers and also for their wives because they seemed to have forgotten all about her.

Sometimes she compared herself to a headstrong bitch that is tethered at the neck by a chain to a stake planted in the old house. Or she compares herself, drying up day by day, to the creatures she sees in her life around her. She realizes that she has been totally defeated as a result of mastering her own rebellious spirit. There are pages and pages along these lines. They caught my eye when I first browsed through the diary and I have recorded them earlier.

Auntie was more preoccupied with herself than with anything that was going on around her. She even showed little interest in the Second World War, which shook the whole world. It receives only a passing mention in the diary, such as when there was a blackout or when there was a sharp inflation and the rent from the store was no longer enough for her father and herself to live on without economies. I was already an adolescent at the end of the war and used to like visiting her from time to time on my way home from school. I think she was very fond of me and enjoyed my visits. She would tell me of her concerns and was more at ease with me than with anyone else in the family. She even gave me a room to myself on the upper floor. I would escape there, regardless of what my mother said, and concentrate of my schoolwork, because I could not put up with Mother's chatter and her rows with Father.

I felt sorry for Auntie in her isolation and the way she was cut off from the world. I would divert her with news I had heard of the war that everybody was talking about. She would listen with great interest, or rather with a grim satisfaction, when she heard of a defeat for the Allies who had colonized our country.

"Have you heard, Auntie?" I said one day. "Yesterday the Germans sank two huge British battleships. The German air force has been making some horrendous air raids on London and Hitler has made a speech lasting three hours. People listened to it in German on the wireless without understanding a word."

She turned to me.

"I don't know what people here see in this tyrant Hitler. Is it good to occupy countries that don't belong to you, to kill innocent men and women and to take away their liberties?"

"Isn't it enough that Hitler is the enemy of the French and the English and also the Zionists for us to like him?"

"And what would we gain from this enmity?" She smiled. "If the French left, we would have Hitler or Mussolini here. We would jump out of the frying pan and into the fire."

I looked at her in astonishment and wondered why my aunt liked to be so contrary.

It did not occur to me at the time that Auntie was right and that her isolation helped her independent mind to think clearly and reach sound conclusions. She could tell right from wrong sooner than those who followed current affairs and jumped to mindless, emotional conclusions.

The day we celebrated the evacuation of the French from Syria, Auntie wrote those words in her diary:

Is our Damascus plunged into a dream or is it all true?
I can hardly believe that the day dawned for which we have dreamt

since we were first conscious of this world. It was the dream of our fathers and our grandfathers. We made huge sacrifices for it.

For a long time I have not wanted to leave the house so much as I have today. I put on my shawl and left Father in a virtual coma. It was as if he was already in the throes of death. I picked all the lilacs and went out of the house with them. I lifted up my veil and went off with my face uncovered. I feasted on the happiness in people's smiling faces. Everyone was smiling. The heavens were raining happiness. The earth was awash with joy. I think everybody had left their houses to go into the street to sing and dance as if they were possessed. They went to the western part of the city, where the main celebrations were being held.

I went to the east, to the Dahdah cemetery.

The cemetery was deserted. There weren't even any gravediggers. It was as if death was also on holiday. For a few minutes I stood humbly among the graves in silent respect. I went to Adil's grave and covered it with lilacs. I embraced the headstone and wept. Had you been alive, I would have put my hand in yours and we would be dancing with everybody else.

I looked out to the Ghuta. I recited the opening verse of the Qur'an and dedicated it to the spirit of Sami and to the souls of the martyrs.

The last page of her diary was written in a shaky hand. It was written for me:

I write these words before I pass on from this world. I have tried to spare you a sight of this tragedy out of sympathy for you, Salma. But you have insisted on staying at my side to be an eyewitness of these events.

I had intended to burn these memoirs before I passed on. But at the last moment I have decided to present them to you.

Read them carefully so you do not fall as your aunt fell. Do not let your life be in vain.

About the author

Ulfat Idilbi was born in 1912 in Damascus, Syria. She was married at the age of seventeen before she could complete her education. She started writing in the 1940s and, early in her career, won a BBC prize for short stories in the Arab World. She has published two novels, four collections of short stories, and a study of *The Arabian Nights*. She is now the doyenne of Syrian women authors, and *Sabriya* has been dramatized for Syrian television.

About the translator

Peter Clark has translated a number of books from the Arabic, including *Karari*, the Sudanese Account of the Battle of Omdurman by Ismat Hasan Zulfo (1980), *Dubai Tales* by Muhammad al-Murr (1991), and *A Balcony over the Fakihani* by Liyana Badr (1993). He has also written biographical works on Marmaduke Pickthall and Wilfred Thesiger. He has had a distinguished career in the British Council and is now their representative in Damascus.

About the series

The "Emerging Voices: New International Fiction" series is designed to bring to North American readers the once-unheard voices of writers who have achieved wide acclaim at home, but were not recognized beyond the borders of their native lands.

With special emphasis on women writers, this series publishes the best of the world's contemporary literature in translation or original English.

Titles in the "Emerging Voices" series are available at bookstores everywhere. For a complete catalog please write to us at the following address:

Interlink Publishing Group, Inc.
46 Crosby Street
Northampton, MA 01060

Tel (413) 582–7054
Fax (413) 582–7057
e-mail: interpg@aol.com